RANDOM
HOUSE
LARGE
PRINT

BLOOD DREAMS

Also by Kay Hooper
available from Random House Large Print

Chill of Fear

Sleeping with Fear

BLOOD DREAMS

Kay Hooper

RANDOM HOUSE
LARGE PRINT

Copyright © 2007 Kay Hooper

Published in the United States of America by Random House Large Print in association with Bantam Books, New York.
Distributed by Random House, Inc., New York.

Library of Congress Cataloging-in-Publication Data
Hooper, Kay.
Blood dreams / by Kay Hooper.—1st large print ed.
p. cm.
ISBN 978-0-7393-2716-6
1. Bishop, Noah (Fictitious character)—Fiction.
2. Serial murderers—Fiction. 3. Government investigators—Fiction. 4. Serial murders—Fiction.
5. Boston (Mass.)—Fiction. 6. Suspense fiction.
7. Large type books. I. Title.
PS3558.O587B58 2007
813'.54--dc22
2007045404

www.randomhouse.com/largeprint
FIRST LARGE PRINT EDITION

10 9 8 7 6 5 4 3 2 1

This Large Print edition published in accord with the standards of the N.A.V.H.

Jacket design by Yook Louie
Jacket art © Alan Ayers and Terry Hill

Prologue

IT WAS THE NIGHTMARE brought to life, Dani thought.

The vision.

The smell of blood turned her stomach, the thick, acrid smoke burned her eyes, and what had been for so long a wispy, dreamlike memory was now jarring, throat-clogging reality. For just an instant she was paralyzed.

It was all coming true.

Despite everything she had done, everything she had **tried** to do, despite all the warnings, once again it was all—

"Dani?" Hollis appeared at her side, seemingly out of the smoke, gun drawn, blue eyes sharp even squinted against the stench. "Where is it?"

"I—I can't. I mean, I don't think I can—"

"Dani, you're all we've got. You're all **they've** got. Do you understand that?"

Reaching desperately for strength she wasn't at all sure she had, Dani said, "If somebody had just listened to me when it mattered—"

"Stop looking back. There's no sense in it. Now is all that counts. Which way, Dani?"

Impossible as it was, Dani had to force herself to concentrate on the stench of blood she knew neither of the others could smell. A blood trail that was all they had to guide them. She nearly gagged, then pointed. "That way. Toward the back. But . . ."

"But what?"

"Down. Lower. There's a basement level." Stairs. She remembered stairs. Going down them. Down into hell.

"It isn't on the blueprints."

"I know."

"Bad place to get trapped in a burning building," Hollis noted. "The roof could fall in on us. Easily."

Bishop appeared out of the smoke as suddenly as Hollis had, weapon in hand, his face stone, eyes haunted. "We have to hurry."

"Yeah," Hollis replied, "we get that. Burning building. Maniacal killer. Good seriously outnumbered by evil. Bad situation." Her words and tone were flippant, but her gaze on his face was anything but, intent and measuring.

"You forgot potential victim in maniacal killer's hands," her boss said, not even trying to match her tone.

"Never. Dani, did you see the basement, or are you feeling it?"

"Stairs. I saw them." The weight on her shoulders felt like the world, so maybe that was what was pressing her down. Or . . . "And what I feel now . . . He's lower. He's underneath us."

"Then we look for stairs."

Dani coughed. She was trying to think, trying to remember. But dreams recalled were such dim, insubstantial things, even vision dreams sometimes, and there was no way for her to be **sure** she was remembering clearly. She was overwhelmingly conscious of precious time passing and looked at her wrist, at the bulky digital watch that told her it was 2:47 P.M. on Tuesday, October 28.

Odd. She never wore a watch. Why was she wearing one now? And why a watch that looked so . . . alien on her thin wrist?

"Dani?"

She shook off the momentary confusion. "The stairs. Not where you'd expect them to be," she managed finally, coughing again. "They're in a closet or something like that. A small office. Room. Not a hallway. Hallways—" **A flash of endless, featureless hallways, brightly lit . . .**

"What?"

The image in her mind vanished as quickly as it had come, and Dani dismissed it as unimportant because an absolute certainty had replaced it. "Shit. The basement is divided. By a solid wall. Two big rooms. And accessed from this main level by two different stairways, one at each side of the building, in the back."

"What kind of crazy-ass design is that?" Hollis demanded.

"If we get out of this alive, you can ask the architect." The smell of blood was almost overpowering, and Dani's head was beginning to hurt. Badly. **Hallways. No, not hallways, two separate spaces, distinct sides . . .** She had never before pushed herself for so long without a break, especially with this level of intensity.

It was Bishop who said, "You don't know which side they're in."

"No. I'm sorry." She felt as if she'd been apologizing to this man since she met him. Hell, she had been.

Hollis was scowling. To Bishop, she said, "Great. That's just great. You're psychically blind, the storm has all my senses scrambled, and we're in a huge burning building without a freakin' map."

"Which is why Dani is here." Those pale sentry eyes were fixed on her face.

Dani felt wholly inadequate. "I—I don't— All I know is that he's down there somewhere."

"And Miranda?"

The name caused her a queer little shock, and for no more than a heartbeat, Dani had the dizzy sense of something out of place, out of sync somehow. But she had an answer for

5

him. Of sorts. "She isn't—dead. Yet. She's bait, you know that. She was always bait, to lure you."

"And you," Bishop said.

Dani didn't want to think about that. Couldn't, for some reason she was unable to explain, think about that. "We have to go, now. He won't wait, not this time." **And he's not the only one.**

The conversation had taken only brief minutes, but even so the smoke was thicker, the crackling roar of the fire louder, and the heat growing ever more intense.

Bitterly, Hollis said, "We're on **his** timetable, just like before, like always, carried along without the chance to stop and think."

Bishop turned and started toward the rear of the building and the south corner. "I'll go down on this side. You two head for the east corner."

Dani wondered if instinct was guiding him as well, but all she said, to Hollis, was, "He wouldn't take the chance if he had it, would he? To stop and think, I mean."

"If it meant a minute lost in getting to Miranda? No way in hell. That alone would be enough, but on top of that he blames himself for this mess."

"He couldn't have known—"

"Yes. He could have. Maybe he even did. That's why he believes it's his fault. Come on, let's go."

Dani followed but had to ask, "Do you believe it's his fault?"

Hollis paused for only an instant, looking back over her shoulder, and there was something hard and bright in her eyes. "Yes. I do. He played God one time too many. And we're paying the price for his arrogance."

Again, Dani followed the other woman, her throat tighter despite the fact that, as they reached the rear half of the building, the smoke wasn't nearly as thick. They very quickly discovered, in the back of what might once have been a small office, a door that opened smoothly and silently to reveal a stairwell.

The stairwell was already lighted.

"Bingo," Hollis breathed.

A part of Dani wanted to suggest that they wait, at least long enough for Bishop to check out the other side of the building, but every instinct as well as the waves of heat at her back told her there simply wasn't time to wait.

Hollis shifted her weapon to a steady two-handed grip and sent Dani a quick look. "Ready?"

Dani didn't spare the energy to wonder how anyone on earth could ever be ready for this. Instead, she concentrated on the only weapon she had, the one inside her aching head, and nodded.

Hollis had only taken one step when a thunderous crash sounded behind them and a new wave of almost intolerable heat threatened to shove them bodily into the stairwell.

The roof was falling in.

They exchanged glances and then, without emotion, Hollis said, "Close the door behind us."

Dani gathered all the courage she could find, and if her response wasn't as emotionless as the other woman's, at least it was steady.

"Right," she said, and closed the door behind them as they began their descent into hell.

1

YOU HAD THAT dream again last night, didn't you?"

Dani kept her gaze fixed on her coffee cup until the silence dragged on a minute longer than it should have, then looked at her sister's face. "Yeah. I had that dream."

Paris sat down on the other side of the table, her own cup cradled in both hands. "Same as before?"

"Pretty much."

"Then **not** the same as before. What was different?"

It was an answer Dani didn't want to offer,

9

but she knew her sister too well to fight the inevitable; Paris determined was as unstoppable as the tides. "It was placed in time. Two forty-seven in the afternoon, October twenty-eighth."

Paris turned her head to study the wall calendar stuck to her refrigerator with **South Park** character magnets. "The twenty-eighth, huh? This year?"

"Yeah."

"That's three weeks from today."

"I noticed that."

"Same people?"

Dani nodded. "Same people. Same conversations. Same burning warehouse. Same feeling of doom."

"Except for the time being fixed, it was exactly the same?"

"It's never **exactly** the same, you know that. Some of it's probably symbolic, and I have no way of knowing which parts aren't literal. I only know what I see, and there are always small, sometimes weird changes in that. A word different here or there, a gesture. I think the gun Hollis carried wasn't the same one as before. And Bishop was wearing a black leather jacket this time; before, it was a dark windbreaker."

"But they're always the same. Those two people are always a part of the dream."

"Always."

"People you don't know."

"People I don't know—yet." Dani frowned down at her coffee for a moment, then shook her head and met her sister's steady gaze again. "In the dream, I feel I know them awfully well. I understand them in a way that's difficult to explain."

"Maybe because they're psychic too."

Dani hunched her shoulders. "Maybe."

"And it ended . . ."

"Just like it always ends. That doesn't change. I shut the door behind us and we go down the stairs. I know the roof has started collapsing. I know we won't be able to get out the same way we went in. I know something terrible and evil is waiting for us in that basement, that it's a trap."

"But you go down there anyway."

"I don't seem to have a choice."

"Or maybe it's a choice you made before you ever set foot in that building," Paris said.

"Maybe it's a choice you're making now. The date. How did you see it?"

"Watch."

"On you? Neither of us can wear a watch."

Still reluctant, Dani said, "And it wasn't the sort of watch I'd wear even if I could wear one."

"What sort of watch was it?"

"It was . . . military-looking. Big, black, digital. Lots of buttons, more than one display. Looked like it could give me the time in Beijing and the latitude and longitude as well. Hell, maybe it could translate Sanskrit into English, for all I know."

"What do you think that means?"

Dani sighed. "One year of psychology under your belt, so naturally everything has to mean something, I guess."

"When it comes to your dreams, yes, everything means something. We both know that. Come on, Dani. How many times now have you dreamed this same dream?"

"A few."

"A half dozen times that I know of—and I'm betting you didn't tell me about it right away."

"So?"

"Dani."

"Look, it doesn't matter how many times I've had the dream. It doesn't matter because it isn't a premonition."

"Could have fooled me."

Dani got up and carried her coffee cup to the sink. "Yeah, well, it wasn't your dream."

Paris turned in her chair but remained where she was. "Dani, is that why you came down here, to Venture? Not to offer me a shoulder to cry on while I go through a messy divorce, but because of that dream?"

"I don't know what you're talking about."

"The hell you don't."

"Paris—"

"I want the truth. Don't make me get it for myself."

Dani turned around, leaning back against the counter as she once again ruefully faced the knowledge that she would never be able to keep the truth from her sister, not for long.

It was partly the twin thing.

Paris wore her burnished copper hair in a shorter style these days—she called it her divorce rebirth—and she was a bit too thin, but otherwise looking at her was like looking into a mirror. Dani had long since grown accustomed to that and in fact viewed it as an advantage; watching the play of emotions across Paris's expressive face had taught her to hide her own.

At least from everyone except Paris.

"We promised," her sister reminded her. "To leave each other our personal lives, our own thoughts and feelings. And we've gotten very good at keeping that door closed. But I remember how to open it, Dani. We both do."

It wasn't unusual, of course, for identical twins to have a special connection, but for Dani and Paris that bond had been, in the words of one childhood friend, "sort of spooky." It had been more than closeness, more than finishing each other's sentences or dressing alike or playing the twin game of exchanging identities.

Dani and Paris, especially in early childhood, had felt more like two halves of one person rather than separate individuals. Paris was the sunnier half, quick to laugh and joke, invariably cheerful, open and trusting, the extrovert. Dani was quieter, more still and watchful, even secretive. She was slow to anger and to trust and far more introspective than her sister.

Night and Day, their father had called them—and he hadn't been the only one to misunderstand what he saw.

Dani and Paris preferred it that way, confiding the truth only to each other. They learned early to hide or disguise the easy mental and emotional link they shared, eventually discovering how to fashion the "door" Paris spoke of.

It gave them the privacy of being alone in their own minds, something most people never learned to value. For the twins, it had finally enabled them to at least begin to experience life as unique individuals rather than two halves of a whole.

Dani missed that former closeness, though. It might now be only a door away—but that door did mostly stay closed these days, with the twins in their early thirties and having chosen very different life paths.

Nodding slowly, Dani said, "Okay. The dream started a few months ago, back in the summer. When the senator's daughter was murdered by that serial killer in Boston."

"The one they haven't caught yet?"

"Yeah."

Paris was frowning. "I'm missing the connection."

"I didn't think there was one. Absolutely no connection between me and those murders, not with the victims and not with any of the investigators. And I never have visions about anything not involving me or the people in my life. Which is why I didn't think this dream was a premonition."

Without pouncing on that admission, her sister said, "Until something changed. What?"

"I saw a news report. The federal agent in charge of the investigation in Boston is the man in my dream. Bishop."

"I still don't see—"

"His wife is Miranda Bishop."

Paris sat up straighter. "Jeez. She's the one who told us about Haven."

"Yeah." It had been in Atlanta nearly a year and a half before. Paris and her husband were one argument away from splitting up, and Dani was between jobs and at loose ends. Neither one of them was interested in becoming a fed, even to join the Special

Crimes Unit Miranda Bishop had told them about.

They didn't want to carry guns, didn't want to be cops. But working for Haven, a privately run civilian organization of investigators with unique abilities—that had sounded interesting.

Absently, Paris said, "That was the last straw for Danny, you know. When I wanted to use my abilities, when I got a job that actually required them. I saw how creeped-out he was. How could I stay with someone who felt that way about any part of me?"

"Yeah, I know. Been there. Most of the guys I've met couldn't get past the fact that I was an identical twin; having dreams that literally came true hasn't exactly been seen as a fun bonus."

"Especially when you dreamed about them?"

"Well, anybody who gets close takes that risk. And since I never dream about sunshine and puppies, most of the guys in my life haven't stuck around long enough to hear about their own personal-doom scenario."

"There was one who never ran."

Dani frowned. "Yeah, well. He would have. Sooner or later."

"Do you know that, or are you only guessing?"

"Can we get back to the dream, please?"

Since a solemn pact made in girlhood, each of them had been scrupulous about staying out of the other's love life. And because her own very rocky marriage had recently left her hypersensitive to that, Paris could hardly push. "Okay. Getting back to your dream—are you saying it has something to do with that serial killer?"

"I think so."

"Why?"

"A feeling."

Paris watched her steadily. "What else?"

Dani didn't want to answer but finally did. "Whatever was down in that basement was— is—evil. A kind of evil I've never felt before. A kind that scares the hell out of me. And one thing that has been the same in every single version of my dream is the fact that it has Miranda."

"She's a hostage?"

"She's bait."

_____

She was my only child."

"Yes. I know."

Senator Abe LeMott looked up from the framed photograph he had been studying and directed his attention across the desk to a face that had become, these last months, almost as familiar to him as the one that had belonged to his daughter, Annie.

Special Agent Noah Bishop, Chief of the FBI's Special Crimes Unit, possessed an unforgettable face anyway, LeMott thought. Because it was an unusually handsome face but, even more, because the pale silver-gray eyes missed nothing, and because the faint but wicked scar twisting down his left cheek was mute evidence of a violent past. Add to that a streak of pure white hair at his left temple, shocking against the jet-black all around it, and you had a man who was not likely to be overlooked, much less easily forgotten.

"You and your wife don't have children." LeMott set the photograph aside carefully, in its accustomed place to the right of the blotter.

"No."

The senator summoned a smile. "And yet you do. Brothers and sisters, at least. Family. Your unit. Your team."

Bishop nodded.

"Have you ever lost one of them?"

"No. A few close calls, but no."

Not yet.

The unspoken hung in the air between them, and LeMott nodded somberly. "Bound to happen. The work you people do, the evil you face. Sooner or later, there'll be a . . . an unbearable price demanded. There always is."

Choosing not to respond to that, Bishop said instead, "As I told you, we lost what faint trail we had near Atlanta. Whether he's in the city or somewhere nearby, that's the area. But until he makes a move . . ."

"Until he kills again, you mean."

"He's gone to ground, and he isn't likely to surface again until he feels less threatened. Less hunted. Or until his needs drive him to act despite that."

"It's gotten personal, hasn't it? Between you and him. The hunter and the hunted."

"I'm a cop. It's my job to hunt scum like him."

LeMott shook his head. "No, it was always more than that for you. I could see it. Hell, anybody could see it. I'm betting he knew it, knew you were hunting him and knew you'd crawled inside his head."

"Not far enough inside his head," Bishop said, a tinge of bitterness creeping into his voice. "He was still able to get Annie, he was still able to get at least eleven other young women, and all I know for certain is that he isn't finished yet."

"It's been months. Is it likely that's why he's been waiting, for the heat to die down? Is that why he left Boston?"

"I believe that's at least part of it. It wasn't the spotlight he was after, the attention. He never wanted to engage the police, to test his skills and will against ours. That's not the kind of killer he is, not what it's about for him."

"What is it about for him?"

"I wish I could answer that with any kind of certainty, but you know I can't. That's the hell of hunting serials: The facts come only after we've caught him. Until then, we have only speculation and guesswork. So all I **know** is bits and pieces, and precious few of those. Despite all the bodies, he hasn't left us much to work with."

"But you know Annie was a mistake, wasn't she?"

Bishop hesitated, then nodded. "I think she was. He hunts a type, a physical look, and Annie fit like all the others fit. If he needed to go deeper than looks, needed to know anything else about his targets because knowing more than the surface was important to him, he would have known who she was, known the extreme risks in targeting her. The way she was living, quietly, like any other young woman in Boston, the ordinary surface appearance of her life, didn't warn him that the response to her disappearance would be so immediate and so intense."

"That's why he stopped, after her?"

Bishop was only too aware that the grieving father he was talking to had spent years as a prosecutor in a major city and so knew the horrors men could do, perhaps as well as Bishop himself, but it was still difficult to forget the father and think only of the fellow professional, to discuss this calmly without emotion.

This killer isn't the only man I've been

profiling, Senator. I've been studying you as well. And I'm very much afraid that you'll take a hand in this investigation yourself before too much longer.

A deadly hand.

"Bishop? That is why he stopped?"

"I think it was part of the reason, yes. Too many cops, too much media, too much attention. It interfered with his plans, with his ability to hunt. Put his intended prey too much on guard, made them too wary. And it became a distraction for him, one he couldn't afford, especially not at that stage. He needed to be able to concentrate on what he was doing, because he was practicing, for want of a better word. Exploring and perfecting his ritual. That's why—"

When the other man broke off, LeMott finished the observation stoically. "That's why each murder was different, the weapons, the degree of brutality. He was experimenting. Trying to figure out what gave him the most . . . satisfaction."

You have to hear this over and over again, don't you? Like picking at a scab, keeping the pain alive because it's all you've got left.

23

"Yes."

"Has he figured it out yet?"

"You know I can't answer that. Too little to work with."

"I'll settle for an educated guess. From you."

Because you know it's much more than an educated guess. And I know now I made a mistake in telling you what's really special about the SCU.

Bishop also knew too well how utterly useless regrets like that one tended to be. The mistake had been made. Now he had to deal with the fallout.

He drew a breath and let it out slowly. "My guess, my belief, is that the response to Annie's abduction and murder threw him off balance. Badly. Until then, he had been almost blindly intent on satisfying the urges driving him. To kill a dozen victims in less than a month means something triggered his rampage, something very traumatic, and whatever it was, the trigger event either destroyed the person he had been until then, or else it freed something long dormant inside him."

"Something evil."

"About that, I have no doubts."

LeMott was frowning. "But even evil has a sense of self-preservation. The brightness of the unexpected spotlight following Annie's murder woke up that part of him. Or, at least, put it in control."

"Yes."

"And so he retreated. Found a safe place to hide."

"For now. To regroup, rethink. Consider his options. Perhaps even find a way to alter his developing rituals to fit this new dynamic."

"Because now he knows he's hunted."

Bishop nodded.

LeMott had given himself a crash course in the psychology of serial killers, immersing himself in the art and science of profiling despite Bishop's warnings, and his frown deepened now.

"Even if he was testing his limits or just figuring out what he needed to satisfy his cravings, to kill so many over such a short period of time and then just stop has to be unusual. How long can he possibly resist the sort of urges driving him?"

"Not long, I would have said."

"But it's been more than two months."

Bishop was silent.

"Or maybe it hasn't been," LeMott said slowly. "Maybe he's done a lot more than go to ground. Maybe he's adapted to being the hunted as well as hunter and changed his M.O. already. Dropped out of sight for a while, yes, but moved and began killing elsewhere. Killing differently than before. Altered his ritual. That's what you're thinking?"

Shit.

Weighing his words carefully, Bishop said, "Most serial killers have been active for months, even years, by the time law enforcement recognizes them for what they are, so there's more to work with in mapping the active and inactive cycles over time, the patterns and phases of behavior. We don't have that with this bastard. Not yet. He moved too fast. Appeared, slaughtered, and then disappeared back into whatever hell he crawled out of. We had no time to really study him. The only way we even pegged him as a serial was the undeniable fact that the young women he killed could have been sisters, they looked so alike.

"That was all we had, all we still have: that

he targeted women who were smaller than average, petite, almost waifish, with big eyes and short dark hair."

"Childlike," LeMott said, his voice holding steady.

Bishop nodded.

"I know I've asked you before, but—"

"Do I believe he could begin to target children? The accepted profile says he might. I say it isn't likely. He's killing the same woman over and over again, and **that** is the experience he's re-creating every time. Whatever else changes, he needs her to remain the same."

LeMott frowned. "But if he **is** changing or has already changed his ritual, if he knows he's being hunted and is as smart as you believe him to be, he must know what commonalities the police will be looking for in any murder case. He must know his M.O. is noted and flagged in every law-enforcement database in the country. Can we afford to assume he'll still target women who fit that victim profile?"

Bishop wasn't particularly reassured by the senator's calm expression and his matter-of-fact, professional tone; if anything, those were worrying signs.

Like nitroglycerin in a paper cup, looks could be terribly deceiving.

LeMott had kept a lid on his emotions for a long time now, and Bishop knew the pressure inside was going to blow that lid sky-high sooner or later.

A grieving father was bad enough. A grieving father with little left to lose was worse. And a grieving father who was also a powerful United States senator and former prosecutor with a reputation for having a tough stance on crime as well as a ruthless belief that justice be served no matter what was something way, way beyond worse.

But all Bishop said was, "He can't change who he is no matter how hard he tries. He'll try, of course. Try to overcome his urges and impulses, or just try to satisfy them in some way that won't betray who he is. But he'll give himself away somehow. They always do."

"At least to hunters who know what to look for."

"The problem isn't knowing what to look

for, it's the sickening knowledge that he has to kill again to give us something to look **at**."

"Always assuming he hasn't killed again and the murder was just different enough to fly under the radar." LeMott wasn't about to let that idea go, it was clear.

Bishop said, "That is a possibility, of course. Maybe even a probability. So I can't say with any certainty that he has or hasn't killed again since he murdered your daughter."

If he had hoped to distract LeMott, back him away, shake him somehow with those last three very deliberate words, Bishop was disappointed, because the senator didn't flinch. He didn't even blink. He just responded to the information Bishop had provided earlier.

"And yet you know he headed south. That he's somewhere near Atlanta."

Shit.

"And you know how I can be certain of that—without any real evidence—when the federal and police task force is still combing Boston for any sign of him."

"You **are** certain?"

"In my own mind, yes. He's not in Boston anymore. He's somewhere near Atlanta. Probably not the city itself, though it's certainly large enough to get lost in."

"You have someone there?"

"Senator, I've spent years building a network, and it's still growing. We have people just about everywhere."

"Human people. Fallible people."

Bishop heard the bitterness. "Yes, I'm afraid so. We believe he's in the area. We suspect he may have killed again. But we have no hard evidence of either belief—and the visible trail ends in Boston."

"How can you know so much—and yet so little of value?"

Bishop was silent.

LeMott shook his head, his mouth twisting. Blinking for the first time in too long, even looking away, however briefly. "Sorry. God knows and I know you've poured more than your energy and time into trying to find this bastard and stop him. Just . . . help me to understand how it's possible for us to do nothing except sit and wait for him to kill again."

Once more, Bishop chose his words with care. "Officially, there isn't much else I can do. All the hard evidence we've been able to find on this killer has been in Boston; all the victims we can be certain died by his hand lived and worked in Boston; all the tips and leads generated have been in Boston, and the task force is still following up on those, probably will be for months.

"My team has been ordered to remain in Boston and continue working with the task force for the duration. Unless and until we have strong evidence, solid evidence, that he's surfaced elsewhere, Boston is where we stay."

"I'd call that a waste of Bureau resources."

"Officially, it's being called the opposite. The city is still on edge, the national media is still there in force, and all the media—from TV and newspaper editorials to Internet blogs—call daily for more to be done to catch this killer before he targets another young woman. And the fact that his most recent victim was the daughter of a U.S. senator is virtually guaranteed to keep that spotlight very bright and that fire burning hot. For a very long time."

"Jobs are at stake."

"Yes."

"There's a new Director," LeMott said.

"Yes." Bishop's wide shoulders rose and fell in a faint shrug. "Politics. He's been brought in to fix what's wrong with the Bureau, to improve the very negative image a string of disastrous circumstances has left in the public's mind. Removing top agents from an investigation the entire country is watching wouldn't, from his point of view, be the best of moves."

"I could—"

"I'd rather you didn't. We may well need your influence at some point, but using it now isn't likely to help us—or the investigation."

LeMott nodded slowly. "I have to defer to your judgment on that."

Whether you want to or not. "Thank you."

"But why would the Director object to exchanging some of your people for more-conventional agents?"

"He doesn't really see the difference."

"Ah. The crux of the matter. He doesn't believe in psychic abilities."

"No. He doesn't." With another faint shrug, Bishop added, "We've weathered a changing of the guard before. We will again; our success record is too good to easily dismiss, no matter what the Director may or may not think about our methods. But in the interim . . ."

"You have to follow orders."

"If I want the SCU to continue, yes, I do. For now. At least officially."

"And unofficially?"

Reluctant for too many reasons to list, Bishop said, "Unofficially, there's Haven."

2

THE BOX CUTTER'S blade was new and sharp, so he used it with care as he cut around the part of the photo's image containing the girl.

She was pretty.

She was always pretty.

He enjoyed her curves. It was one reason he took such care in cutting the images out of the photographs and newspapers, because his knife could slowly—so slowly—caress the curves.

He was careful even with her face, though the curves of nose and chin and jaw barely caused a ripple inside him.

But her throat. The very slight, gentle curves of her breasts, just that faint hint of womanliness. The delicate flare of hips. Those his knife lingered on.

Sometimes he scanned the pictures into his computer and manipulated the images to suit a variety of fantasies. He could replace clothed flesh with naked, change all the different hairstyles to the short, dark, nearly boyish look she almost always wore. He could pose her any way he liked, do wild things with color and texture. He had even found autopsy photos and superimposed her head onto those bodies that were laid out, their exposed organs gleaming in the cold, clinical light.

But that sort of thing, he had discovered, gave him little satisfaction. It was too . . . remote.

Maybe that was it. Or maybe it was something else.

All he knew was that the computer, while useful as a research tool, had proved worse than useless in satisfying his urges.

But the photos . . .

He finished the last cut on this particular

photo and carefully lifted her out. A candid shot, it showed her coming out of a pharmacy, juggling bags, her face preoccupied.

Though it was October, the day was warm enough that she was wearing short sleeves and a light summer skirt, with sandals.

He thought her toenails were painted. Deep red, or perhaps bright pink. He was almost sure of it, though the picture didn't confirm that pleasant suspicion.

He held the cutout in his cupped hands for a moment, just enjoying it. His thumb rubbed the glossy paper gently, tracing the flare of her skirt, the bare thighs below.

He studied every detail, memorizing.

He closed his eyes.

And in his mind he touched her.

Soft skin. Warm. Almost humming with life.

The blade cold in his other hand.

His lips parted, breath coming faster.

Soft skin. Warm. A jerk now. The hum becoming a primal sound of terror and pain that sent fire licking through his body.

Soft skin. Wet. Slick.

Red.

He smeared the red over her jerking breast. Watched it glisten in the light as she moved. Listened to the **un . . . un . . . un . . .** grunts that were primitive sounds of agony. They thrummed in his ears like wings, like a heartbeat, like his own quickening pulse.

The fire in his body burned hotter and hotter, his breath came faster, the blade in his hand penetrating in forceful thrusts, again and again and again—

He barely heard his own hoarse cry of release above the wordless, keening sounds she made dying.

Soft skin.

Wet.

Slick.

Red.

3

COMING BACK TO Venture, Georgia, a relatively small town not far outside Atlanta, was not something Dani had wanted to do, so she hadn't exactly planned for it. Her apartment was still in Atlanta, along with most of her clothes and other belongings; she had packed as if for a weeklong vacation somewhere.

That had been nearly a month ago.

Not that clothing was a problem, given that she was living with her twin sister. But she and Paris had both worked very hard to have separate lives as adults, and living in the same house again wasn't really helping sustain that determination.

In fact, it made it all too easy to slip back into girlhood habits and routines. Like this weekly trip to Smith's Pharmacy downtown, because it was the only place in Venture that sold honest-to-God homemade ice cream from the lunch counter, which still did brisk business, and the twins had a lifetime habit of ice cream before bed every night.

Dani had missed this in Atlanta. Not that she hadn't continued the habit; she literally couldn't sleep without at least a small bowl of ice cream at night. But she'd had to substitute brand names for the homemade stuff, and there was simply no comparison in her mind.

Jeez.

Ice cream.

Thirty-one years old, and the treat she looked forward to all day long was ice cream shared with her twin sister before bedtime.

Bedtime at eleven o'clock most nights.

"I'm pathetic," she muttered, and dropped two of the bags she was juggling while trying to dig her car keys from the bottom of her purse.

"Let me."

Dani froze, watching a pair of very male hands pick up the dropped bags. Her gaze tracked upward slowly, following as he straightened to note that he was still whipcord-lean, that his shoulders were still wide and powerful, that he was still the sort of good-looking they wrote about in romance novels.

His dark hair was just beginning to gray at the temples, and there might have been a few more laugh lines at the corners of his steady blue eyes, but he still had the face of a heartbreaker.

Marcus Purcell.

Venture was a small-enough town that she had expected to run into him sooner or later. She had hoped for later.

Much later.

"Hey, Dani. How's tricks?"

The old childhood greeting brought an unexpected lump to her throat, but she thought her voice was calm enough to hide that when she replied as she always had.

"The rabbit ran away, but I still have the top hat. How're things in your magic show?"

"Not much of an act these days, I'm afraid.

The beautiful assistant got a better offer, and after that there didn't seem to be much point."

And there it was.

Trust Marc not to pussyfoot around a subject she would have avoided as long as necessary.

Avoidance was her defense mechanism, but hardly his.

"It wasn't a better offer," she heard herself say. "It was just . . . a change I needed. We both needed. You wanted to stay here, and I didn't."

"You never asked, Dani."

That shook her, but only for a moment. "Your roots were always here. I didn't have to ask. And you knew once Paris decided to stay here, I—"

"Wouldn't." He shrugged. "And yet here you are."

"Visiting. Because Paris needs me."

"Yeah, who's getting divorced is always a hot topic around here, so I heard. Tough on her. But she's better off without him."

"Oh? And why is that?" She was willing to talk about anything else, even her sister's painful divorce. Which told her something unsettling about her own feelings.

"Because there are just some things a man shouldn't say about his wife. Not even when he's drunk. Maybe especially not when he's drunk. And never to another man."

Dani couldn't bring herself to ask out loud but knew the question showed.

"Not much I'm willing to repeat, Dani. But he talked a lot, and probably in bars up and down the East Coast since he traveled so much. He said she was a literal ball and chain. Holding him down. Said he couldn't have anything to himself. Not his thoughts, not even his dreams. No private space she couldn't get into. He said she made his skin crawl sometimes."

"I knew he had trouble handling it, but . . ."

"There was no handling, believe me. Not for Dan. It was something he never accepted, never even got used to. Something he hated. Which is bad enough, considering he married Paris anyway. Telling strangers in bars that your wife really does know what you're thinking and dreaming and it makes you sick to your stomach is stepping way over the line." Marc shrugged. "Whether anybody ever listened to him or just chalked it up to drunken ramblings doesn't mitigate the fact that he acted like a jerk. He was drunk a lot toward the end. Spent more than one night in my jail, sobering up."

Paris had told her that Marc was sheriff now, but Dani felt the need to comment. And to change the subject. "I never thought you'd end up in law enforcement."

"Yeah, well, things change."

Not everything changed, Dani thought, but she felt unnerved and uncertain and was very aware that they were standing on the sidewalk in front of the pharmacy in downtown Venture, in full view of God and half the town's citizens, and that everybody south of God was taking it all in with interest.

"I should be going," she said abruptly. "My ice cream is melting."

To her utter relief, he didn't respond to that lame comment as it probably deserved, but merely said, "You were digging for your keys, I think. Find them?"

Dani produced the keys, used the remote to unlock the Jeep parked only a few yards away, and, as its headlights flashed in acknowledgment, accepted the bags he held out to her.

"Take care, Dani."

It held the sound of finality, something she should have accepted gratefully, but he hadn't moved more than a few steps away from her when she heard herself speak. And even as she did, she was aware of a fatalistic certainty that she was turning a critical corner in her life.

And had no idea what lay ahead.

"Marc?"

He paused and looked back at her, eyebrows lifting but otherwise expressionless.

"Has anything . . . bad happened in Venture lately? In the county? I mean, anything really bad? I read the paper, but—"

"Are you talking about a crime?"

"Yeah."

He was frowning now. "Nothing really out of the ordinary. A few robberies, domestic disturbances, possession, a couple of meth labs busted."

"Nothing else?"

Slowly, he replied, "Two missing persons I've been uneasy about."

"Women?"

"One teenage girl; her parents believe she ran away a couple of weeks ago. One wife

45

whose very scared husband insists would never have left him of her own free will."

"How long ago was that?"

"Last week. And no sign of her yet. What do you know, Dani?"

"Nothing. I don't . . . know . . . anything. Just . . . be careful, that's all."

He took a step back toward her and kept his voice low even though nobody else was near. "What have you dreamed, Dani?"

She couldn't look away from him. And she couldn't lie.

Not to Marc.

"There's nothing concrete. No name or face. Not even a crime I can be sure of, except . . . except that it's bad." She thought of a missing teenager, a missing wife, and felt cold despite the warm early-afternoon October sun. "I know that it's bad, that it's a poison here. Somebody evil, I don't know who."

"Dani, we both know evil doesn't wear horns and a tail to signal that it's with us. If there's anything else you can tell me—"

"There isn't. Not yet, at least."

Marc's frown deepened, and he took another step toward her. "You've had this dream more than once?"

She nodded, unwilling to admit that it was pretty much a nightly occurrence now.

"Okay. Tonight, come get me. Take me in with you."

Dani realized only later that she wasn't nearly as shocked by the idea as she should have been. In that moment, however, she just shook her head and said, "I can't do that."

"Sure you can. You've done it before."

"That was years ago, Marc. Another lifetime ago." **And I had no idea how dangerous it was.**

He took another step, and now he was standing in front of her, so close she had to tilt her head to look up at his face.

"It never made **my** skin crawl, Dani," he said softly. "It never creeped me out. It was never something I hated. It never made me think of you as anything other than the unique and remarkable woman I loved. Just in case you didn't know that."

She had the vague suspicion that her mouth was open.

47

"Come get me tonight," Marc repeated. He turned and walked away.

Somehow Dani managed to get herself and her bags into the Jeep. She thought the home-made raisin cake she'd bought was probably crushed, because she'd been holding on to those bags for dear life, and she was sure now that the ice cream was melting. She didn't much care about either.

Just in case she didn't know.

Just in case she didn't know.

Jesus Christ Almighty.

She was still rattled when her cell phone rang, and it took several rings for her to dig it out of her purse. Making a mental note to get another damn purse or at least to better organize this one, she answered, knowing without the need for caller I.D. that it was Paris.

"We have visitors," Paris announced without preamble.

Dani closed her eyes. "Don't tell me."

"Afraid so. Miranda Bishop is here. With John."

———

Deputy Jordan Swain prided himself on his professionalism. His dedication and intelligence. His rapier wit. And his ability to look like a cool stud in his uniform, thanks to the kind genetics of blond good looks and a rigorous morning workout routine.

He was also well known for his cast-iron stomach, and it was that which failed him late Wednesday afternoon.

"Sorry about that," he muttered, as he returned from his hasty visit to the bushes a few yards away and well outside the yellow crime-scene tape.

With a grunt, the sheriff said, "Well, at least you made it outside the tape. I would have been pissed if you'd contaminated the scene, Jordan."

"How could I possibly have contaminated it any more than it already is?"

"Funny."

"Actually, it isn't." Jordan swallowed and tried not to think about all the blood and viscera spattered and scattered around them. Which was more than difficult since it **was** all around them and pretty damn well impossible to miss.

The house—vacant and with a FOR SALE sign in the neat front yard—was at the end of a long driveway and on considerable acreage, which was probably why nobody had noticed the butchery that had taken place in the well-maintained, previously very lovely and peaceful backyard patio/pool area.

Nobody, that is, until the gardener had shown up for his routine maintenance work and rounded the back corner of the house, his wheelbarrow filled with the tools and implements he needed to begin getting the plantings ready for the coming winter.

The wheelbarrow, overturned, lay where he had abandoned it just outside the pool area, when he had fled after his first glimpse of the carnage.

And it was a scene of carnage. The comparison that had sent Jordan fleeing into the bushes to lose his lunch was that it looked rather like someone had fed a medium-size cow into a wood chipper.

"Jesus, Marc, what kind of animal would do something like this?"

"The kind we have to catch." Marc held up a clear plastic evidence bag containing a very large, very bloody hunting knife with a serrated edge. He studied it with a frown. "How many places you figure sell these?"

"Oh, hell, at least a dozen or more in the county. Not counting pawnshops."

Marc nodded. "That was my take. We're not likely to get any kind of useful lead from this. Plus, leaving it right here at the scene marks the perp as either very stupid—or very sure we won't be able to trace the knife back to him."

"I hate to think of anybody this vicious being smart too," Jordan said, "but I think we'd regret assuming otherwise."

"Yeah. Still, we'll find out what we can."

"Might get lucky," Jordan agreed somewhat dubiously.

Marc sent him a wry look, then summoned with a gesture one of his two crime-scene technicians and handed over the knife. "Shorty, you or Teresa find anything we can't see for ourselves?"

"Not so far, Sheriff." Shorty, who in the grand tradition of nicknames towered over both other men and, indeed, most people, blinked sleepy eyes and appeared to stifle a yawn. "Might have to move the tape back a few yards, though; I think I've found a couple pieces of her right at the periphery of the area."

Jordan, who had been about to make a caustic demand to know if they were keeping Shorty up, absorbed this new information with another sick twist of his stomach.

Stoic, Marc said, "So the vic **was** a woman."

"Hard to tell without the . . . relevant parts," Shorty said, "but Teresa thinks so. Me too. We found the tip of a finger with a polished acrylic nail still attached. A pinky, I think."

Jordan retired to the bushes again.

Shorty looked after him briefly, then directed his attention back to the sheriff's expressionless face. "My excuse is five years of morgue duty in Atlanta," he said. "What's yours?"

"Rage," Marc Purcell said.

"Ah. You wear your mad like a shield. I've known other cops could do that." Shorty nodded, studying the sheriff openly. This fairly rural county tended to see few murder cases, and most of those were the domestic or grudge type, where the killer was as obvious as the victim was, as like as not still standing over the body, looking bewildered, smoking gun or bloody knife in hand.

Not so hard to solve, those cases.

In the two years Shorty had been with the Prophet County Sheriff's Department, this was the first real murder scene he had worked with Purcell.

Interesting guy, Shorty thought. Born here, raised here. Went to a top university in North Carolina, earned a law degree, and returned to Venture to practice. Word around the department was that he'd always been slated to hold some kind of elected office, that it was a family thing going back generations, but everybody seemed a bit surprised he'd chosen law enforcement over other political opportunities.

Shorty wasn't surprised. He'd spent his entire adult life around cops, and this guy was a cop down to his bones. There were some like that, maybe with an innate sense of justice or just outrage—as Purcell had admitted—that the world was chaotic and needed somebody to at least try to impose order. Somebody to wear the white hat and fight the good fight.

A lost cause, Shorty thought, because the bad guys these days were well funded and had access to way too many dangerous toys. But, hey, there were sure as hell worse things to live your life in pursuit of. He was quite aware of that, since his own ambitions usually went no further than a warm and willing piece of ass for the upcoming weekend.

Apparently oblivious to the scrutiny, the sheriff said, "Am I wrong in thinking she was killed here, not just butchered here?"

"There's some arterial spray over there by the pool, so, yeah, I'd say so. Dunno if she was conscious, but I think she was alive for quite a while from the time she first started bleeding."

"You're saying he tortured her?"

"I'm saying he wanted her to bleed, Sheriff. And from all the bloody drag marks, he moved her around while he was doing it."

"Why, for Christ's sake?"

"Maybe he was painting a picture for us." Shorty grimaced when the sheriff stared at him. "Sorry. But I'm not being flippant about that. Most of the drag marks show she was a deadweight—no pun intended—when he was moving her around." He gestured to one area of the stamped concrete nearest them that even a layman would have defined as a bloody drag mark.

"Like that one. And the one on the other side of the pool. I'm no profiler, but I've seen more than my share of bloody murder scenes and this one is . . . really, really weird."

"I wish you'd just said grisly and horrible."

Shorty looked at him curiously and then offered a shrug. "Like I said, I've seen bloody crime scenes before. But most of 'em, they're the result of somebody getting pissed beyond belief and going nuts. If a knife is the weapon, they stab, they slash, they chase after the vic as long as he or she is still moving. But the only reason they move the body afterward is to get rid of it.

"This guy, either he couldn't make up his mind where he intended to leave the body or . . . or he was just having fun. Maybe posing her. Cutting off a piece of her here and there. I'd swear at least a few of the internal organs were placed, arranged, and very carefully."

With no discernible emotion, Purcell said,

"Like the heart on the end of the diving board?"

"Yeah. I imagine a shrink could have a field day with that. Just like they could write a paper or two on why he decided to wrap twelve inches of her small intestine around that rosebush and why exactly half her liver is lying in the center of the birdbath over there. We haven't found the other half yet."

Purcell drew a breath. "Shorty, how much of her **isn't** here?"

"Well, a lot, really. The tip of that one finger is the only bone we've found. A lot of skin, but it's in pieces, like everything else. Most of the internal organs are here, including some brain matter."

"He gutted her **and** opened her head."

"Looks like. We haven't found any scalp so far, but there's what looks to me like an ax or hatchet mark in the stone of the pool coping, and that's where we found the brain matter."

"The knife couldn't have . . . ?"

"Nah, it would have taken something with a lot more heft and a solid edge. Hatchet is about as small as I'd go, and it would have to be a good sharp one. Could be something larger, but the cut in the stone is only about four inches from end to end, and the edges are distinct, so I wouldn't think it's any sort of long, curved blade. My money's on an ax or a hatchet."

"We didn't find either."

"Not so far. Maybe that was his personal toy and he didn't want to leave it behind."

"Yeah. Yeah, maybe."

"There were a couple hairs in that cut as well, not obvious because of the gore. Too bloody to make out the color now, but, well, once we get back to the lab, at least we'll know a bit more about her. Again, I'm no profiler, but I think he probably didn't mean to leave any hair at all, so the little we found may turn out to be important."

Purcell stared rather fixedly at the end of the diving board over the red-tinted pool, where the heart of a murdered woman still lay, and Shorty thought he was holding on to his mad with both hands and a hellacious willpower.

"The fingertip," the sheriff said at last. "Enough for a print?"

"It's enough."

"Good. Get me that print, Shorty. And every other bit of information you can, including your own theories and suppositions. I even want to hear your guesses. Understood?"

Shorty didn't bother with a verbal okay, just nodded and moved a bit quicker than was normal for him to get back to doing his job. Mad made a dandy shield, he thought, but Marc Purcell's mad was beginning to smolder.

He didn't want to be close when it finally exploded.

She knew.

Marc wondered if this was what Dani had dreamed, and hoped to hell it wasn't. Not this.

But she had known something bad would happen, or had already happened, and this was about as bad as Marc ever wanted to see.

Except that he had a leaden feeling in the pit of his stomach that told him this was just the beginning, that things were going to get a lot worse before they got better. Dani had looked worried, which was unusual enough;

she didn't give away much and never had. But, even more, he had felt her anxiety, like a jolt to the gut, and the sudden reawakening of that old connection had caught him off guard.

So off guard that he had said more than he'd intended to about his own feelings.

"Marc? Sorry about that." Jordan sounded as queasy as he looked, his complexion pasty and his eyes sick. "But I just don't think—"

"Go back to the station," Marc told him, pushing aside everything but the job he had to do. "Check if we have prints on either Bob Norvell's wife, Karen, or the Huntley girl, Becky. If we don't have them on file, send a couple of teams with kits to their homes and get them there."

If anything, Jordan looked sicker. "The families are bound to ask why. What do I say to them?"

Marc didn't hesitate. "That we need all the information we can get to find missing persons, and prints are more valuable than photos in some cases." This time he did hesitate, before adding steadily, "Tell the teams to find something with DNA. Hairbrush, razor, toothbrush, whatever might give us what we need. And tell them to be subtle about it."

"So we don't tell the families about . . . this?"

"Not until we know something for sure. Until then, I want this kept as quiet as possible, Jordan, understand? Anybody talks to the media is going to be looking for a new job tomorrow, and it won't be with a reference."

"I understand, Marc, and so will the rest here. But you know as well as I do that we won't keep it quiet for long."

"As long as we can." His cell phone rang, and he answered it before the second ring. "Yeah?"

"Marc, it's Dani. I know you're busy, but—"

"You know where I am? What I'm looking at?" Marc realized that his voice was too harsh, but there didn't seem to be anything he could do about it.

The silence on the other end of the line was brief, and then she said quietly, "I know. There are some people you need to meet. Here, at Paris's house. Can you come?"

"I'm on my way," Marc said.

4

H E HAD TO CUT HER image from another photograph because the first one got all crumpled, but that was okay.

He always made copies.

With some of his tension eased, the jagged edge of his need blunted, he was able to carefully remove all the uninteresting bits from the picture, leaving only her.

He set her aside and reached for the next picture, this time cutting her out from the background of a gas station where she'd been standing by her car, pumping gas.

The next was of her walking a dog in the park. He debated but in the end cut the dog out as well.

Huh. He hadn't really thought about dogs, but—

His mind shied, and he frowned to himself. No, not dogs. Not animals.

She didn't even like animals. Could never bear to have them in the yard, much less in the house. Dirty things.

"Dirty, dirty things!"

"No. Not dogs. Not animals. They don't matter."

He cut the dog from the shot and dropped it in his trash can.

Just her, then.

Just her.

He worked steadily through the stack of photos until he'd done them all, cutting her meticulously from each shot and tossing the remainder of each photo into the trash.

When he was done, he gently gathered up the pictures of her and carried them into the next room.

The room was large, and the thick concrete walls made it both chilly and something of an echo chamber. He enjoyed both attributes, though his recent work had diminished the echo effect at least a bit.

There was a bright spotlight beaming down onto a stainless-steel table in the center of the room, but he ignored that for the moment. Instead, he went to one of the walls, where a long strip of halogen track lighting on one of the beams above provided smaller spotlights, which were carefully aimed and focused on the precise geometric arrangement of squares of corkboard that lined the entire long wall from concrete floor to open-beamed ceiling.

Everything lined up perfectly.

He had used a laser level. Nifty thing, very helpful.

Each square of corkboard was two feet by two feet, and each was framed by a thick line of black paint that served to separate it from the adjoining squares. Three of the squares were nearly filled with cutouts of women, each individual woman getting her own square, and no two of the squares side by side or even near each other.

"We live alone," he murmured. "We die alone."

He stood back for a moment, then chose a square near the center of the room, again making sure it was isolated from the others.

He pulled a wheeled stainless-steel work cart nearer the square, placed his pictures carefully on the shiny surface, and opened a waiting plastic box holding white pushpins.

It took him at least fifteen minutes to place the pictures carefully, to pin them onto the corkboard. He left space, of course, for other pictures. There would be others.

These pictures came first. The hunting.

And then her.

And then pictures of her metamorphosis would join the others on her board. Until at last it was complete. Until she was complete.

He turned finally from his display wall and went to the center of the room, and to the table.

She was secure, of course. He was always careful about that. And the drugs had done their work; she was only now coming out of it, eyes fluttering, trying to focus.

He waited until they did, until she saw him. Watched those eyes widen and grow terrified.

He smiled down at her.

"Hello, sweetheart. We're going to have so much fun."

5

EVEN WITH DAYLIGHT savings time still in effect, the sun was going down and the air had grown decidedly chillier by the time Marc pulled his unmarked cruiser into the driveway of Paris Kincaid's rehabbed farmhouse on the edge of town. He assumed Paris's BMW was in the garage, since he didn't see it and since she was known to be finicky about leaving it out in the weather.

Dani's Jeep was in the drive ahead of Marc's cruiser. And parked beside it was an innocuous black SUV.

Innocuous, my ass. Why not just use plates that say FED?

Standard Georgia license plates or not, Marc knew a federal vehicle when he was staring at one.

And because he didn't really want to think about why federal agents would be here now, on this particular day, unsummoned and, please God, unneeded, he chose to focus instead on the irritatingly neon choice of vehicle.

Even with all the SUVs on the road, there was just something about this one that screamed out what it was. Way too obvious for his taste. Marc never wore a uniform, did not carry his weapon openly if he could avoid it, and had made certain his "unmarked" cruiser looked more like a businessman's nice car than one belonging to a law-enforcement official.

He didn't like to be all that visible while he kept an eye on his town; his might be a political position in some minds, but not in his, and he probably knew more about what went on in Venture than any sheriff before him could have claimed.

Not that it was always a pleasure to be so well informed.

Like now. Knowing that at least one citizen of Venture had died horribly and they had so far found only pieces of her made his stomach churn in a way his chief deputy would have recognized. The difference was that Jordan could get physically sick and pretty much rid himself of the poisons—and sleep like a baby tonight.

Marc would be having nightmares for weeks.

Assuming he could even sleep.

Dani met him on the front porch, her face pale and drawn, the earlier worry now even more obvious. "I'm sorry," she said immediately. "When we talked before, in town, I didn't know."

"You knew something." It wasn't—quite—an accusation.

"Something. But not that. What I knew—what I know or think I know—hasn't happened yet."

Marc considered that briefly, then shrugged it off to be dealt with later. Right now he had to be concerned with what had happened, not what might. "When you called a few minutes ago, you knew."

"Because somebody told me. Come in, Marc. There are people here you need to meet."

Feds. But why come like this? Why so . . . unofficially? He didn't budge. "So you said. What people?"

Dani didn't seem surprised or put out by his stubbornness, and answered readily. "John Garrett, for one. You've probably heard of him."

"I've heard he's a very wealthy man and a very powerful one. I don't know what the hell he'd be doing in Venture."

"He's also a good man, trying to make a difference. He and his wife, Maggie, run the . . . company Paris and I work for. You know about Haven?"

"I know it's not federal."

"No. Privately run."

"I don't know much more than that. I knew Paris traveled some for work, but far as I can recall she never said much about her job, other than mentioning the name one day in passing. She did seem to have very flexible hours and workdays."

"I guess people have noticed that," Dani murmured.

"When you're gone for a week and then don't seem to work again for a month or more, yeah, people do notice. Honestly, though, most assumed, at least this last year or so, that Paris was still being supported by her ex."

"Damn. She'll hate that if she finds out."

"I'd be real surprised if she didn't already know. The gossip in Venture is hardly a furtive thing; it's a recreational activity. Want me to tell you how many cities Dan's job has taken him to in the last year? I understand there was some betting as to whether he and Paris met up at least twice for reconciliation attempts."

"I hope you bet against that."

"As a matter of fact, I did." Quite deliberately, he added, "I'm a bit better than the average Venture citizen at reading the Justice twins."

For an instant he thought she would challenge him on that point, but in the end Dani pushed it aside with a gesture. "But the town doesn't know much about Haven. Do you know any more than that?"

"I admit I got curious. Asked around. Police scuttlebutt says it's a civilian organization of mavericks, supposedly psychics, people just barely this side of the lunatic fringe."

"Thanks a lot."

"I'm just telling you what I've heard."

Despite her words, Dani didn't appear to be offended, and just nodded. "Okay. What else have you heard?"

"That the services Haven offers run the gamut from advising on police cases and running independent investigations of things like insurance fraud to going undercover in big companies to find evidence of industrial and corporate espionage. And that you guys will investigate just about anything—for a price."

Half under her breath, Dani said, "John was right. We need to work on our image."

"Does the scuttlebutt have it wrong?"

"The bare bones of it, no. We are mostly psychic, varying abilities and degrees of strength and control. A lot of us are . . . a bit out of the norm even among psychics, with abilities you won't find named in any of the reference books. We have extremely flexible hours because each of us has an ability that may be useful to a particular case or investigation but certainly not all of them. Paris and me . . . well, you of all people must know that what we can do wouldn't be all that handy in investigating anything under ordinary circumstances."

"Considering you're precognitive only when dreaming, and Paris's abilities barely register unless you two team up, yeah, I can see how that could be a drawback in using the abilities as tools."

"Exactly."

"And yet you get work."

She nodded. "You'd be surprised how many **extra**ordinary circumstances there are. Or maybe you wouldn't be. I was."

Instead of asking about particulars, Marc said, "Was the gossip right about what Haven offers?"

"We do advise and investigate. Work with police as well as private companies and individuals. We do go undercover, if the situation calls for it."

"Services for sale to the highest bidder?"

She shook her head. "No, that part's wrong. Really wrong. Look, do you know about the FBI's Special Crimes Unit?"

Ahhhh.

The presence of the federal vehicle in

Paris's driveway now began to make sense—though he was still suspicious of and very much worried about the timing.

"I've heard of it," Marc replied. "Gained a rep in the last few years for solid police work and a very high solved-case percentage. Also considered by local law enforcement wherever they've worked to be trustworthy, because they do what they say they do—advise and aid, not take over. And they don't want the credit, not publicly. In fact, they stay as far out of the spotlight as they can get."

"Haven is basically a civilian offshoot of the SCU. John Garrett has a good friend in the unit, and there was an investigation he became a part of—and one thing led to another. The idea for a civilian organization made sense, if only to make use of talent going to waste. In putting together the unit, its chief had located any number of strong psychics who just weren't suited to be cops, federal or any other kind."

"Mavericks?"

Dani began to shake her head, then shrugged. "Some, sure. People who don't like rules, who don't . . . play well with others.

Emotional baggage is probably the norm rather than the exception, and that can get in the way, more for some than others. I mean, using psychic abilities can look a lot like conning somebody, and plenty of us have had bad experiences with the police. Plus, just being psychic seems to make some of us . . . fragile. Difficult to work with, or at least unable to work within certain rigid structures such as law enforcement."

"So you work outside the law."

"We're not crooks or con artists, Marc."

"No?"

"No." She let out a little breath, and added, "I didn't think I'd have to convince you. Not you."

"Convince me of what, Dani? That psychic ability is real? We both know I'm in the believer's camp on that one. That doesn't mean I can automatically agree that mixing unstable psychics with a killer who has to be the poster boy for unstable is a good idea."

She flinched visibly. "Miranda said it was bad, but—"

"Who's Miranda? A fed or part of Haven?"

"She's SCU. Her husband, Noah Bishop,

created the Special Crimes Unit, fought for it, recruited the right people. He's officially the unit chief, but they run it together. They share . . . a unique connection. Come inside, Marc. Listen to what we have to tell you."

He still didn't budge. "I don't recall asking for help."

Dani hesitated, then said steadily, "I think most sheriffs in your position would wait. Investigate this one murder **as** a single murder. And then the next one. And maybe, before the third one or just after, he'd realize he had a serial killer on his hands. That's when he'd ask for help. And by then it would be too late."

"Most sheriffs."

"Yes. But not you."

"Because?"

"Because it's not about ego with you, it's about justice. Because you have a better sense than most that there are dark forces all around us—all the time. And because what you saw today was only the tip of the iceberg, and that's something you feel. Something you know deep inside yourself."

"Dani—"

"It's evil, Marc. What's underneath the surface you saw today is pure, raw evil. Something no amount of conventional police work can even begin to handle."

She drew a breath and added, "And you know it."

Jordan Swain, in addition to priding himself on his good looks, also prided himself on the fact that he was a good cop. He hadn't joined the sheriff's department just because it was better than a job selling insurance or real estate or something.

He genuinely wanted to help people.

Until now, he had cruised along his career path pretty much as planned.

Until now.

"The first halfway free day we get," Teresa Miller was telling him grimly, "Shorty and I are teaching all the rest of you how to collect latents and DNA evidence."

"Teresa, I know it's asking a lot, but—"

"A lot? Christ, Jordan, you were the one tossing his cookies at the scene—what was it?—at least twice today."

"I'm not ashamed of it," he said with total honesty. "If I'd wanted to look close-up at blood and guts, I would have gone into your end of police work. But **you** went into that end, Teresa. And until we get that halfway free day, I need you to lead one team and Shorty the other to collect prints and DNA from the Norvell and Huntley homes."

"Shit."

"Today."

"There's no day left in today, Jordan. And why does it have to be now?"

"Because the sheriff said so. Because it should have been done already, when we got the missing-persons reports."

"That's not SOP, not for every missing person."

"It is now. Look, Teresa, I'm sorry. But I need you and Shorty to do this. You're both getting double overtime, if that helps."

She sighed and for the first time looked simply weary. "It doesn't help much. I don't know how I'm going to face either of those families, knowing I've probably been picking up pieces of their loved one half the afternoon."

"Yeah. Yeah, I know."

She squared her shoulders. "Okay, I'll tell Shorty and we'll pick our teams. They can print family members for elimination while we collect all the latents we can find. And DNA, if we can find that."

"Sheriff said to try not to alert the families we're looking for DNA," Jordan reminded her.

"Yeah, I heard you the first time. But you can tell the sheriff from me that I think he'd better come clean with the families about what we found today—and soon. Because we both know they're going to hear about it."

"We need a positive I.D., Teresa. Maybe we'll be able to spare at least one of the families the certainty that a daughter or a wife was hacked up and left in pieces."

A hollow laugh escaped Teresa. "You think we'll be able to do that?"

The question caught him off guard. "If we get a positive I.D., we'll be able to eliminate—" He broke off, going cold inside, because Teresa was slowly shaking her head. "What?"

"Jordan, I had some preliminary tests run on the early blood and tissue samples we took out there."

"And?" All of a sudden he really wished he could take back that question. But it was too late.

"And I can tell you right now that we have blood and tissue from at least two victims. At least."

If Marc hadn't known before being introduced to the two strangers waiting for him in Paris's living room that Miranda Bishop was with the SCU, he would have pegged the wrong one as the fed.

John Garrett really looked the part.

He was a big man, broad-shouldered and athletic, with dark hair and the level gaze of someone accustomed to command, and the dark suit he wore only intensified that impression.

Miranda Bishop, on the other hand, was casual, in a silk blouse and jeans that did nothing to disguise her centerfold measurements, with her longish jet-black hair pulled back at the nape of her neck—and was the first woman Marc had ever met in the flesh who was absolutely drop-dead gorgeous.

That was his first impression.

Shaking hands with her a moment later, he looked into electric-blue eyes and knew immediately that her stunning exterior was the least important aspect of her. He could easily see her as a federal agent handling herself in any dangerous situation that came along.

But even more—

"You're a telepath," he said. "And not just that. A seer. And you have one hell of a shield."

"Told you," Dani murmured.

Miranda released his hand, smiling faintly. "And you," she said pleasantly, "are a rare bird in our universe. A nonpsychic with the ability to recognize psychic abilities in others. Even shielded abilities."

"It hasn't been much of a gift," Marc told her, avoiding so much as a glance at Dani. "Passive in the extreme."

"But it could be helpful," John Garrett said as the two men were introduced and shook hands. "Under the right circumstances."

"Maybe. Not circumstances I've encountered so far, however."

Paris spoke up then to say dryly, "You just haven't been running with the right crowd, Marc. Have a seat."

"I have a murder to investigate," he said.

"You wouldn't have come this far if you hadn't been willing to listen. Have a seat."

She was right. Dammit.

Marc sat down.

The room was spacious for a relatively small house, but not so spacious that there was much real distance between any of the five people in it. Except for two of them.

Dani was sitting in a chair not three feet away from the one Marc chose, but he thought she was nevertheless far away from him, despite the faint connection he could still feel. She seemed shut in herself, withdrawn, and he knew it was deliberate.

Even as a kid she had done that, isolating herself from those closest to her when something went wrong. Not because she didn't care, but because she felt things a lot more deeply than she ever wanted to show. Because she didn't want to see some of the things her ties to people allowed her to see. And it was probably the twin thing, too, Marc had decided, the need to be her own person, apart from Paris.

Maybe that was why she had grown up resisting anybody getting too close, resisting attachments. Marc had wondered many times since if, in trying to hold on to her ten years ago, he had actually driven her away by grabbing and holding too tightly.

He caught a glance from Paris and realized that even Dani's twin was worried about her. Which was not a good sign. The question in Marc's mind was whether it was the situation that was affecting Dani—or the people involved.

Was she still trying to pull away from him, him in particular, especially in light of his impulsive words on a very public sidewalk today?

John Garrett said matter-of-factly, "You know I'm not psychic."

Marc didn't even have to concentrate, though he did have to shift his focus back to the matter at hand, and it was more difficult to do that than he had expected. "I do know that. And yet you run an organization designed to make use of the psychic abilities of your people."

"My wife is an empath, and my best friend a seer." Garrett shrugged with a rueful smile. "I'm the one with the business-oriented mind. Somehow it all made sense."

"I can understand that. What I can't understand is what you're doing here. In Venture. You or Agent Bishop."

A faint laugh escaped Miranda Bishop. "Miranda, please. Most people call my husband by his surname alone, so there's really only one Bishop in the family. And in the unit."

"Okay, Miranda it is. I'm Marc."

She nodded, exchanged glances with Garrett, then said, "We're here because of the predator hunting in Venture. You found the partial remains of one or more of his victims today."

"One or **more**?" It wasn't as much of a surprise as Marc wished it was; the leaden feeling in his gut had been telling him for some time that both the missing women were already dead.

"There are probably two victims so far," Miranda said. "At least."

"Am I supposed to assume you know all this because you're a seer?"

"If you're wondering whether I knew in advance that he'd strike here, the answer is no. We'd been tracking him from his last hunting field, using a network of agents and John's people."

"A network?"

Garrett said, "Bishop had the idea, the goal, of building a network of psychics, who could be activated at a moment's notice in any given area to aid police in especially difficult investigations. He started with his unit—with federal agents—of course, and built on that base. There are other law-enforcement officers he's reached out to, people scattered across the country, working their own cases but available and willing to help us if we need them. And I've been building the civilian branches of the network. Haven. We aren't cops, but all of our active investigators are trained and licensed P.I.s."

Marc looked at Dani. "You're a private investigator?"

She looked at him directly for the first time

since they'd entered the house, if only fleet-ingly. "No. I'm not an active investigator."

"Dani's abilities," Garrett said, "are specialized, as you know."

"Passive," she said, with another glance at Marc. "Even psychics can have totally passive abilities."

Marc saw both Paris and Miranda frown slightly, but neither of them challenged Dani's statement. Instead, the federal agent got them back on topic.

"Between the SCU, others in law enforcement, and Haven, our network of available psychics has grown even more quickly than we anticipated. Recently, we've been . . . experimenting somewhat."

"By tracking killers?" Marc asked.

"More or less."

"Successfully?"

"Results have been spotty," she admitted readily. "Probably not surprising, given the varying strengths and abilities of our people."

"But you feel confident that you know who butchered at least one young woman here in Venture sometime in the last twenty-four hours?"

"Who—yes. But not in the helpful sense of knowing his name or even what he looks like."

"So what you **know** is that he's a serial you've tracked from a prior hunting ground." He didn't make it a question, because he had no doubt that was the answer.

Miranda nodded. "Afraid so."

"And you're absolutely sure?"

"Marc, I'm not **absolutely** sure the sun will rise tomorrow. Pretty sure, mind you, but not absolutely sure." She shrugged. "Could I testify under oath in a courtroom? Not with facts. But feelings? Psychic certainty? Am I sure in my own mind who this bastard is? Yes."

"Because you had a vision?"

"No. Because another of our psychics got a hit. And she's very accurate. It's the same killer."

"You haven't even studied the scene," Marc said, knowing the objection was purely a matter of form.

"Yes," Miranda said. "I have. I just wasn't there at the time."

6

THE FACT THAT JORDAN chose, in the end, to accompany Teresa and her team out to the Norvell home had less to do with any urge to learn how to collect forensic evidence and more to do with his feeling that while he might not be strong in science, he understood people. And he had learned early as a cop that there were few things more helpful in any investigation than gathering information from people rather than from paperwork.

But this was his first experience with a missing and probably dead victim—and a distraught husband.

A distraught husband he'd gone to school with.

"You're **sure** there's no word about Karen?" Bob Norvell waved the forensics team toward the bedrooms at the rear of the small, well-kept house but kept his gaze fixed on Jordan.

"We're doing everything we can to find her, Bob, you know that." Jordan was a lot more uncomfortable than he'd expected and had to concentrate to keep his expression professional—and impassive.

"She wouldn't have left me, Jordan. You know that, right? That she wouldn't have left me?"

"Yeah, Bob, I know that. Everybody says you guys were—are—happy together."

If Norvell noticed the slip, he ignored it. "She wouldn't have left me, and there was no reason anybody would want to hurt her. Not Karen. Karen's a sweetheart, she really is. Everybody likes her."

"Bob, why don't we sit down? It may take a few minutes for the team to do its work, so . . ."

"Yeah, sure, I'm sorry." Norvell led the way into the living room, adding, "Can I get you anything? Coffee or something?"

"No, thanks." Jordan regretted that almost immediately, realizing that giving Norvell something to do probably would have been a good idea, at least to the extent of giving the deputy a break from that anxious gaze.

Coward! Do your job, for Christ's sake!

As they sat down, Jordan made a determined effort to be professional. "I've read the report, of course, Bob, but I wanted to ask if there was anything else you could tell me, anything you might have thought of in the last few days."

"Like what?"

"Before she disappeared, was Karen different in any way? Did she seem nervous or worried?"

Norvell shook his head. "No, she was just the same as always. I kissed her good-bye and went to work—she had a day off from the bank, but I didn't—and when I got home she wasn't here." His face crumpled suddenly. "I should have got her that dog. She wanted a little dog to keep her company when I wasn't here, especially when I was gone overnight for business. I really should have got her that dog."

Wary of the emotional storm he could see

looming, Jordan said quickly, "Had you noticed anything different yourself? I mean, had you seen anybody hanging around in the neighborhood, a stranger or just somebody who made the hair on the back of your neck stand up for no reason you could be sure of?"

"Around here? No."

"And Karen didn't mention anything? She hadn't seen anything or anyone that made her uneasy?"

Norvell frowned suddenly. "Wait a minute. She did say the girls at the bank teased her about somebody taking pictures of her, that she had a secret admirer. She laughed it off, said she thought they were pulling her leg, because she never saw anybody."

"When was this?"

"Oh, hell, Jordan, it was back in the summer. I remember because she hadn't mentioned it to me until we were at the beach on vacation. To be honest, it sort of **did** make the hair on the back of my neck stand up, if just for a second or two. You remember how it was back in the summer; you couldn't turn on the news without hearing about this killer or that stalker, like the whole country was full of psychos, so I was worried. But she laughed it off. And by the time we got home . . ."

By the time they returned home, both suspicion and uneasiness had been forgotten. Understandably.

"I'll talk to the girls at the bank," Jordan said briskly, "and see if they remember anything that might help us. It's probably nothing, Bob, but it won't hurt to check."

"You'll let me know if you find out anything?"

"Of course. Of course I will." Jordan felt like a bastard, a part of him wanting to warn Bob Norvell to start his grieving now. But the cop, of course, kept the man silent.

"I should have got her that dog," Norvell mumbled.

You can go the formal route, of course," Miranda Bishop told Marc. "Contact the FBI, report the crime and your suspicion that you could have a serial operating here in Venture."

"And?"

"And the Bureau, following procedure, would have Behavioral Science study all the crime-scene information, possibly contact and interview some of your people, and formulate a profile of the unknown subject. Your killer."

Nobody had ever accused Marc of being slow on the uptake. "Bureaucratic red tape. Which would take how long?"

"You might get a preliminary profile in a week, more likely two or three weeks given the Bureau's current workload. And it would of course be based only on what's happened here, treating this killer and this hunting ground as unique."

Marc leaned forward, elbows on knees, and kept his gaze on Miranda, despite his growing awareness of Dani and her utter stillness only a few feet away. Why was she so damn silent? He wasn't vain enough to believe it was all about him, so what was it?

Staring at the agent, he asked, "Is that why you're here? To warn me that the FBI is not going to be much help to me in this investigation?"

"No, I'm here to warn you that for political and bureaucratic reasons too numerous to go into, the FBI is having internal issues of its own, and those unfortunately affect the

SCU. Ideally, an SCU team would be sent here immediately, especially given the viciousness of the crime, to aid you and your people in every way possible."

"But that won't happen this time. Officially."

Miranda nodded. "Noah is very good at playing the political game when he has to, and right now he has to if the SCU is going to survive. So the unit's top agents, including him, have to remain in Boston, working with a task force set up this summer to investigate a series of murders in that city. I'm sure you remember."

It was his turn to nod, slowly. "Murdered a senator's daughter, the final victim of a dozen, and then just stopped."

Miranda looked at him steadily.

"Ah, shit. He's here? It's the same killer? The **hunting ground** you tracked him from was Boston?"

"I'm afraid so."

"So why the hell isn't the task force breathing down my neck?" He held up a hand before she could begin to answer. "Don't tell me. Because no matter what you know or believe you know, there's not a shred of evidence either of us could take to court."

"Or even to the Director of the FBI. This Director, at least. And by the time there is . . . Well, let's just say that the one thing Noah and I are sure of about this killer is that he's fast. He killed a dozen women in Boston in less than a month. If he **is** here, as we believe he is, then he'll strike quickly and viciously—and then probably move on to his next hunting ground."

John Garrett said, "This is exactly the sort of situation Bishop anticipated, and one of the reasons Haven was formed. To . . . circumvent any political or practical situation that might hamstring the SCU. We have a very short chain of command and no bureaucratic red tape."

"You also don't have badges," Marc pointed out.

"No, but we do have friends in very high places."

Marc was already nodding. "Senator Abe LeMott."

"He's the latest high-ranking supporter to come on board, yes. He believes very strongly in what the SCU and Haven can accomplish, working together or independently of each other."

"Why can't he cut through the red tape and get the SCU here—officially?"

Miranda said, "We don't want to use his influence unless we have to. Especially since he and the new Director don't exactly see eye to eye politically. If the Director bowed to pressure, as he surely would given the country's sympathies for Senator LeMott, then he'd resent it. And sooner or later, the price demanded for that would be high."

"Jesus, I hate politics," Marc said under his breath. And before anyone could remind him that he was himself an elected official, he added, "Okay, so **officially** the SCU can't help me, and anything from the FBI itself is probably going to be too little too late."

"That's about the size of it."

"Which, I gather, explains what Mr. Garrett is doing here."

"John," Garrett said. "And, yes, it does. Senator LeMott has hired the services of Haven, for the duration. He wants this killer stopped, obviously. He doesn't particularly

care how that's accomplished. In fact—"
John looked at Miranda, his slanted brows
rising in a silent question.

She sighed. "Marc, there's a very real concern that if we don't make some progress in
stopping this killer, LeMott will . . . take
matters into his own hands. Right now he's a
ticking time bomb and doesn't feel he has
much to lose, especially since his wife's sui-
cide a couple of months ago. Annie was
barely in the ground before her mother swallowed a handful of pills. LeMott's career has
been important to him, but since he lost his
daughter and wife he's kept working, we believe, only because his is a position of power
and he intends to use that power eventually.
All he has left is his . . . crusade to find the
killer who destroyed his family.

"He's a former prosecutor. He's also a former marine. He could do serious damage, and
a lot of people could be hurt needlessly. Right
now he's in D.C., and we need to keep him
there. Which means we need to make some
tangible progress in this investigation, ASAP."

"With all due respect to the senator and
his grief," Marc said politely, "I want to catch

this bastard as soon as possible because he's butchering young women." His hard gaze shifted to John Garrett. "And I don't care who's picking up the tab, just as long as we all have the same goal in sight."

"We do," John said immediately.

Dani spoke for the first time in a long time to say rather tightly, "But the SCU isn't part of this. Miranda isn't staying. Are you, Miranda?"

So that's part of it. She's worried about Miranda. Something must have happened to her in the vision dream. He had wondered if these last years had taught Dani at least that she could no more control fate than anyone else could, despite her glimpses into an often grim future. Now he had his answer; she was still fighting that inescapable truth.

The federal agent looked at Dani with, Marc thought, an oddly compassionate little smile, and said, "It might not make a difference, Dani. Whether I go or stay. You know that."

Miranda knows it too. That fate does what it will, despite everything we do to try to change it.

"I know you need to go. Back to Boston, or to Quantico, or somewhere. Anywhere but here. Because if he's here—you can't be."

"What am I missing?" Marc demanded, intent on confirming his suspicions.

Paris stirred and also spoke up for the first time in a while. "It's about Dani's dream, Marc. The one she told you about earlier this afternoon."

Marc turned his gaze to Dani and waited until she finally looked back at him. "What about the dream?" he asked.

Dani drew a deep breath, let it out slowly. And told him.

Marie Goode wasn't a fanciful girl. Never had been. She wasn't the type to jump at shadows or thrill to ghost stories, and if she heard a strange sound in her apartment late at night, she'd grab a can of pepper spray and go see what, if anything, was there.

Usually nothing was, though once she had discovered a raccoon on her deck, raiding her bird feeder. The pepper spray hadn't been necessary on that occasion, since the creature had been as wary of her as she was of it, and fled.

Her father kept saying he didn't like it that her apartment was on the ground floor of the complex, and Marie was on the waiting list for a larger apartment on an upper floor, but she'd never felt particularly vulnerable where she was. There were good locks on the doors, and while the complex **was** on the outskirts of town, it was still a safe, well-lit area.

Which was doubly a good thing right now, since her old car was in the shop, hopefully being fixed, and she had to walk from her job at the small restaurant several blocks away. If she couldn't get a ride, at least.

On Wednesday night, no ride was available. And a private party celebrating an upcoming wedding had stayed late, which meant it was later than usual when Marie helped close up and set off on foot toward home.

She wasn't nervous.

At first.

It hadn't really cooled off much in early October, but the summer had been brutally hot and too dry, so, in defeat, a lot of the trees had simply dropped dead brown leaves without the customary colorful show first. During the daytime, the dead leaves everywhere were a depressing sight; at night, with a fitful breeze, it was a bit creepy.

The leaves rustled and whispered as the air currents caught them and slid them along the sidewalk and against the buildings Marie walked past. It was as though a small crowd of people followed her, just out of sight, and whispered among themselves, keeping their secrets.

Now **that** was a fanciful thought, Marie decided. And why was she thinking such absurd things?

She realized her hand had crept up to the nape of her neck, and she could literally feel the fine hairs there standing straight out.

Her common sense gave her obviously overactive imagination a stern talking-to, and Marie stopped on the sidewalk, turning slowly to study her surroundings. Nothing at all unusual met her gaze.

The breeze died down just then, so the whispering leaves were stilled and silenced. The sidewalk was well lit, as it was all the way to her apartment complex.

A car passed her, then another going in the opposite direction.

An ordinary night in Venture.

See? There's nothing wrong. Just your imagina—

In the moment of absolute silence, after the car passed and before the breeze stirred up again, Marie heard something. A very distinctive sound she recognized.

The click and whir of a camera.

Not the digital cameras so prevalent these days, but the old-fashioned kind that used film and different shutter speeds according to the light, and—

She heard it again. Her mouth went dry, and she could feel her heart begin to thud against her ribs.

Without wasting another second, Marie continued on her way home, one hand diving into her shoulder bag and closing around the slightly reassuring can of pepper spray, while the other fumbled with the keys she was already holding to find the big whistle on the key chain. She walked briskly, head up, just the way her father had taught her.

"Don't look like a victim, Marie. Walk like

you're going somewhere, but make sure your eyes keep moving, keep scanning the area. And listen to your instincts. If they tell you to run, you run like hell. If they tell you to yell, then you yell your head off. Use the whistle. Don't be afraid of being embarrassed if it turns out to be nothing. Embarrassment isn't permanent. Being dead is."

A truth he, as a doctor, certainly knew.

Marie brought the whistle halfway up to her lips but no farther. Because as suddenly as the fear had gripped her, it let her go. She felt no sense of menace, no threat, no anxiety. Still, she didn't slow her brisk pace or cease scanning her surroundings continually.

And she didn't relax even a bit until she was inside her apartment, the timer-activated lights welcoming and the door triple-locked behind her.

She didn't truly relax until she had gone methodically through her apartment, checking every window and door, every closet. Even under her bed and inside the bathtub and shower.

Only then did she sink down on the foot

of her bed with a shaky sigh, relaxing her death grip on the pepper spray and whistle.

That's when she saw the necklace lying on her dresser.

It was the nightmare brought to life, Dani thought.

The vision.

The smell of blood turned her stomach, the thick, acrid smoke burned her eyes, and what had been for so long a wispy, dreamlike memory now was jarring, throat-clogging reality. For just an instant she was paralyzed.

It was all coming true.

Despite everything she had done, everything she had **tried** to do, despite all the warnings, once again it was all—

Wait. This isn't—

"Dani?" Hollis appeared at her side, seemingly out of the smoke, gun drawn, blue eyes sharp even squinted against the stench. "Where is it?"

"I—I can't. I mean, I don't think I can—" **Why do I feel so confused? I've been here** before. I've done this before. So why does it all feel . . . different?

"Dani, you're all we've got. You're all they've got. Do you understand that?"

Dani said, "If somebody had just listened to me when it mattered—"

But they did listen. I know they did.

I remember that much.

Don't I?

"Stop looking back. There's no sense in it. Now is all that counts. Which way, Dani?"

Impossible as it was, Dani had to force herself to concentrate on the stench of blood she knew none of the others could smell. A blood trail that was all they had to guide them. She nearly gagged, then pointed. "That way. Toward the back. But . . ."

"But what?"

"Down. Lower. There's a basement level."

"It isn't on the blueprints."

"I know."

I told you all this before. Didn't I?

Didn't I?

"Bad place to get trapped in a burning building," Hollis noted. "The roof could fall in on us. Easily."

Bishop appeared out of the smoke as suddenly as Hollis had, weapon in hand, his face stone, eyes haunted. "We have to hurry."

"Yeah," Hollis replied, "we get that. Burning building. Maniacal killer. Good seriously outnumbered by evil. Bad situation." Her words and tone were flippant, but her gaze on his face was anything but, intent and measuring.

"You forgot potential victim in maniacal killer's hands," her boss said, not even trying to match her tone.

"Never. Dani, did you see the basement, or are you feeling it?"

Feeling? Wait. That's not the way my abilities work. I just dream things. I'm not clairvoyant.

Paris is.

Paris . . .

"Stairs. I saw them." The weight on her shoulders felt like the world, so maybe that was what was pressing her down. Or . . . "And what I feel now . . . He's lower. He's underneath us."

"Then we look for stairs."

Dani coughed. She was trying to think,

trying to remember. But dreams recalled were such dim, insubstantial things, even vision dreams sometimes, and there was no way for her to be **sure** she was remembering clearly.

But this is the vision dream. I know it is. It's the vision dream, and for the first time I know that's what it is even while I'm in the middle of it.

While I'm dreaming.

Because I am dreaming.

I have to be dreaming.

She was overwhelmingly conscious of precious time passing and looked at her wrist, at the shiny Rolex watch that told her it was 1:34 P.M. on Tuesday, October 28.

Wait. Why is the watch different? And why is the time different? More than an hour earlier. Why would it be earlier?

"Dani?"

She shook off the momentary confusion, or at least attempted to. "The stairs. Not where you'd expect them to be," she managed finally, coughing again. "They're in a closet or something like that. A small office. Room. Not a hallway. Hallways——"

"What?"

The instant of certainty was fleeting but absolute. "Shit. The basement is divided. By a solid wall. Two big rooms. And accessed from this main level by two different stairways, one at each side of the building, in the back."

"What kind of crazy-ass design is that?" Hollis demanded.

"If we get out of this alive, you can ask the architect." The smell of blood was almost overpowering, and Dani's head was beginning to hurt. Badly. She had never before pushed herself for so long without a break, especially with this level of intensity.

Marc appeared out of the smoke as abruptly as the other two had and took her hand in his free one. In his other hand was a big automatic handgun.

Wait. The sheriff's department personnel carry revolvers, don't they?

"Where to now?" he asked. "I can't see shit for all this smoke."

And why is that bugging me when Marc shouldn't even be here?

What the hell is Marc doing here?

Hollis replied to his question. "Dani is guiding us."

He looked down at her, his expression totally professional but his eyes worried and gentle. "I always knew the beautiful assistant was the real magician," he said. "Like the man behind the wizard's curtain. Where to, Dani?"

She felt a wave of dizziness, of almost wild uncertainty. This was wrong, so wrong in so many ways.

This isn't the way it's supposed to happen!

It was Bishop who said, "You don't know which side they're in."

"No. I'm sorry." She felt as if she'd been apologizing to this man since she met him. Hell, she had been.

Hollis was scowling. To Bishop, she said, "Great. That's just great. You're psychically blind, the storm has all my senses scrambled, and we're in a huge burning building without a freakin' map."

"Which is why Dani is here." Those pale sentry eyes were fixed on her face.

Dani felt wholly inadequate and terribly confused. "I—I don't—All I know is that he's down there somewhere."

"And Miranda?"

The name caused her a queer little shock, and for no more than a heartbeat, Dani had the dizzy sense of something out of place, out of sync somehow.

How could it be Miranda? I warned her. I warned her, and she went back to Boston to be with Bishop. But he's here, he was always part of this. Only she shouldn't be.

And . . . where is Paris?

Where is Paris, and why do I have her abilities?

"Dani?" Bishop's face was even more strained.

Miranda. He asked about Miranda.

And she had an answer for him. Of sorts. "She isn't—dead. Yet. She's bait, you know that. She was always bait, to lure you."

"And you," Bishop said.

Dani didn't want to think about that. Couldn't, for some reason she was unable to explain, think about that.

Why can't I think about it? What did I do to change so much—and all the wrong things?

"We have to go, now," she heard herself

say urgently. "He won't wait, not this time."
And he's not the only one.

The conversation had taken only brief minutes, but even so the smoke was thicker, the crackling roar of the fire louder, and the heat growing ever more intense.

"We're running out of time on every level," Marc said, his fingers tightening around Dani's. "It's been dry as hell for weeks, and this place is going up like a match. I've called it in."

Bishop swore under his breath. "Marc—"

"Don't worry, they know it's a hostage situation, and they won't come in. But they can damn well aim their hoses outside and try to save the nearby buildings." He paused, then added, "Am I the only one who suspects this bastard planned out every last detail, including this place being a tinderbox?"

Bitterly, Hollis said, "No, you aren't the only one. We're on **his** timetable, just like before, like always, doing everything he expects us to do like good little soldiers."

Did she say that before? I don't think she said that before.

Bishop turned and started toward the rear of the building and the south corner. "I'll go down on this side. You three head for the east corner."

Dani wondered if instinct was guiding him as well, but all she said, to Hollis, was, "He doesn't care whose timetable we're on, does he?"

"If fighting it means a minute lost in getting to Miranda? No way in hell. That alone would be enough, but on top of that he blames himself for this mess."

It's not his fault.

Oh, God, I think it's mine.

"He couldn't have known—"

"Yes. He could have. Maybe he even did. That's why he believes it's his fault. Come on, let's go."

Dani and Marc followed, but she had to ask, "Do you believe it's his fault?"

Hollis paused for only an instant, looking back over her shoulder, and there was something hard and bright in her eyes. "Yes. I do. He played God one time too many. And we're paying the price for his arrogance."

But it's not his fault. I'm almost sure . . .

Dani held on to Marc's hand even tighter as they followed the other woman. She could hardly breathe, her throat tighter despite the fact that, as they reached the rear half of the building, the smoke wasn't nearly as thick. They very quickly discovered, in the back of what might once have been a small office, a door that opened smoothly and silently to reveal a stairwell.

The stairwell was already lighted.

"Bingo," Hollis breathed.

But it's a trap. We all know it's a trap. Why are we just walking into it?

This doesn't make any sense!

Paris . . . where's Paris?

Dani wanted to suggest that they wait, at least long enough for Bishop to check out the other side of the building, but every instinct as well as the waves of heat at her back told her there simply wasn't time to wait.

It's a trap and none of us cares.

Why not?

Hollis shifted her weapon to a steady two-handed grip and sent Dani and Marc a quick look. "Ready?"

Dani didn't spare the energy to wonder how anyone on earth could ever be ready for this. Instead, she just nodded.

Marc squeezed her hand, then released it and took a half step closer to Hollis, saying to Dani, "Stay behind me. You're the only one of us without a gun."

"She doesn't need a gun," Hollis said.

I don't? Why don't I?

"I still want her behind me," Marc said in a tone that not many would have argued with. "Let's go if we're going."

Hollis had only taken one step when a thunderous crash sounded behind them and a new wave of almost intolerable heat threatened to shove them bodily into the stairwell.

The roof was falling in.

They exchanged glances and then, without emotion, Hollis said, "Close the door behind us."

Oh, shit.

It always ends this way.

Dani gathered all the courage she could find, and if her response wasn't as emotionless as the other woman's, at least it was steady.

"Right," she said, and closed the door behind them as they began their descent into hell.

Dani sat up in bed with a jerk, unable to breathe for a moment, feeling that her lungs were still clogged with smoke. But that feeling passed quickly, and she was left staring around the pleasant guest bedroom of Paris's house, familiar to her even in the postmidnight darkness.

"Tonight, come get me. Take me in with you."

That was what he'd said. Before he had really known anything about what they faced, that's what he'd told her.

To come get him and bring him into her dream.

"But I didn't," Dani heard herself murmur in the quiet of the room. "I didn't take him with me. He was there. When it happens, in the future. He's part of it now."

What had she done?

Dear God, what have I done?

7

THE PREPARATIONS were as enjoyable as anything that followed, he had discovered.

Maybe the most enjoyable, in fact.

The first time, he had made the mistake of leaving her conscious, which had caused him all sorts of problems, not the least of which had been the mess.

The second time, he had drugged her so completely that she was a deadweight quite difficult to manage and, worse, her eyes had remained closed.

It wasn't nearly as satisfying if she couldn't see him.

This time, he was experimenting with a certain drug, one very similar to the infamous "date rape" drug. The version he was using, if administered properly, kept the patient in a sort of biddable twilight state, able to move and follow directions but with virtually no physical strength.

His one reservation had been that there was no way to tell how her mind would be affected, not until he actually used it.

He really didn't want her to be dopey and unaware of what was happening to her.

That would take all the enjoyment out of it.

"Can you hear me, sweetheart?" he almost crooned.

She blinked sleepy eyes, a little puzzled, and she sounded rather like she'd just returned from a trip to the dentist when she murmured, "I hear you. Where ith—is—thith place?"

"This is my secret laboratory, and I'm Doctor Frankenstein." He laughed. "No, sweetheart, this is home. My home. And now your home. I've been working hard to get it ready for you."

Her brow furrowed. "Real—really?"

"Of course."

She tried to move, and the first hint of panic showed in her widening eyes. "I—I can't—"

"You have to be still for me, sweetheart." He checked the carefully padded leather restraints on her wrists and ankles, then returned to the head of the table.

And her head.

He frowned down at her and carefully adjusted the curved block at the base of her neck, then repositioned the basin in the sink underneath the cascading long blond hair.

Her hair was too long. Much too long.

"You should have had this cut months ago," he scolded her, picking up the scissors from the utility cart beside him.

"I—I don't—"

"Oh, it's all right. I realize you didn't have me there to remind you. But that's all changed now." A bit gingerly, fighting his dislike of the sensations, he gathered up a handful of her hair and began cutting.

"Oh—oh, don't—"

"Don't be ridiculous, sweetheart. You know I have always preferred your hair short."

Tears were leaking from the corners of her eyes, and he paused a moment to enjoy the way they sparkled in the glare of the spotlight high above her.

Then he went back to cutting her long hair short, saying cheerfully, "You know, I had no idea there were so many shades of dark brown. And I couldn't really remember which one I preferred. So I bought half a dozen. We'll find just the right one."

"Oh, God," she whispered.

"Just the right one. You'll see."

He continued with his work, and long blond hair began to fill the basin underneath her changing head.

Bishop sat up in bed with a jerk, his heart pounding, breath rasping as though he'd run miles. There was a leaden queasiness in the pit of his stomach, and for a few moments he thought the only way to rid himself of the poison was the literal one.

But no.

That wouldn't work. Not this time.

He finally slid from the bed and went into

the bathroom, without turning on a light. He rinsed the sour taste from his mouth, splashed cool water on his face.

He didn't look into the mirror even to see the darkness.

When he returned to the bedroom, it was to go to the window, standing to one side out of habit as he pulled the edge of the heavy curtains aside far enough to look out.

Nothing moved out in the motel's parking lot. Or beyond. And Bishop had the odd sense that it was more than the usual middle-of-the-night stillness. That it was something unnatural, a threat beyond his ability to sense it.

You need to rest, Noah. Sleep.

His wife's voice in his mind, as natural and familiar as his own thoughts and far more soothing.

I need to catch this bastard. Before he does that to another woman. Before he does it to you.

I'm safe.

Are you? Then why is Dani still dreaming you aren't?

You know the answer to that. We both know.

Bishop rested his temple against the hard window frame and continued to stare out at the still, still night, this time without really seeing it at all.

I couldn't risk you.

I know. I understand.

But will Dani? Will any of them?

Yes. When it's over. When that animal is dead or caged and the world is a safer place without him. They'll understand then. They'll understand, Noah.

"I hope so," Bishop murmured aloud. "I hope so."

8

DON'T UNDERSTAND why Bishop and Miranda sent you," Dani said.

"Careful, or you'll hurt my feelings." Hollis Templeton was on her feet, leaning forward with her hands on the conference table as she stared grimly down at crime-scene photos taken the previous day.

"You know what I mean. I told Miranda all about the dream, all the details I could remember. She told you, didn't she?" Dani was too worried to be able to hide it.

"Yeah."

"Then what the hell are you doing here? I

121

mean you instead of another agent. If what I saw is how this thing ends, then you're there. In a burning building with the roof caving in. Going down into a certain trap, to confront a—a deadly evil. Don't tell me you signed on for something like that."

Hollis straightened and offered the other woman a rueful smile. "I didn't know what I was signing on for when I joined the SCU. I don't think any of us did. And it has certainly been an adventure I could never have imagined back when my life was normal."

"An adventure is one thing," Dani pointed out, "but willingly stepping into a situation that will likely end in your violent death is just—just—"

"Stupid?"

Dani lifted her hands in a helpless gesture. "Well, isn't it?"

"I don't see you going anywhere."

"That's different."

"Is it? Why?"

"Because it's my dream, dammit."

Hollis was still smiling faintly. "And do your dreams always come true?"

"The precognitive ones do."

"All the time? Absolutely, one hundred percent the way you dreamed them?"

"Well . . . there are always little things different."

"And some things are symbolic?"

"Sometimes. All right, a lot of the time. But the major elements, the ones that don't change, are almost always literal. And one thing that's been utterly consistent in this dream every single time is the way it ends. We go down into the basement of that warehouse with the roof caving in behind us."

"And then?"

Dani blinked. "Like I said, that's where the dream ends."

"So you have no idea what happens next?"

"Well . . . no."

"Then you've really just seen the stage set. All the players in their parts, the atmosphere thick with smoke and menace, everything primed for a really tragic ending."

"That's not enough for you?"

Hollis smiled. "Believe me, I have strong feelings about not dying. Very strong feelings. I'll tell you all about it someday. In the meantime, if I've learned anything during my stint with the SCU, it's that the universe puts us where we need to be, when we need to be there. As for your vision dream, the warning is duly noted. Clearly it's a bad situation all the way around. Unless we can change it, of course."

Dani frowned at her.

Hollis took a chair on her side of the conference table. "Dani, I know you guys inside Haven don't have the same rules, the same watchwords, hell, maybe not even the same beliefs as we do in the SCU. But there's a truth we've learned to rely on, one I'm pretty sure you know as well as I do."

Reluctantly, Dani said, "That some things have to happen just the way they happen."

"Exactly."

"And our fiery deaths are on that list?"

"I don't know. And as you've just admitted, you don't really know either. Not for sure. Because if you knew **for sure** that's the way this whole thing would end, you wouldn't still be here."

It was true, but that hardly helped. Dani hated feeling responsible for the fate of others and was already regretting that she had shared her vision dream with anyone other than Paris.

Except . . .

Miranda had known without having to be told. Oh, she had asked Dani for details but also made it clear that she and Bishop had seen something with their shared precognitive ability, and whatever they had seen had brought her to Dani.

That didn't really help Dani's worry or her sense of guilt either. The weight she had been aware of during the vision dream, the pressure bearing down on her, had become a conscious thing now, a waking thing, as though something dark and heavy loomed just above her head.

She was afraid to look up, afraid she would actually see something there.

Trying to ignore that oppressive sensation, she said to Hollis, "Okay, then. Why did Miranda go back to Boston and send you down here?"

"Because those were the logical next steps to make if she knew nothing of your vision, if she just continued along the path she was on before coming to Venture and talking to you.

She couldn't stay here, obviously; no prominent member of the SCU could be here, not officially, not with the Director watching like a hawk."

"I get that. That she couldn't stay."

Hollis nodded. "If she'd been missing from the task force in Boston more than twenty-four hours, it would have been noticed. Questions would have been asked. And her and Bishop's quiet maneuvering to track this killer all these weeks without the Director realizing what they were doing would have been for nothing."

"And you're here because . . ."

"Because I was the logical team member to send. I haven't been a full-fledged agent for all that long, so I'm well under the Director's radar. I wasn't on another case. I haven't been with the task force. As a matter of fact, I'm still officially on leave, after the last case I was on ended . . . painfully."

Dani asked a silent question with lifted brows.

"I got shot."

"You—"

Hollis waved away concern. "I'm fine. I

heal fast. Which is a good thing, apparently, because I hold the distinction of being the member of the SCU wounded the most times in the line of duty. Technically, the only member ahead of me on the list is Bishop, because he died. Death trumps multi-wounded."

Dani blinked. "You're not serious."

"No, being dead really does top being multi-wounded. Quentin decided. You draw even with dead only when you've been wounded a dozen times or else spend at least a month in a coma."

Dani hadn't met Quentin, though since he was one of the more infamous members of the SCU she had certainly heard things about him. She really wanted to meet him. "That's not what I meant. Bishop died?"

"Well, just for a little while. A few minutes. I'll have to tell you that story sometime too. It's a doozy."

"I'll bet."

Paris came into the conference room and closed the door behind her. "Marc's on his way," she reported. "The preliminary forensics from the crime scene are just coming in, so he's bringing them."

"Oh, joy," Hollis said. "I just love starting out my day with crime-scene photos and forensics reports on a grisly murder." She half-stood to reach into an open box of donuts placed incongruously beside the photos. "And a jelly donut. I can handle most anything as long as I start my day with a jelly donut. Or cold pizza."

Dani hadn't spent much time with Hollis—in the flesh, so to speak—but she had quickly realized that the other woman's seemingly flippant attitude was a combination of genuine humor and the darker gallows type common among cops and soldiers.

One could summon a grim laugh, or one could drown in the horror of an unspeakable crime. Hollis would always summon a laugh.

So would Paris.

"Are there any left with sprinkles?" Paris asked, going to the coffee station set up on one side of the conference room. "I need caffeine and sprinkles to get going. And Dani got me up and out of the house too early for either."

"Two left with sprinkles. Dani?"

Feeling her stomach twist, Dani shook her head. "I'm good, thanks."

"No, you aren't," Paris said as she joined them at the table. "Your nerves on an empty stomach are never a good thing." She produced, as if from thin air, a tall lidded paper cup and a straw. "One of Marc's obliging deputies got this for you. A vanilla milk shake."

"I hope you thanked him for me."

"I did. Drink up."

"Interesting breakfast," Hollis commented, preparing to bite into her donut.

"Her vision dreams come with a touchy stomach," Paris explained.

Dani said, "Miranda told us most of the psychics they've found over the years tend to pay some price, physically, for the abilities they have."

Hollis nodded. "True enough. Lots have headaches, some blackouts, even short-term memory loss. A few use up energy so fast it's like their abilities are more powerful than their own bodies. Scary stuff."

"Do you pay a price?" Dani asked.

"Headaches, though usually not bad ones. And when there's a storm, I feel like one giant exposed nerve. All that electrical energy, according to Bishop."

"Not fun."

"No."

Dani shrugged. "I get off pretty easy."

Paris said, "With the vision dreams, maybe. But it sure as hell drains you when you do the dream-walk thing."

Hollis looked interested. "You can dream-project? That's rare."

"What I do isn't really dream-projecting. I mean, I can't enter other people's dreams," Dani explained. "Just pull them into mine. Sometimes. But I'm not very strong at it."

"Want to qualify that a little more?" Paris asked dryly.

"Well, it's true and you know it. I can't pull just anybody in: There has to be a connection of some kind. Besides, I'm out of practice."

"Just because you spent ten years trying to deny—"

"Paris."

Her sister lifted her hands in a helpless gesture directed at Hollis. "She doesn't like to talk about it. But the truth is that until we teamed back up to work with Haven, Dani went out of her way to avoid . . . connecting . . . with anybody. So she is out of practice, and that ability is a rusty one; we've only been able to use it a couple of times in the last year or so."

Dani concentrated on drinking her milk shake, hoping to quiet the uneasy rumblings of her stomach.

"But the abilities still affect you physically," Hollis noted, watching her.

Dani shrugged. "It's a nuisance, mostly. But it's a temporary nuisance, not a regular occurrence."

"So you usually don't have the same vision dream more than once?"

"Oh, I've had them more than once. And the third time, as they say, is the charm."

"Then it comes true?"

"Then it comes true. But I've never before had the same one nearly every night for weeks on end." Dani lifted her milk shake in a slightly mocking toast. "Which also explains why I take very, very seriously the feeling of doom this particular vision dream creates in me."

————

Marc, you'd better take a look at this."

"I've just about hit my quota of sickening this morning, Jordan," the sheriff said as he rose from the chair behind his desk. "Forensics reports. Teresa was right, dammit; we have pieces of two vics, not one. We won't get a DNA match for a while, but . . . Shit. Just tell me you don't have more of the same to show me."

"What I've got to show you is just plain weird," his deputy told him flatly.

"Christ. What is it?"

"Shorty said he made the comment to you that maybe this killer was drawing us a picture or something out there. With the blood and—everything else at the scene."

"Yeah, I remember."

"Well, he got to thinking, apparently. Even before he talked to you about it. Wondered if maybe there was a pattern in that mess none of us could see—at ground level."

After a moment, Marc said, "I'm all for initiative. So where did he take the shot?"

"The roof. There was a ladder in the garage, he said. I didn't ask too many questions."

"Because he got something?"

Jordan took another step into the office and held out a photograph. "It wasn't obvious until he did some digital work this morning, removing all of us, the equipment, everything that altered the scene from how the killer actually left it. But it's obvious as hell now."

Marc studied the photo for only a moment, then swore under his breath and picked up the closed folder on his blotter. "Come on. Time for you to meet the rest of the team."

"There's a team?" Jordan followed the sheriff from his office and down the hallway toward the conference room, adding in a lowered tone, "I'm not going to like this, am I?"

"You'll like the team. You won't like what they have to say."

"I saw Paris out here a little while ago."

"Yeah."

"Dani too?"

Marc nodded.

"Since when do we work with civilians?"

"Since now." Marc paused at the door of

the conference room and gave his chief deputy a steady look. "Remember all those stories your grandmother used to tell you?"

The sick feeling that had been twisting in Jordan's gut since he'd first seen Shorty's overhead shot of the crime scene intensified. "Yeah, I remember. Are you telling me—"

"I'm telling you to keep an open mind." Marc opened the conference-room door, adding, "And brace yourself."

That's a good forensics guy you've got there," Hollis said absently about ten minutes later as she studied the photo pinned to the bulletin board on one side of the conference room. "He thought outside the box."

"But how far outside the box?" Dani realized everyone was looking at her inquiringly, and added, "Could the killer know somebody would have the bright idea of getting an overhead shot? I mean, could he count on that?"

"And did he need to." Hollis nodded. "Could be it was a little secret just for himself he thought nobody would discover. Something he could gloat over in private. I'm betting when we catch this guy, he'll have lots of pictures. Maybe other trophies, but definitely photographs of his . . . work."

Marc asked, "Because this scene was so obviously staged?"

"Because it's staged so well. So precisely. In my former life I was an artist, and I can tell you this scene was composed, for want of a better word. The natural elements already present, the hardscape and landscape, have been used to balance and enhance his . . . embellishments."

Jordan, sitting at one end of the conference table and trying hard to avoid looking at the crime-scene photos spread out too close to him, said, "Is how or why he left the message as important as the message itself? I mean, **look** at it. And somebody please tell me it doesn't mean what I think it means."

He had been introduced to the federal agent but was still trying to figure out why the FBI would have someone here unofficially rather than officially. If, that is, the "sign" left by the killer meant what he thought it meant.

What he really, really hoped it didn't mean.

Dani said to Hollis, "It still isn't enough, is it? To take to the Director? To bring the task force down here?"

Hollis picked up a marker from the table and went to the bulletin board. With quick, sure strokes, she highlighted what they could all see, a message left for them in blood and viscera.

The shape was a bit rough but unmistakable: a five-pointed star. And in the center was a ragged but all-too-clear number: 14.

Paris murmured, "Guess he wants to be a star."

"He already is," Hollis said. "In his own sick, unspeakably twisted way."

"He must have picked that place, that particular backyard, very carefully," Marc said. "And not just because it belonged to a vacant house. The hardscape and landscape there almost formed a star without his . . . additions, just like you said. He didn't have to do much to connect the dots."

"So it's a message?" Dani ventured. "I mean, besides the obvious one?"

Jordan drew a deep breath and let it out very slowly and quite loudly, not speaking until he was absolutely sure everybody in the room was looking at him. Then, displaying what he felt was the patience of a saint, he said, "Speaking of messages. The number. Fourteen. Somebody please tell me it doesn't mean what I'm afraid it means, that he doesn't have another twelve victims lined up."

The first thing Marc had told the others in the room was the information that forensics placed blood and tissue from two separate victims at the scene, so everyone was aware of that.

Hollis cleared her throat and looked steadily at the deputy. "I'm afraid it's worse than that. He's giving us his box score—so far. The two victims here make fourteen."

"He's killed twelve other women? In Venture?"

"No, he killed the first twelve somewhere else. In Boston, we believe."

"Jesus. This is the same killer? The one all over the news who went on a rampage this summer and ended by butchering a senator's daughter?"

"We believe so, yes."

Jordan blinked, but before he could ask the obvious question, Marc said, "Unfortunately, we can't call on the task force set up to hunt this animal down."

"Why the hell not?"

Hollis said, "Because it isn't the same M.O. Because we have no proof it's the same killer."

Jordan gestured wordlessly at the photo pinned to the bulletin board.

She shook her head. "He never numbered them before, as far as we know. Not the crime scenes, not the victims. In fact, we never had a crime scene before, just . . . dumping grounds where he left his victims. Nobody ever saw him, and the task force was never able to find any forensic evidence pointing to even a potential suspect.

"So, to an . . . unbiased . . . investigator,

that number could mean anything. It could mean, as you guessed, that he plans on killing at least another dozen victims. It could also be a number important to him and him alone, for reasons we can't possibly know yet. Hell, it could be his birthday, or an anniversary, or no more than a number he picked out of the air just to have fun with the cops."

"You don't believe any of that," Jordan said.

"I told you what I believe."

Jordan cocked his head slightly to one side, never taking his gaze off the federal agent. She was very attractive, which he had of course noticed immediately, but there was something else, a quality about her he couldn't quite put his finger on. A kind of serenity, perhaps, as if nothing in life ever would or ever could surprise her. Or maybe it was the sense he had that her sharp blue eyes saw the things around her with a clarity he could only imagine.

Whatever it was, he found it intriguing.

Very intriguing.

"Okay," he said slowly, "so **why** do you believe it? If the M.O. here is different, if there isn't enough evidence to convince the task force or, I gather, the Director of the FBI that this is the same killer, then how come you're so sure?"

Hollis turned her head and looked at the sheriff, lifting a brow.

"He'll believe you."

"Well, that'll make for a nice change." Hollis looked back at Jordan and said matter-of-factly, "We've been using psychics to track him since Boston. We had placed him in the general area of Atlanta when one of our mediums was contacted two days ago by your first victim, Becky Huntley. When her picture came up on the missing-persons data-base, well . . ."

Dani said, "John and Miranda didn't mention that yesterday."

"They didn't see the need to go into specifics then and there." Hollis shrugged, then offered Dani a faint smile. "I would have gotten around to it eventually, though."

"Because you were the medium," Marc said, his tone not the least bit questioning.

She nodded. "I was the medium. It's another reason I was picked for this job." She looked again at Dani. "Another reason I had to be here. Because Becky contacted me. And when a victim gets in touch, that's pretty much a gilt-edged invitation from the universe to come to the party."

9

THE INFORMATION didn't make Dani any happier, but she knew better than to protest. Instead, she said, "I'm guessing Becky Huntley didn't have anything helpful to offer you?"

"They seldom do, I've discovered. And when they do, it tends to be vague or cryptic. Becky said to pay attention to the signs, that someone was leaving us a trail to follow."

Marc frowned at her. "Someone?"

"Yeah. Unfortunately, she didn't stick around to explain that. Which is a real shame on several counts. As a rule, serials don't leave trails, and the Boston killer certainly didn't."

"Or signs?" Jordan murmured, glancing toward the crime-scene photo on the bulletin board.

"Or signs. With serials, if they get caught it's most often not because of stellar police work but because the bastard slips up. Makes a mistake. Leaves a victim alive, or doesn't clean up after himself, or is otherwise careless."

"But not because he leaves a trail," Dani said.

"No, that's not the norm. It would have been nice to get specifics from Becky, but the contact was just too brief." Hollis grimaced. "Though I have to admit that I'm relatively new at this medium stuff, and I'm only now reaching the point where I can—sometimes—hear them."

"Do you see them?" Jordan asked. As Marc had promised, he seemed to have no difficulty in accepting, without a blink, the reality of psychics and her own claims of being a medium.

She wondered why and made a mental note to find out later. She nodded. "Sometimes as clearly as I see you now. Other times, hardly at all."

"That must be unsettling. Either way."

"You could say that."

With a slightly queasy look crossing his expressive face, Jordan said, "When you see them, they don't look like . . ."

"Like they did when they were killed? Showing me how they were killed, how they died? No. No wounds, no signs of illness, not even especially pale—when I see them clearly, at least."

"Do they ever tell you anything about . . . what comes after?" he asked, clearly genuinely curious.

"No. But something must, right? I mean—they're dead but they still exist, somehow. They communicate. They seem to think, to feel, just as they did when they were alive. Personality intact, as far as I can tell."

"And they stay like that?"

"You mean indefinitely?" Hollis shrugged. "I don't know. All I can tell you is that once we've closed a case, murderer caught or killed, I don't see or hear the victims anymore. Another SCU member, a much stronger medium than I am, says some spirits choose to remain in that state to serve as guides, but not many of them. No idea why."

Before Jordan could do more than open his mouth to ask another question, the sheriff interrupted.

"Jordan, I know you're curious. Hell, I'm curious. But let's get our priorities straight. If this is the same son of a bitch who tore through Boston last summer, we're looking at more victims, and probably sooner rather than later."

"It's the same killer," Hollis said.

"Okay, it's the same killer," the sheriff said. "So, why here? Why pick Venture as his hunting ground? This is a long way from Boston, and a small town makes it far less likely he can disappear into the crowd."

Dani shook her head. "He has to have some connection here, with someone or someplace. Something that drew him here. Isn't that the only reason that makes sense?" There was an itch at the back of her mind that told her she had forgotten or overlooked something important, probably in her vision dream.

Hardly surprising, that. But damned frustrating.

"It's certainly one of the few reasons," Hollis said. "To ditch the anonymity of a big city for a small town, where strangers very likely get noticed, and quickly, is not exactly a smart move, especially if you plan to remain an active serial killer."

"Maybe he panicked," Jordan suggested. "If you guys were getting close—"

It was Hollis's turn to shake her head. "No, the task force wasn't closing in on him. But the media spotlight got awfully bright when Annie LeMott went missing, and brighter still when her body was found. Bishop believes that's what drove the killer from Boston."

"It makes sense," Marc agreed. "But Dani's right. I doubt this bastard picked Venture by sticking a pin in a map."

Jordan said, "So I guess we're looking for a connection."

"Which," Paris said, "is not going to be easy when we have no concrete facts on this man."

"Not going to be easy." Dani sighed. "Masterly understatement, I'd say, at least unless we're able to pick up the right signs and follow this trail supposedly being left for us."

"That's assuming there is a trail," Jordan said, adding to Hollis, "No offense."

"None taken. I'll be very surprised myself if we do find a trail. The universe is usually not so helpful."

"And why would a killer be?" Dani said to the room at large.

Marie Goode, in addition to not being an especially fanciful woman, was also not a stupid woman. So finding a necklace that was not hers very late on Wednesday night in her supposedly safely locked-up apartment had sent her internal alarm bells jangling. **Especially** after the walk home and the creepy sensation of being watched and followed.

So she had done what any rational woman would, under the circumstances, and called the police. And uniformed sheriff's deputies came, and took her statement, and checked all her doors and windows for her, and carried away the necklace, saying they'd look into it and promising that a patrol car would cruise past her complex every hour for the rest of the night, just to make sure there was nobody lurking out there.

That should have been the end of things.

Marie had tossed and turned fitfully nevertheless, leaving lamps on in her living room **and** her second bedroom, plus the outside lights, and getting up at least three times to check the doors and windows again.

By the time morning finally came, she was hardly rested, but it was a workday for her. She dragged herself out of bed and took a quick shower, unable to relax even after she was dried and dressed. She skipped her usual coffee for toast and weak tea, hoping to settle her jumpy stomach. It even worked.

Until she unlocked and opened her front door.

A dozen red roses that had been propped against the door fell over the threshold.

She didn't even have to bend to read the card nestled within the green tissue wrapping. There was no envelope, just a plain white card with two words written in a flowing hand.

Hello, sweetheart.

Maybe another woman would have been

charmed by a secret admirer leaving flowers. Maybe another woman would have enjoyed a much brighter day with that thought in her mind.

Maybe Marie would have. Except for that creepy walk home last night.

And the necklace left inside her locked apartment.

And the fact that the hair on the back of her neck was standing straight up once again.

It was broad daylight, and Marie's apartment was less than a dozen blocks from the sheriff's department.

She closed and locked the door, leaving the flowers outside. She got her pepper spray and her whistle, holding both in shaking hands.

And then she called the sheriff.

All we can do is work with the information we do have," Marc reminded the group in the conference room. "We have crime-scene data, forensics reports, victim profiles. From Boston as well as here. Right?" He looked at Hollis with his brows raised.

She nodded and gestured to a very thick accordion file folder on the conference table. "In there is every bit of information Bishop felt we needed concerning the investigation so far. It's not all the case information, obviously; that would fill boxes. But in there is a complete background and profile of each of the Boston victims.

"And his victim preferences are very important, we believe. In Boston, that was his only really consistent trait, and Bishop believes he won't stray far from it, now or in the future. He always chose the same physical type of woman. Small, delicate, dark brown hair, brown eyes. Almost childlike."

Jordan frowned, but before he could comment, Hollis was adding, "We also have Bishop's latest profile of our killer."

"Latest?" Paris asked.

"He started revising the original as soon as we knew the next hunting ground would be so far from Boston. So different from Boston. Plus . . . well, one other thing I did get from Becky was that the killer had definitely escalated in his sheer brutality but in so doing took a pretty large leap as serial killers go, which is unusual. That alone required a revision of the profile."

Marc frowned. "A leap?"

"In the speed and degree to which he escalated in violence. The twelfth victim, Annie LeMott, was savagely beaten, and she was stabbed multiple times—but her body was left more or less intact. All of the victims in Boston were."

"But not Becky," Marc said. "And not Karen."

"Shit," Jordan muttered. And when everyone looked at him, he added, "I guess we **are** sure Karen's dead too?"

"We're sure there are at least two victims," Marc confirmed. "And I'm willing to accept Hollis's word that Becky is one of them, unless and until DNA results contradict her. Karen's our only other missing person, Jordan."

"Yeah. Yeah, I know. I just really don't want to have to be the one to tell Bob his wife's dead."

"A friend?" Hollis asked.

"Not a close one, though we went to school together." He shrugged. "Small town."

"With the traditional small-town grape-vine?" she wanted to know, shifting the sub-ject. Maybe.

It was Marc who said, "People around here tend to keep their business to themselves when it comes to outsiders, but that isn't to say that they don't know what's going on around them and talk about it among themselves."

"But they'll be slow to do anything like alert the media?"

"That's been the rule around here as long as I can remember. At least for most of the lo-cals. But we have a crop of relative newcom-ers in the area, and I have no idea what their tolerance for media scrutiny would be. Some people do love the spotlight."

Hollis sighed. "Ain't that the truth. So we don't have much time before the news breaks."

"I'd guess not much, no." Marc shook his head and directed the conversation back a step. "You said this killer escalated to an un-usual degree?"

"Yeah." Hollis frowned. "The time gap could explain the intensity of the escalation, at least in part. If he wanted to kill, needed to kill, but couldn't, for whatever reason. Sheer frustration could easily make a killer more savage."

"Assuming there actually was a time gap."

She nodded. "Always possible he's killed somewhere else and we missed the signs."

"But you don't believe that."

"No. We believe he's laid low all these weeks, that he didn't kill until he got his hands on Becky Huntley on or after September twenty-second, when she disappeared. Before that . . . maybe he was searching for a place like Venture. Or maybe he came straight here, because of that connection Dani suggested, and has spent all this time since his arrival getting ready."

It was Marc's turn to frown. "He didn't do much advance prep the first time, did he? Grabbed the women usually coming or going from home or work, in areas with little or no security."

Hollis nodded. "Yeah, he was like a vicious animal. Grab and run, and lucky enough or smart enough to time every grab perfectly. Never any witnesses, which means we haven't even the vaguest description of him."

"He could be anyone," Dani murmured. "We could walk right past him on the street and never know."

"Probably," Hollis agreed. "If monsters looked the part, they'd be a hell of a lot easier to catch."

Marc circled once again back to the point, saying, "But if he **did** spend all the time between the last murder in Boston and the first one here somehow getting ready, that's new."

"One of the many potential differences, yes."

"An important difference?"

"Bishop believes so. And I agree. Think about it. What he risks most in a smaller area with fewer people is discovery. He can't grab and then butcher a dozen victims in a dozen different locations over a short span of time, not in a place like Venture. He might be able to do that once, maybe twice if he's really lucky, but not more than that. He needs a base. Somewhere safe, somewhere isolated, somewhere he can do what he wants to do with little or no fear of discovery."

Dani stirred and said, "Like a warehouse.

Like the basement of an otherwise deserted warehouse."

Hollis nodded. "Like a warehouse. When the universe offers you a signpost, you pay attention."

"But is that part of the trail we're meant to follow?" Dani's uneasiness grew. "Or something entirely separate?"

"Actually," Hollis said in a slow tone of realization, "it's an even more complicated question. Because Becky didn't say we were **supposed** to follow the trail. She just said someone was leaving us a trail to follow."

There was a long silence, and then Dani said, "And in my dream, we're walking into a trap."

Before anybody could comment on that, an older deputy tapped on the door and stuck his head in, addressing Marc apologetically.

"Something we thought you ought to know, Sheriff."

"What?"

"We got a call late last night from a young lady who suspected she was being followed home from work and that somebody had gotten into her locked apartment."

"Steal anything?"

"No, that's the weird thing. He left something behind. A necklace. Shorty's looking it over now."

Marc frowned. "I take it she's sure it wasn't left by a boyfriend or something like that."

"She's absolutely positive, Sheriff. She's also shook up and not the sort to get that way without reason. A while ago, when she opened her apartment door to leave for work, she found a dozen red roses leaning against her door—with a note that spooked her even more. She called it in, and this time the deputies responding decided you should talk to her."

Eyeing his deputy, Marc said, "I take it you were one of those deputies?"

"Yes, sir."

"You were out at the crime scene yesterday, weren't you, Harry?"

"Yes, sir." With clearly forced calm, Deputy Walker added, "I know Bob Norvell, and I know Becky Huntley's parents. And I really think you should meet Marie Goode and talk to her. I think maybe she's got reason to be scared."

Gabriel Wolf parked the Jeep well back from the abrupt end of the old dirt access road and got out. He didn't get too close to the edge, just close enough to peer over and note that a spring flood sometime in the past had changed the course of a wide creek and allowed it to wash out a long stretch of the old road.

It was no Grand Canyon but still a long way down to the sluggishly moving creek.

"Well, shit," he said. "Have to be close enough, I guess."

He got his binoculars from a large duffel bag in the backseat and returned warily to the best vantage point he'd been able to find overlooking most of Prophet County, at least without climbing a fucking mountain. This time, he not only kept well back from the unstable edge but also in the dubious cover of a cluster of trees only now beginning to assume this year's muted fall colors.

He did not want to be seen up here.

He adjusted the focus of the binoculars and swept the distant area first, where the small town of Venture was visible, sprawling more than he had expected. It had once existed as a fairly important stop along the railroad from Atlanta heading north; the line had run through Venture and continued along the eastern slopes of the Blue Ridge Mountains, transporting cotton, tobacco, pecans, and whatever other crops and goods the state produced, as well as the stone and other minerals quarried farther to the south.

Gabriel studied what he could see of Venture, frowning a little. He'd seen small towns left by the wayside of progress, abandoned when railroads closed down lines and unwise timber harvesting practices left scarred hillsides and crops like cotton and tobacco failed or moved elsewhere, and this particular small town had either recovered from such economic hits long ago or else had never experienced them.

And yet . . . trains no longer even paused here, slowing a little as they passed Venture only because the line then wended its way into the mountains, where speed could be deadly. As far as Gabriel could see, there were no major industries in the area, barring one lone paper mill up on the river miles outside town.

Several tidy farms boasted dairy cows, some beef cattle, and other small livestock, and he'd noted at least three other farms where horses and riders were from all appearances trained in show jumping and cross-country eventing. Some timber was being cut to the west of the town, but not on a large scale despite the proximity of the paper mill. He spotted a couple of tobacco fields, but most of the agriculture he saw consisted of little more than backyard vegetable gardens intended only to supplement or supply much of the diet of the families that owned and worked them.

"Where's the money coming from," he murmured.

You're a suspicious bastard.

"Yeah. Yeah. It's my job to ask the tough questions."

Actually, it isn't. It's your job to find that warehouse. Or at least eliminate as many dead ends as we can.

Gabriel visually swept the area again, and sighed. "This used to be a major stop for at least two railroads, and one very large textile mill operated in the area for generations; there are abandoned warehouses, deserted buildings, and defunct storage facilities all over the damn place."

Defunct?

"Yeah, don't you like that word?"

I'm just wondering how come such a prosperous little town hasn't torn down all those abandoned buildings.

"It does give one pause, doesn't it?"

They don't seem to clutter up the land-scape too much. Maybe that's why.

"If it ain't ugly, leave it be?"

Well, even demo costs money.

"You calling me a suspicious bastard again?"

No, I'm sharing your suspicion. But I don't know that it gets us anywhere.

"Now you're just being a pessimist." Gabriel continued to study Venture through his binoculars, sharpening the focus on the neat and very attractive downtown area. "Huh."

What?

He sighed and lowered the binoculars.

"Either the right hand doesn't know what the left hand is doing—No, that's not it, that's never it, even when it looks that way."

What are you muttering about?

"I think we're dealing with that need-to-know shit again. We aren't alone in Prophet County."

Well, we knew that.

"I'm not just talking about Dani and Paris. Or Hollis Templeton."

Who, then?

"Somebody unexpected. Somebody who really shouldn't be here, not for this one."

Who do you—Oh. Oh, shit.

"Exactly," Gabriel murmured, raising the binoculars to his eyes once again to watch a surprisingly inconspicuous figure strolling along the quaint downtown sidewalk. "I guess he's taking the predicted threat to Miranda very, very seriously."

10

MARC DIDN'T HAVE any logical reason for taking Dani with him when he went to talk to Marie Goode in his office, so he didn't bother trying to invent one.

He was just relieved Dani didn't ask.

That emotion lasted only until they went into his office and Marie Goode rose from one of his visitor's chairs.

She was petite, almost waifish, with short dark hair and big dark eyes, and looked almost childlike in her waitress uniform.

Shit.

Marc exchanged a quick glance with Dani, and then they continued on into the room and he introduced the two women, offering no information as to who Dani was or why she was part of the interview.

Marie Goode was clearly too upset to worry about it. "Sheriff, did Deputy Walker tell you? About the necklace and the flowers? About somebody following me last night?"

"He told me, Ms. Goode. But I haven't had a chance to read your statement, so if you wouldn't mind going through it all again for me now? You believe someone began following you when you left work last night?"

"Well, I thought it was my imagination at first, but . . ."

Dani watched the younger woman continue to relate her experience to Marc, but a chill shivered over her skin when she realized that Marie's voice had faded, within a matter of seconds, into silence.

It had happened to Dani before—but only in her vision dreams. Then, while she slept, her mind seemed to accept these abrupt silences of the people and places and things around her, because something deeper than her dreams, deeper than her visions, understood that it needed to listen to whatever was happening far beneath the surface. To something more important. And it was almost always something vital to her understanding of the vision dream's true meaning.

But now her waking mind scrambled in panic, the knee-jerk, fearful reaction so quick that she very nearly missed that whisper of sound beneath the voices in the room, beneath the light, beneath what she could touch. Beneath what seemed real.

I want you.

She went still inside, the instinctive focus barely holding panic at bay. Her gaze shifted to Marc, and she wished desperately that it was his whisper she heard in her head. That she could believe it was his whisper.

It wasn't.

It was cold. It was hard. It was implacable.

And it was evil.

I want you, Dani. I'll have you. Even if you run. Even if you hide. No matter what he does to protect you. No matter what you dream. No matter—

"Dani?"

She realized she was on her feet in front of Marc's desk, half-turned toward the door. She also realized that Marie Goode was gone, that Marc must have just shown her out, because he was coming back from the door, frowning at her.

Dani sat down abruptly and fought to pull air into her lungs, as though she had been holding her breath for a long, long time.

"Dani, what the hell's wrong?"

"I—I don't—" She pulled herself together and did her best to hold her voice steady. "I thought I heard something, that's all. Did you assign a guard for Marie Goode? She's the right type, and if he's already watching her—"

"Of course I assigned a guard." He sat down in the other visitor's chair, still frowning at her. "What did you hear?"

"I said I **thought** I heard—" Again, she got a grip on herself, on the panic that was doing its best to overwhelm her. "I'm not sure. Maybe my imagination. I thought I heard a whisper, that's all."

"A whisper? Someone trying to reach you? Psychically?"

"My abilities don't work that way."

"Just because they never have," he said

slowly, "doesn't mean they can't. Psychic ability grows and evolves just like any other human ability does. What did the whisper say?"

"Marc, I don't—"

"What did it say, Dani?"

She didn't want to answer, but things were
already so strained between them that she
didn't want to make the situation worse. "He
said . . . he wanted me. That he'd have me."

"Who?"

"I don't know who. Even if I'd heard his
voice before, who can recognize a whisper?"

"All I know," Marc said deliberately, "is
that it scared the hell out of you. So I'm
guessing that even if you aren't sure, you suspect what you heard came from the killer."

"That's not possible."

Marc's frown was gone, yet his face managed to be harder than ever. "You're already . . .
keyed on to this killer, right? Dreaming about
him?"

She had never heard that particular termi-
nology, but it did make sense to her. "In a
manner of speaking."

"We both know it's all about connections
with you. I assumed you were having the vi-

sion dreams because Miranda's a friend and there was a threat against her."

Dani hesitated, then nodded. "So did I."

"Any chance the killer keyed on you **because** of the vision dream? That he somehow caught one end of a connection straight back to you?"

"I don't know." **God, I hope not.** "Maybe. Or maybe, if it happened at all, it was somehow through Marie Goode. If he's watching her—"

"She isn't psychic," Marc said. "What if he is?"

Dani drew a breath and said, "I don't have to be an experienced investigator to know that if this killer is psychic, we're in very big trouble."

"Either way, if he is or isn't, you're still scared as hell, Dani. Because he's touched a part of you not many people have touched. Whether you made the connection or he did, it's real. It exists. Do you think I can't see that? Do you think I can't feel it?"

"Marc . . ."

"We both know those kinds of connections aren't easily severed once they're made. And he could hurt you, couldn't he? He could come after you in a way that no physical barrier, no wall or locked door or bodyguard with a gun could stop."

Not something she wanted to think about, because it did scare the hell out of her. Especially since it eerily echoed the whisper she had heard.

Still, with forced lightness, she said, "I'm safe. At least until we find that warehouse." She heard herself say it.

She only wished she could believe it.

Gabriel pulled the Jeep off the otherwise deserted road and behind a tangle of some kind of vine he didn't recognize. "I hate it when somebody changes the rules," he grumbled.

We don't know that anybody did.

"Bullshit, we don't know. The SCU is supposed to be all but invisible here in this investigation, and he's about as visible as it gets."

You said he seemed inconspicuous.

"**Seemed** being the operative word. **Temporary** being a better one. Just as soon as this town wakes up to the knowledge that two of their own have been murdered, have been **butchered,** you can bet strangers are going to get noticed. And probably shot."

I think you're exaggerating. But best we keep a low profile and work as fast as we can.

"I hear that." He got out of the Jeep and paused beside it only long enough to dig a smaller backpack from the big duffel bag in the backseat, then locked up the vehicle. He moved through the woods along the road for twenty or thirty yards, then came upon the disintegrating blacktop drive leading to a fair-size cluster of buildings that had once housed some kind of manufacturing plant.

What was manufactured?

"Details, details."

They might be important, you know that.

Gabriel sighed and shrugged the backpack off one shoulder. He opened a pocket and pulled out a map of the county that boasted numerous areas circled in red. He studied the notes scrawled in the margin for several moments. "Plastics."

Nothing more specific than that?

"Not on the map. But if I remember the research from yesterday, it was plastic hangers, something innocuous like that. Just a place that made useful things."

And got closed during a downsizing of the company. I remember now.

He replaced the map in the backpack and continued on his way, following the old blacktop all the way to the buildings. The first one he came to was so featureless he didn't have a clue what it might originally have been designed to house; all he saw was the big rusting padlock on the windowless door.

Gabriel turned the heavy padlock up so he could see the bottom and knew from the amount of rust that his picks would be useless; a hammer and chisel, he thought, wouldn't be able to cut through the years of rust.

"Hey, a little help here."

Sorry. My mind wandered.

"Well, wander it back, will you? Lock. And not one I can pick without a chisel. Or maybe some C-4."

Just a sec. Wait . . . There.

He heard the sharp **click** and found the padlock opening in his hand. It was still rusty and unwilling, but it opened.

"Still got the magic touch, Rox."

Yeah, yeah. Check this place out and let's leave.

"You getting antsy?"

I also don't like it when somebody changes the rules. Be careful, Gabe. I have a bad feeling.

There were few things in the world Gabriel respected as much as his sister's bad feelings, so he paused at the unlocked door long enough to get both a flashlight and a gun from his backpack. Then he put his shoulder to the door and forced his way into the derelict building.

Back in the conference room, Marc filled the others in on both the interview with Marie Goode and Dani's experience.

"I don't like this," Hollis said.

"Which?" Paris demanded. "And join the club. Marc, I hope you don't mean to leave Dani unguarded."

"I don't."

Dani didn't protest, just looked at Hollis and waited. She was trying very hard to pretend that she was unconcerned, that the slimy voice of a killer in her mind didn't terrify her to her marrow, and knew all too well that at least two people in the room were perfectly aware of exactly what she was feeling.

Three, really, as Hollis's words made clear.

"Having that sort of contact with evil is about as bad as it gets," she said to Dani, her tone matter-of-fact even though there was sympathy in her expression. "Did the connection feel solid?"

Dani forced herself to think about it and finally shook her head. "Not really. As a matter of fact, it ended very abruptly." **When Marc said my name.**

"You've never been telepathic," Paris noted. "Even within an established connection, it's more feelings than thoughts."

Dani carefully avoided looking at Marc. "This was both—sort of. Cold, hard, complete sentences. But sort of like an echo." She shook her head. "I can't remember all the details of my vision dream; maybe this was just that, a leftover echo of something I hadn't consciously remembered."

Marc looked at Hollis, brows raised. "Possible?"

"Sure. It could also be possible that Dani's abilities are evolving, or that either she or the killer somehow established a connection between them. Or . . ."

"Or what?" Marc demanded.

Dani knew what he was asking and also knew he didn't want to suggest to Hollis—**to anyone**—that the killer might be psychic, as he had speculated. She was grateful when the other woman frowned and shook her head.

"Or . . . let me think about that for a while."

"Do I have a choice?" Marc asked wryly.

"Not really." She softened that with a smile, which quickly faded. "The other thing I don't like is the increasing evidence that our killer is changing or has changed, fundamentally. Marie Goode is the right physical type, right age, right everything he likes. But to . . . make his interest in her so obvious strikes me as a completely new element. Letting her hear his camera, leaving the roses, and—" She frowned at Marc. "What about the necklace?"

"Shorty reported in as we were leaving my office. It looks like the necklace might be the one Becky Huntley was wearing when she disappeared. No prints. In fact, chemical traces show it was recently cleaned, with ammonia or one of those jewelry-cleaning solutions you can buy in any jewelry store. Description fits. Her parents will have to I.D. it to be sure."

"Please don't give me that job," Jordan murmured.

"Harry's going. Hollis, if it is Becky's necklace, what does it say about this bastard? Leaving a trophy from one victim in the home of a potential victim he's stalking?"

She was frowning, and her tone was almost absent when she said, "I'm no profiler, remember. Not officially, anyway, though Bishop has made sure most of us know more than the average shrink about the psychology of killers. I'll have to fill him in on the latest, and quickly. In the meantime, what this twist tells me about the killer is what I said, that he's continuing to change, to evolve."

"His M.O.?"

She nodded. "And that means something happened to change **him**. Something's different in him, in his life, the way he thinks and feels. Assuming he can feel, that is."

Marc suggested, "Maybe he changed because he was forced to leave Boston. Maybe the experience of becoming hunted himself made it more . . . imperative . . . for him to see himself as the hunter again."

Dani said, "So more care in that part of his ritual. More-elaborate steps before catching his prey. Following, taking pictures, maybe even, in his mind, courting her."

"Yuck," Paris muttered.

"It may help us," Hollis pointed out. "Until that necklace is identified by Becky's parents, we won't have a strong tie between Marie Goode and the killer. But if it **is** identified as hers, then for the first time we may be a step ahead of this bastard."

"Do we make that obvious?" Jordan wondered. "I mean, have our watchdog presence around her obvious to the killer?"

"It's a risk either way," Marc said. "For my part, I'd rather err on the side of protecting a potential victim."

Hollis looked at him steadily for a moment, then nodded. "Your call."

"And I run the risk of him just moving on to another potential victim. That being the case, I say we find him before he moves on. So, what do we know about him?"

"We know the type of victims he chooses."

Jordan said, "Um . . . I started to bring this up earlier, but if you saw Karen—"

"I know. A blonde, with blue eyes. And according to her missing-persons report, Becky Huntley was a blue-eyed redhead."

"Both the right type otherwise, though," Marc said slowly. "Small, delicate in build. Becky was barely eighteen."

Paris said, "You can change hair color with dye or a wig. And tinted contact lenses are usually enough to change eye color. Would he go that far?"

"To fulfill his fantasy, satisfy whatever need is driving him? I'd guess yes," Hollis said.

Marc said, "And Bishop's guess?"

"That's it." With a sigh, Hollis added, "Bishop is a gifted profiler in more ways than one, but even he's struggling to reconcile the differences between these first two murders in Venture and the previous dozen in Boston. And the new information is not going to help clarify things."

"He hasn't had much time, after all," Dani commented.

Hollis shrugged. "He's had a couple of days since I saw Becky. That's usually enough time for him to at least get a sense of a killer or a change in one, especially a killer he's already spent months studying. But this monster is off the charts. Off even Bishop's charts."

To the room at large, Jordan said, "I don't know Agent Bishop, but for some reason that little nugget of information scares me more than anything else."

"Then you have good instincts," Hollis told him soberly. "Because Bishop has seen evil up close and personal more times than any of us would even want to know about—and this guy, this killer, is something new."

"New how?" Marc asked intently. "In viciousness? In cunning?"

Jordan offered, "Even given the carnage we saw yesterday, and granting it was as bad as I ever personally want to see, there are countless books and, hell, Web sites devoted to serial killers who were pretty damn vicious and cunning. Cannibals, necrophiles, and animals who did things to their victims so incredibly evil I hope there aren't names for them."

Hollis was nodding. "Yeah, the law-enforcement and psychological case studies are full of their work."

Repeating his question, Marc asked, "So what about this killer is new? What makes **this** killer so unusual that even a huge task force headed up by the FBI's top monster hunter hasn't gotten close in months of trying?"

Hollis hesitated for a long moment, then said slowly, "The belief has always been that when we do I.D. this killer, we'll discover in his background, his past, what we find in the personal histories of virtually all serial killers. Abuse, dysfunction, possibly some sort of head trauma early in life, things like that."

"If you want me to feel sorry for this bastard—"

Hollis waved that away. "No, no. Most of us also believe that serial killers are born with something missing, whether you call it a conscience or a soul, which enables them to be far more monster than man. We don't know whether that missing component is all it takes or whether the individual could live a perfectly normal life—at least outwardly—without hurting anyone at all. If his or her childhood environment was nurturing and positive, and there was no trauma, there's at least the possibility that the person would never commit evil acts."

"But?" Marc was still watching her intently.

"But. What we are fairly sure of is that the missing component, coupled with either childhood trauma and abuse, a head injury, or some kind of intense emotional and psychological shock, virtually always produces something evil. A serial killer, rapist, pedophile, arsonist—even a terrorist. The inclinations were there, the instincts, the needs. And something happened, over time or in a single traumatic event, to bring them to the surface."

"I'm still waiting for the other shoe to drop," Marc said.

"Sorry to take so long getting to it. Here's the thing. From this point on, we're in that off-the-charts territory. We have theories. We have a few SCU case studies of situations we felt were borderline or that didn't allow us enough time for any real examination or understanding of the personalities involved. But we don't have proof. Hell, we don't have anything close to proof."

"Hollis—"

She held up a hand. "Marc, trauma—in childhood or as an adult—can also trigger psychic abilities. In fact, some studies have shown definitively that the areas of the brain inexplicably energized in most psychics are the same as those inexplicably active in serial killers."

He drew a deep breath and let it out slowly. "You're telling me we've got a serial killer operating in my town and he's **psychic**?"

As if, Dani thought with brief, dim amusement, he had not already considered the idea himself.

"It gets worse," Hollis said. "The SCU has psychics who are extremely sensitive to fluctuations in electromagnetic fields and can detect unusual psychic activity, even at a distance; we call it being very plugged in to the universe."

"Okay. And so?"

"And so, from reports he's received from those psychics in this general area, Bishop suspects our unknown subject is one of only a handful of psychics we've ever encountered who has more than one primary ability. Not secondary or ancillary abilities, but each as powerful and fully developed as any of the others. We don't even know how many abilities are possible or which ones he might have. Maybe he's a telepath and a seer **and** telekinetic with the ability to heal. Maybe less. Maybe more. He could be a living, breathing miracle, created out of the same unknown horror that triggered his compulsion to kill. Undiluted evil—times ten. And none of us, not even Bishop, has ever faced anything like that."

11

IT HAD TAKEN HIM HOURS to get her hair cut just right, but he didn't mind that. There was little sense of night or day in this place, so he paid little attention to clocks and simply rested when he was tired. In any case, he was just a bit obsessive when it came to her hair, he knew that. It had to be perfect. The length and style, the color.

That was important.

He got mad if any of the details were wrong.

The ugly yellow hair he had removed from her head was neatly bagged and put aside; he would incinerate it later, just as he would burn the clothes she had been wearing.

While the hair color was processing, he carefully cut away her jeans and blouse, pausing often to listen to her sobs, to watch the way the small mounds of her breasts jerked and quivered. He left her underwear for last, taking his time, enjoying himself.

He slid the very sharp lower blade of the scissors slowly against her skin, gathering one thin bra shoulder strap and slicing it with a single neat cut. Then the other strap.

He watched for a little while, smiling, as her breasts rose and fell, listened as she sobbed pitifully. He rested just the tips of his fingers on her belly, closing his eyes for a moment to better feel the soft, warm skin and quivering muscles.

He could feel himself stirring, and savored those sensations as well, but reminded himself these were just the preliminaries.

He wanted to make it last.

Her bra was the usual flimsy thing, and it required only a single easy snip of the scissors to part the satiny material between her breasts. He watched again for a few moments, almost holding his breath, because every jerky breath she took caused the cups to slide farther to the sides, oh so slowly releasing her captive flesh.

He waited until a rosy nipple began to emerge, then impatiently removed the bra himself, casting it into the nearby garbage bag holding the rest of her clothing.

His hand reached out, greedy to touch her, and he had to force himself to use only the tips of his fingers to trace the shape of her small breasts, to slowly circle the pebbled surface of her nipples.

"You like this, don't you, sweetheart?"

She made a wild, muffled sound, straining against the restraints at her wrists and ankles, and he frowned at the strip of tape across her mouth.

"I didn't want to tape your mouth. It's ugly, that tape. But you were talking nonsense, and I didn't want to hear that." He used his index finger to circle her nipple again and again and rub back and forth across the stiff tip. "I want you to tell me how good this is, though. I want to hear that. Will you be naughty if I take away the tape, or have you learned your lesson?"

She made another unintelligible sound, this one less wild.

"Will you behave? Will you tell me how much you love me touching you?"

She closed her eyes briefly, more tears leaking from the corners, then opened them and nodded.

He pinched the tip of her nipple before releasing it, then used the same hand to reach over and slowly peel the tape from her mouth.

"Please—"

"I told you before, sweetheart, begging is for later." His voice was patient, but he let her see the closed scissors in his other hand. "Don't worry, I'll remind you when. For now I just want to hear how much you love me touching you."

She closed her eyes, again just for a moment, then opened them and nodded jerkily. "Oh—Okay. I can do that."

He glanced aside at the stainless-steel work cart, which held several prepared syringes, and frowned a little. She was very lucid, he thought. Maybe too much so. It had been hours since the last injection; he might need to give her another soon.

"Touch me," she whispered, and drew in a

shuddering breath. "I—I love the way it feels when—when you touch me."

He smiled and carefully lay the scissors low on her belly, pointing toward her legs, with the tip of the blades barely touching the low-cut waistband of her panties. He watched her jerking response, listened to the little moan she tried hard to muffle, and his smile widened.

He put both hands on her breasts, squeezing, rubbing his palms back and forth over her stiff nipples.

"Yes." Her voice was little more than a murmur, thick and raspy. "Touch me. Like that. I love it."

He found the sensations pleasurable but not so much that he didn't keep glancing toward the timer on his work cart, the timer that was ticking down the few minutes left until he could rinse her hair, and blow it dry, and make sure the rich brown color promised on the box was the right shade.

It had to be just right.

She made a choked sound. "I—I won't—tell anybody. Please don't hurt me! Please, oh, please don't—"

The timer finally dinged, and he smiled.

"Good. Time to see if this color is the right one."

"Oh, God, please don't hurt me!"

"Now, Audrey, I've warned you about that. I decide when it's time for you to beg, remember?"

"Audrey? I'm not—my name isn't Audrey."

He stared at her.

She wet her lips and said quickly, "Okay. Okay. I can be whoever you want me to be."

"Don't be ridiculous, Audrey. Who could you be but yourself?"

"Right. I'm sorry. I—I just forgot." Her gaze flitted to the worktable. "It must be those shots you keep giving me. I forget things."

"Really? Hmmm. I'll have to note that side effect. For next time."

"What?"

He bent slightly and used a control at the side of the table to begin tilting it hydraulically, so that the Y-shaped lower half where her ankles were restrained rose and the upper half lowered slightly.

She shivered and bit her bottom lip but remained silent.

He went to the now-lowered head of the

table, made sure the specially designed sink was stable beneath her head, and turned on the water. He adjusted the temperature, made it as hot as he could stand, and began rinsing her hair.

She gasped and stiffened but didn't cry out.

"Sorry, sweetheart, but it has to be hot water. To get all the color solution out." He rinsed her hair, his gaze wandering from that automatic task after a few moments to roam over her body.

He liked the way she looked on his special table. Each of her naked legs lay in its individual stainless-steel channel, the ankle lovingly restrained by a sheepskin-lined, thick leather strap. The two channels met, more in a U shape than a Y, about eight inches from her crotch, though he had designed that area of the table with a drop flap to allow him complete access to her body. The table was made to fit Audrey, and it fit her well.

It always fit her well.

From the hip to the breast areas, the sides of the table were straight and close in, with only about five inches of stainless steel showing on either side. And then, just at her shoulders, the table branched out straight in a **T**, so that her arms also lay in individual channels, the wrists restrained just as the ankles were.

Above the crosspiece of the **T**, there was only enough stainless-steel surface for the neck block that held her head up above the sink.

He looked at Audrey secured lovingly to his table, and his smile widened. Perfect. Just perfect. Well, it would be once she was squeaky-clean and shaved smooth in all the right places.

"Mister, please, you—"

"Audrey, don't make me angry with you. You never call me **Mister,** for heaven's sake."

She stared up at him, her eyes wide. "Uh . . . the shots. I c–can't remember."

"Darling. You call me darling, Audrey. Always."

"I'm sorry. I'm sorry—darling. I won't forget again, I promise."

"I certainly hope not." He reached for the shampoo. "I don't want to get angry with you, Audrey. I really don't."

"No, darling," she whispered. "The last thing I want . . . is to make you angry with me."

12

A VICIOUS SERIAL KILLER was bad enough, Dani thought; a vicious serial killer in possession of an unknown number of psychic abilities was, literally, the stuff of nightmares.

Her nightmares.

Everyone's nightmares.

Finally, Marc moved his shoulders as though casting things off, and said, "Okay, we deal with that possibility—or probability—when we have to. For now we work the case, get up to speed on the investigation in Boston so far, and continue our investigation here. Any arguments?"

None were offered.

It wasn't really a question when Marc asked Hollis, "You'll be reporting in to Agent Bishop ASAP?"

"With your permission, in about five minutes. It'll be on the QT, of course, at least unless—or until—we find enough evidence to convince the Director this is the same killer. Or until the media gets wind of it and he starts taking heat that way."

Paris asked, "How much time do we have, realistically, before all that media attention starts?"

Marc shrugged. "You know we don't have a local TV station, and our daily newspaper isn't exactly known for its hard-hitting journalism. Plus, geographically we're fairly isolated, so we don't get many strangers or people just passing through. There's a lot going on in Atlanta right now, as well as in the other major cities surrounding us, so plenty of news elsewhere."

"But two victims of a brutal killer," Dani said, "is news no matter how small the town. Especially these days, the way the media latches on to anything sensational. Once word starts to spread . . ."

Hollis looked at the sheriff with raised brows. "Hard to really tell from the photos, but I gather the crime scene was fairly remote, to say the least. How secure was it? How soon before word **does** leak out?"

"My people won't talk. The families of the victims are going to be in shock for a while once they're told. Bob and Karen didn't have any kids; Becky's parents are older and tend to keep to themselves. I don't see any of them going to the media—or being very receptive if the media comes to them."

"Even to make a public appeal for justice? That seems to be the thing these days."

"Maybe in a few weeks or months. Not for a while."

Hollis nodded. "Are they likely to go public in a smaller way, reach out to the community maybe for emotional support? Churches, that sort of thing?"

Marc looked at Jordan, who shook his head and replied, "The Huntleys don't even belong to a church, far as I know. And Bob Norvell was never known as a joiner. Surprised me when he married."

The room was silent for a few moments, and then Paris stirred and said, "Am I the only one who feels guilty because I know what happened to two missing women before their own families know?"

"You get used to it," Hollis said. Then she shook her head. "Actually, no, you don't. At least, I never have. Who **is** informing the families?"

"I am," Marc said. "Or I will, when we have some kind of positive I.D. Either the DNA results or . . ."

. . . **or we find the rest of them.**

Not that he needed to say that.

Why didn't you take me into the dream last night, Dani?"

Dani looked up with a start from the file she was studying, realizing only then that she and Marc were alone in the conference room.

"Don't panic," he said. "Jordan took Hollis out to the crime scene, but I'm sure Paris will be back in here any minute. The dream, Dani. You had it again last night."

"I wasn't going to panic." She was about to remind him that they'd been alone together in his office but then fought a shiver as she wondered if they really had been.

"Dani?"

He saw too much—even without the benefit of psychic abilities. There was, she thought, probably something profound in that.

"It's just . . . even though I didn't take you in, you were there this time. You were part of the vision dream. You were there, and Hollis, and Bishop. And I had Paris's abilities."

"What?"

Dani nodded. "I think I did before, it's just that last night I became aware of it. That she wasn't there, when she should have been. That I had her abilities. More than her abilities, I think. Hollis seemed to feel that I . . . had some kind of weapon, that I didn't need a gun."

"Wait. You had Paris's abilities? I wasn't aware you and Paris could share abilities; I thought you could just enhance each other's."

"We can't share them. At least, we never have. I've never been clairvoyant or had her secondary ability. And she's never had precognitive dreams or visions."

"Or been able to pull other people into her dreams?"

"No. She's never been able to do that. And we tried, as kids."

"Not since?"

Dani conjured a smile. "Somewhere along the way, it stopped being a fun secret we shared and started being our lives. Exploring our own psychic limits wasn't really the priority, not for a long time. Since we started working for Haven, we've done more of that, of course, especially because John and Maggie believe siblings can make the best partners and they needed to know if we could be."

"Found out yet?"

"Not really. We knew that we were always stronger individually when we worked together, just as you said, that my vision dreams are more vivid and Paris is more clairvoyant."

"But no ability-sharing."

"I wouldn't even know how to try to do that."

"But there are signs that your abilities, at least, are evolving."

"Maybe. Okay, probably." Dani managed a shrug, despite the tension she felt. "The sort of high-stress situations we get involved in can be life-altering in every way."

"What do you mean?"

It was not a conversation Dani had wanted to have with Marc, but she found herself going on. "Just like the SCU team, members of Haven are seldom called in except when all the more conventional methods have failed. And the stakes are usually very, very high. So we push ourselves."

"You always did do that."

"Not the way I've pushed myself since signing on with Haven. The truth is that we don't know what our limits are, none of us. Investigations, situations like this one . . . test the limits we believe are there. Maybe push us past them."

"But?" He was watching her intently.

"But sometimes the results aren't all that positive. We get pushed into unknown territory, Marc. We're dealing with electrical energy, remember, and there's a lot of it in the human body, in the human brain. Trying to control that doesn't always work or doesn't work the way we expect it to."

"Is that why you didn't take me into your dream? Because you've discovered it's dangerous?"

She half-nodded. "It's a rare ability, apparently, dream-walking, so there isn't much concrete information on it. Hell, there's almost no information on it. But the theory developed by the SCU and all their doctors and research is that because I'm bringing someone else's consciousness into my mind—where the level of electromagnetic energy is higher than normal—it could damage that person. Non-psychics aren't used to that kind of energy; their own brains aren't hardwired to handle it the way ours are."

"Are you saying someone **has** been hurt because you brought them into your dreams? Or is it all just theory?"

"**Just** theory is all most psychics have to go on. To live with. At least until something very bad happens to change theory into reality. And that theory makes sense. So the only one

I've taken into my dreams since I joined Haven has been Paris. She's psychic **and** my identical twin. We figured if anybody could handle it without being hurt, it would be her."

"It didn't seem to affect me," he pointed out.

Dani managed another shrug, this one jerky. "Maybe for the same reason you can recognize psychic abilities in others." **Or maybe because there was always a different kind of connection between us.**

"Or maybe because we were lovers," Marc said calmly.

"Maybe," she said, striving to match his calm.

"The connection between us is still there, Dani."

"Yes," she said. "I know."

Hollis stood in the backyard of the vacant house, at the edge of what had been a lovely pool area before a monster had turned it into a scene of carnage now encircled by yellow crime-scene tape. The organs and other body parts had been removed, but bloodstains baked to a rusty tint by the hot Georgia sun still marred the lovely tile and stone, and the red-tinted pool was only partially drained.

She could hear flies buzzing.

Jordan cleared his throat when he noticed the direction of her gaze, and said, "The drain's clogged. We have a call in to the pool-maintenance company. They may want to call a biohazard-removal company."

"Everybody's a specialist these days," Hollis murmured.

"And your specialty is being a medium."

Hollis was tempted to go into the whole most-wounded-in-the-unit thing but decided not to. Mostly because she hadn't yet judged the tolerance level of the (really very good-looking) deputy; he had certainly handled everything thrown at him so far with apparent acceptance, but you just never knew what the tipping point might be.

"Yeah," she said, "that's my ability."

"Is that why you wanted to come out here? Because you hope one of the victims will—will appear to you?"

"Well, don't make it sound like it would be from behind a magic curtain," she said dryly.

"I didn't mean it like that. Honestly, I didn't. Just wasn't quite sure how to put it."

Hollis thought about it, then shrugged. "As good a way as any, I guess. And, yes, I thought I might see something. Or someone. I tend to, at crime scenes. Not always, mind you, but often enough to sort of expect it."

Jordan looked around them somewhat warily. "So . . . do you? See anyone?"

"Not so far."

"Huh. We wait, then, I take it?"

Hollis was conscious of both amusement and curiosity. "Tell me something, Deputy."

"Jordan, please. I thought we'd gotten past that part, at least."

"We have. Tell me something, Jordan. How come you're so tolerant of all the psychic stuff? Most cops aren't."

"You're a cop."

"Yeah. Well, barely. Anyway, I belong to a special unit where being psychic is the rule. What's your excuse?"

"Raised with it," he said.

Hollis turned her head and stared at him. "You're not the seventh son of a seventh son or anything like that, right?"

He smiled. "No, nothing like that. Not the mumbo-jumbo side of the paranormal. My grandmother wasn't a gypsy fortune-teller. But she had the Sight. It's been common in this area for generations." He watched her brows rise, and added, "**Prophet** County, for a reason."

It was her turn to say "Huh. That didn't come up in the research. I wonder if Bishop knows." Then she shook her head. "Oh, hell, of course he knows. Dani and Paris were born here, weren't they?"

"Yep. And their mother was a medium, like you. Marc was born here, too; in his family, the **gift** has always been an interesting kind of variation. Not exactly psychic but with a better-than-average bullshit detector. The Purcells have always known who they could trust and who was lying to them; it's one of the reasons they've been so successful politically. And maybe why Marc has been so successful as sheriff."

Hollis said, "Huh," again, and studied him more intently. "What about you? Your grandmother had the Sight and . . . ?"

"And I don't." He shrugged. "I've never

really decided whether it's a regret or a relief, to be honest. But spending time around some of you who have to deal with it makes me lean a little toward relief. It seems to be more a burden than a gift."

"Well, I've come to the conclusion that it's both. Sometimes a gift, sometimes a burden. But always an adventure."

"That's probably a healthy way to look at it."

The words had hardly left his mouth when Hollis became aware that something was happening. After all this time, her physical reaction was always the same: All the fine hairs on her body stood out as though electrical energy filled the air, and goose bumps rose on her flesh as if someone had abruptly opened a door into winter.

She looked around slowly, **knowing** there was no mist really here but seeing it rising up from the ground. The creepy sight was difficult to ignore, but Hollis was able to when she saw a woman coming out of the pool, walking slowly up the steps out of the water, leaving no ripples behind.

She wore no bathing suit, but casual shorts

and a short-sleeved top, and in fact appeared perfectly dry even though she had seemingly just left the red-tinted water. Her long, pale blond hair even gleamed a bit in the sunlight.

Hollis took a step toward her, so focused on what she was seeing that she totally forgot the deputy standing beside her.

"Who are you?" she asked. "I don't recognize you." She meant from the photos of the two missing women.

The woman glanced back at the pool behind her, and said, "You won't find much else now."

Hollis was surprised that the voice she heard was so normal but pushed that aside as unimportant at the moment. "Who are you?" she repeated.

"You don't know about me yet." She glanced back at the pool again, and her expression turned anxious. "Never mind that. Look for her in the water. And be careful. The trail he's leaving for you isn't what you think it is."

Hollis opened her mouth to ask another question, experience having taught her that these visitations never lasted long, but before she could—

"Hollis?"

She looked down at Jordan's hand on her arm, then at his concerned face, already aware that the temperature was hot again, that the energy in the area was gone. She looked back at the pool only to confirm her suspicions.

No woman or spirit stood at the edge of the red-tinted pool.

"What the hell just happened?" Jordan demanded.

"I'm not really sure," Hollis answered slowly. "When did you say the pool-maintenance people were coming to clear the drain?"

"Supposed to be here tomorrow or Monday."

"Call them," Hollis suggested. "Tell them to be here tomorrow. Early."

And that connection doesn't mean anything to you?" Marc demanded.

"Should it?" She was trying hard to keep her voice level and unemotional. Trying—and failing.

"You tell me."

"What do you want to know, Marc? Whether there's a man waiting for me back in Atlanta? There isn't. Whether I found that **normal** life I wanted so badly? I didn't."

"Dani . . ."

"But I found a kind of peace eventually." Once she got going, Dani couldn't seem to stop herself. "When I accepted the fact that there was no escaping this **gift** of mine, that I couldn't run far enough or fast enough to leave it behind. When I accepted the fact that sleep would never be dreamless for me and night-mares would be the norm. When I accepted the fact that with knowledge comes responsi-bility, that God, or the universe, or just my own damn stupid moral compass won't let me walk away, let alone run away, even when I see things that scare the living hell out of me."

She forced a laugh and heard the brittle-ness in it. "Once I accepted all that, once I made peace with it—"

"Bullshit. You haven't accepted anything. Least of all yourself."

"You don't know what you're talking about."

"Don't I? Dani, I'm the guy who got left

behind, remember? I'm part of what you were running away from."

"Don't flatter yourself."

"Oh, I don't consider it a plus in my life, believe me. In fact, I must have been dumb as hell not to see you already had your bags packed and one foot out the door about the time I was congratulating myself on a relationship so solid you were willing to share your dreams with me. Literally."

"I did not mean to do that," she said tightly.

"Oh, sure you did, Dani. No matter what you believe, you were testing your abilities even back then. And me, I thought it was a sign of trust. But that wasn't it, at least not the kind of trust I wanted. Limits, Dani. Even then you were testing them. You just wanted to find out if there was a connection between lovers even identical twins couldn't know, a bond so strong it would open doors you'd never been able to open before."

Dani stared down at the file open before her, the words—describing a vital life cut short in Boston—blurring. Her chest ached, and she wasn't entirely sure she was breathing.

Softly, Marc added, "You wanted to find out. But when you did, when that connection opened the door, threw it wide, it scared the hell out of you. So much so you wanted to run the first time. But even then you were courageous enough to try again, I know that now. I was . . . awed . . . by the experience, and I asked you to do it again. So you did.

"I didn't know what I was asking, what it was costing you in sheer energy. And you never said a word. Until that last night, when the dream you took me into was one of your visions."

Dani looked up finally, staring across the table at him. "I saw your face when we woke up. I saw the horror."

He shook his head, never breaking eye contact. "The horror was for the dream—not for you. Nobody wants to see their mother die of a terrible disease, and that's what you showed me."

"It's always someone's doom, what I see. Don't you get that?"

"I get it. So what? You're supposed to be to blame for that? Dani, I never blamed you for showing me something that was going to happen, even if it was terrible."

"I don't believe you."

"I know. But you will. When you're brave enough to try again."

She drew a breath. "I am **not** taking you into that dream. Not that one. You're already in it, part of the vision. God knows what would happen if—if—"

"Let's find out."

Dani rose to her feet so abruptly that her chair nearly tipped over behind her. "No. We won't. Not tonight. Not ever."

In her panicked rush to get out of the room, she nearly ran over her sister in the doorway.

"Whew." Paris came in and sat down at the conference table. "Been waiting awhile for that cork to blow. Thank you."

Marc sighed. "You say that like it's a good thing."

"It is. Trust me. Dani needed to let go of some stuff, and she's been so busy giving me my space so I can deal with stuff of my own that I haven't been able to help her. I think maybe you just did."

"Really? Because it looked to me like she was still suppressing and avoiding like crazy."

"I saw her face. She's in the ladies' room having a good cry."

Marc leaned back abruptly in his chair. "Well, that makes me feel like shit. I didn't want to hurt her."

"You didn't hurt her, you just shook her up. Which she needed."

"How the hell do you know that? The clairvoyance?"

"That, and"—Paris made a vague gesture with the fingers of one hand—"the twin thing. Don't worry, she's fine. She was standing paralyzed at a crossroads, and you gave her a shove."

"I don't think I care much for the metaphor."

Paris smiled. "That's okay. I've got a million of 'em. Can you pass me that file, please?"

Hollis waited until she was back in her motel room that evening to report in—and there was a lot to report, even if much of it was unhelpful at best and speculation at worst.

Par for the course when it came to the SCU, Hollis thought.

"If Dani has established a connection," she said to her boss, using the cell's speaker capability to talk to Bishop while she dug through her suitcase to find something to wear for pizza and brainstorming at Paris's house, "it could help us—or be dangerous as hell for her. Or both."

"It could be worse if he's the one who established the connection between them."

"No kidding. Any way for us to determine that? I mean, before it blows up in our faces?"

"We're in unknown territory here, Hollis."

"Are we ever in anything else?" She sighed. "Just tell me. What can I try?"

"If Dani's willing, you can try a dream walk. Between you, you and Paris might be able to sense another connection."

"What if we wind up in her vision dream?"

"Be very careful."

Hollis sighed again. "Anybody ever tell you

that you can be frustrating as hell, boss? Never mind—rhetorical question."

"We need to know if Dani does have a psychic connection with the killer, Hollis."

"Yes, of course we do. And it would be nice to know who my blond ghost was. It was so late by the time Jordan and I got back to the station that I didn't have a chance to talk about that with the others. Though Jordan checked, and there've been no more missing women reported. So there's not much to talk **about**."

"She said to look for her in the water?"

"Yeah. **Her.** Referring to somebody else, or at least that's how it sounded. But she came out of the pool. Which has a clogged drain, I'm sorry to say."

"I doubt that was literal, Hollis. That the remains of whoever she meant will be found in the pool."

"Well, Jordan was spooked enough that I'll bet he's there at dawn with the pool people—and the forensics unit. So we'll know soon enough what's in that drain."

"Considering what was at the crime scene, I'd expect more of the same."

"Yeah. Dammit." Hollis brooded, then said, "All these obvious changes in his M.O. Either he's getting sloppy or . . . or what?"

"Or something's happened, either to him or in his life. It could be the move from Boston. It could be something else. But whatever it is, it's having a profound effect on him and could influence both who he kills and how he kills from this point on."

"Hmm. What do you know that you aren't telling me?"

Bishop didn't bother to deny it. "Nothing that could help you in the investigation."

"Uh-huh. You do realize that secrecy of yours is going to come back and bite you on the ass one of these days?"

"Maybe. But not today."

Hollis was tempted to say that today was almost over and what about tomorrow, but she didn't push it—even while she was wryly amused by her own trust in him.

She didn't trust easily these days.

"You'll have the new profile ASAP," Bishop was saying. "In the meantime, be careful. You might not fit the victim profile so far, but neither does Dani, and he's made it

213

clear he wants her. Everything we think we know about him could be changing—or be just plain wrong."

"Gotcha." It was, Hollis decided as she ended the call and closed her phone, not the most reassuring of reminders.

Especially given Dani's vision dream.

13

DANI DIDN'T REALLY want to sleep that night, mostly because she didn't want to dream. The brainstorming session with Hollis and Paris had produced nothing useful, as far as they could tell, and the knowledge that Bishop was completely rewriting his profile of the killer had done nothing to help.

The opposite, in fact.

Maybe that was why both Paris and Hollis suggested that she bring them into her dreams.

"Have you ever taken two people in at once?" Hollis asked curiously.

Dani shook her head. "I'm not sure I can even do that."

Hollis sipped her wine and then lifted the glass in a little salute. "Well, I'm game if you decide to try. If you happen to pull us into the vision dream, we can at least try to remember all the details we can, maybe some you've missed."

"And if it's just an ordinary, everyday dream?"

Paris said with a grin, "Then we get to be voyeurs."

"Dammit, Paris!"

Hollis said, "Let me guess. Marc?"

Dani cleared her throat. "Paris thinks she's being funny. It was just one time; I don't even know why I dreamed about him that night, because I hadn't seen him in years."

"Did it ever occur to you," Paris said, "that it might be my doing? That you dreamed about Marc that night, I mean."

"What? How could it be?"

"Something Maggie suggested I try, not long after we first signed on with Haven." Paris held up a hand before Dani could find the words she was obviously seeking. "Don't blame her. The suggestion was that I think of something or someone you had a strong connection to and hold that in my mind as I went to sleep on a night when we had planned to dream-walk. So I did."

"Marc?"

"Well, you were so determined **not** to talk about him that I knew you still had feelings for him. So I thought about him." She smiled slightly. "Didn't quite expect to find myself in such a passionate dream, but—"

"Jesus, Paris." Dani felt her face get hot and silently thanked the universe that she had been able to bring that dream to an end rather quickly. Or, at least, shove Paris out of it. And why **had** she been dreaming erotic dreams about Marc, anyway? She'd gotten him out of her system by then.

She **had**.

Hollis said, "Let's **not** think about Marc tonight, okay? It's not that I'd deprive you, Dani, it's just—"

Dani held up a hand. "No explanations necessary, really. Look, guys, I don't even know if I can take both of you in."

"Give it a try," Hollis suggested. She

drained her wineglass and added, "One of Bishop's many theories is that when you have enough psychics in the same small area, especially if they're all focused on the same case, their energies sort of . . . overlap. All kinds of weird things can happen, but what usually **does,** in our experience, is that abilities begin to shift, to change. So, even if you aren't successful in taking us into your dreams, the effort itself might help us or might help your abilities to evolve."

Serious now, Paris said, "Help us how?"

"Well, we're all involved in this investigation. Trying to figure out who our killer is, where he is. The subconscious is damn powerful, especially a psychic's subconscious, and when it's set free of the arbitrary restraints and limitations we put on our minds and abilities while we're awake . . . anything can happen."

Limits. What are mine? Dani wondered. It was a question she hadn't really considered, even when asked to do so.

Paris said, "When you say **anything,** I have to wonder if it's always a good thing."

Hollis shook her head without hesitation. "No, there's a risk. There's always a risk when we use our abilities. And dreams are a kind of no-man's land, especially for psychics. Energies can interact in ways we can't predict."

Dani sighed. "Tell me again how that could ever be viewed as a good thing?"

"You know how," Hollis replied promptly. "Whether we like it or not, our abilities evolve. As we use them, as we **try** to use them, as we test our limits. Now, personally, I don't like walking in cemeteries. Anymore. But I do it now and then, because I don't want there to be a place where I'm afraid to use my abilities."

"I dream whether I want to or not," Dani said.

"But you choose whether to take others into your dreams. I'm betting you haven't done it very many times in your entire life. True?"

"True enough."

"And most of those when we were kids," Paris offered.

With a shrug, Hollis said, "If you don't use a muscle, it atrophies. Not something you want to happen to a muscle that could save your life one day. Your decision, of course, but it's all about control for most of us."

"I don't know," Dani said finally. "I'll think about it."

She hadn't wanted to admit that the very idea of bringing anyone else into a vision dream—especially **this** one—scared her in a way she couldn't really explain.

Still, as she tossed and turned that night, she was very aware of the sheriff's department cruiser that had escorted them home and would remain parked outside, with Marc's deputies keeping watch over her despite her protests. That reminder of potential danger was added incentive to test her limits.

Plus, Dani admitted to herself that Hollis's challenge had made her uneasy, and not just because she didn't want to lose an ability she hardly understood. There was also that creepy voice in her mind and the very important question of who—or what—it belonged to.

Maybe Paris and Hollis could help her figure that out somewhere in the depths of her own sleeping mind.

And what if dream-walking somehow

helped them to identify or even find this killer and avert the fiery ending of Dani's nightmare vision? Wasn't that worth taking a chance?

Would she ever be able to forgive herself if she **didn't** take the chance and what she had seen came true?

No.

And they were both psychics, both unlikely to be harmed by her energies. Right?

Right.

Dani stopped tossing and turning, forcing herself to relax. She closed her eyes and began going through the relaxation and meditation techniques she had been taught, all the while holding in her mind the questions of who and where the killer was.

Ready or not, guys, here we go.

Okay, this is new." Dani found herself standing at the intersection of two seemingly endless corridors. Each corridor was hospital-like in its gleaming cleanliness, and each was lined with closed doors.

"Hey," Paris said, beside her on the right,

"I thought you always started someplace familiar, to ground the dream. This doesn't look like anyplace I've ever been."

"Me either," Hollis said from Dani's left side.

"I do always start somewhere familiar," Dani said, a faint uneasiness stirring inside her. "But I've never been here before."

"Well, your subconscious brought us here for a reason," Hollis said with a shrug. "There are four corridors and three of us, so I say we split up."

"No," Dani said. "We stay together, always in sight of each other."

"It's one of her rules," Paris said to Hollis. "She's afraid somebody could get lost in her dreams."

"Well, do you **know** it couldn't happen?" Dani demanded of her twin.

"All I said was that the sense of self-preservation would probably pull the visitor out even if you weren't near to give them a shove," Paris said.

"Yeah, but you don't know that for sure. And I'd really rather not have somebody else's consciousness taking up residence in my dreams, thank you very much."

"Okay, okay."

Hollis said, "I'm sort of glad I don't have siblings. Look, if we're not going to split up, then somebody flip a coin or something. I know dream time is different from real time, but my dreams usually end right at the good parts, so let's not waste time arguing when we could be looking for some sign of this creep—and any connection to Dani."

"I **knew** you had at least one more motive for trying this," Dani said.

"Bishop's suggestion. But he's right; we might be able to find the connection, assuming one exists."

Dani shrugged, aware that, as was often the case in her dreams, she was calm, that initial uneasiness fading. She chose the corridor she had been facing. "This way, then. Not that I have any idea what we're looking for. I doubt it'll be him."

"Some representation of him, maybe." Hollis tested the first door on the left. "Locked. Damn."

"This one too," Paris reported from the right side.

Dani hesitated but then kept walking. "Maybe they're all locked. Maybe my subconscious doesn't have a clue."

"Dani, maybe we should stop and think about this." Paris reached out to touch her sister's arm, and they both jumped.

"Ow! Paris—"

"What just happened?" Hollis wanted to know.

"Sorry, I forgot," Paris said to her sister, then looked at Hollis. "Secondary ability. I channel energy. When I'm awake, it's barely enough to cause static on radios if I hold one in both hands, but when I'm asleep it's a little stronger."

"And when she's asleep and with me," Dani said, "it's a lot stronger. We have no idea why."

Hollis looked interested, but before she could say whatever was on her mind, they were all startled by a scream.

A woman's scream of agony, breaking off with chilling suddenness.

It echoed up and down the corridors,

bouncing off the hard surfaces until it seemed there were dozens of screams, hundreds of them, endless screams pounding against them.

"Where . . .?"

"I can't tell—"

Dani . . .

"Dani, your nose—"

Dani woke this time curled up on her side, her head throbbing in a way it never had before. She tried to push herself up on one elbow, vaguely surprised at how stiff and sore she felt.

Then she felt something else and reached up to find a thick wetness around her nose and mouth.

Her hand came away red with blood. She reached to the nightstand for a tissue and held it to her nose, then looked toward the doorway of the bedroom just as Paris reached it.

Paris didn't look so hot; though there was no nosebleed, she was pale and her eyes had a curiously bruised look to them.

"Marc just called," she said. "We have another missing woman."

It isn't Marie Goode?" Dani asked as soon as Marc came into the conference room.

"No, she's present and accounted for. Still under guard, and considering a trip to Florida to visit her folks, but fine."

"Who's the missing woman?" Hollis asked.

"Her name," Marc said, "is Shirley Arledge. Twenty-four, five-two, a hundred and ten pounds, delicate build. Another blue-eyed blonde. Her husband just got back from a business trip into Atlanta and found her gone. No note, no missing luggage or clothes, her car's still in the driveway, and—most important according to him—her cat's in the house, and she'd never leave without him."

"Do we know how long she's been missing?" Hollis asked. Like Paris, she, too, was visibly tired and had seemed just a bit withdrawn since arriving a few minutes before.

Dani felt guilty as hell.

"Hard to say. Husband left Tuesday, and he said they hadn't scheduled any check-in calls for such a brief trip, that her plans for the week had been working in her garden, getting it ready for winter. She was nesting, he said. They'd been trying to get pregnant."

"Christ," Hollis muttered. She studied the photo of Shirley Arledge and unconsciously shook her head. This was not the woman she had seen at the crime-scene pool.

Marc added, "Jordan just called in and said they've found a basket with some garden tools on a brick pathway behind the house. Evidence she'd been working out there, but nothing to indicate a struggle or any kind of violence. Teresa's on her way out there, but I'm betting we won't have any forensics to speak of."

"How was the cat?" Dani asked. "Hungry or not?"

"Not, but it doesn't tell us much; they have one of those dry-food dispensers that hold enough kibble for at least a week, as a convenience, and her habit was to fill it up every Monday."

Dani started to speak, then thought better of it.

"What?" Marc asked, apparently picking up on undercurrents.

Or simply reading her expression, the probability of which Dani found more than a little unsettling.

"I'm not a cop," she said.

"So? Dani, you're here for what you bring to the table, and that includes any relevant dreams, thoughts, speculation, or hunches and intuition. Let's hear it."

"Okay. I hope to God I'm wrong, but let's assume that Shirley Arledge is or will be the third victim of the serial killer here in Venture."

"Possibly the fourth," Hollis said, and explained what she had seen at the crime scene the previous day.

"You're sure this isn't the woman you saw?" Marc asked, indicating the photograph.

Hollis shook her head and went to pin the photo on the bulletin board beside those of Becky Huntley and Karen Norvell. "I'm positive. I don't know who she is or why nobody's reported her missing—yet—but it's a safe bet she's a victim of our killer."

"Shorty's at the crime scene with the pool-maintenance people," Marc said. "Jordan rousted everybody first thing this morning; whatever you saw must have spooked him."

"Or I did," she said ruefully. "I'm told it's a bit unnerving to watch a medium trying to communicate with a spirit."

"Well, we'll know in the next few hours if there's any real evidence in that pool." Marc looked at Dani. "You were saying, if Shirley is a victim . . . ?"

"Then maybe we know now what the killer's been doing all these weeks. Maybe he came straight here, to Venture, already had or found his safe place, and got it ready. And then started selecting his victims."

"Hunting," Paris said. "But not one at a time, more like a . . . group of potential targets. He had a pretty good I.D. on all of them before he moved on the first one."

"It makes sense," Dani said. "Just like in Boston, these women were grabbed as they went about their lives, and in each case the timing was perfect; they were outside, unprotected, with no witnesses. He never had to break down a door or even shatter a window to get at them."

Hollis said, "No way to chalk that up to chance. Not the three times here, and sure as hell not the dozen times in Boston."

"But in Boston he didn't have the time between victims to do much hunting, and there sure as hell hasn't been much more here," Marc objected—but then nodded. "Of course. The X factor: Is he or isn't he psychic. That's what tipped off Bishop, wasn't it? The hunter was moving too fast to spend much time searching for his prey between attacks, yet there each victim was. Perfect time, perfect place, perfect opportunity. Exactly when and where he wanted them, when and where he expected them to be. Almost like magic."

"Or like he knew," Dani said.

Hollis was nodding. "The more-traditional profilers insisted that the killer had likely selected most if not all of his targets early on, that he knew their habits and routines long before he got his hands on them. And that makes sense, up to a point, but it conveniently ignores the several instances where the victim was alone and vulnerable—and in a situation not a normal part of her routine—when she was taken. Once, maybe, the killer got lucky. Not more than once."

Paris closed a folder and pushed it away from her with a slight grimace, which Dani

knew the others would probably read as dis-
taste rather than what it was: the response to a
pounding headache. "And then there's Annie
LeMott," she said. "If I'm reading the files
right, even the traditional profilers agreed that
the killer wasn't interested in the limelight and
would **not** have grabbed Annie if he had
known who she was."

Marc offered another objection. "But
wouldn't he have known? If he was psychic, if
that was how he was hunting his prey?"

"You'd think." Hollis was scowling at no
one in particular. "Damn, no wonder Bishop's
still trying to get a handle on this guy."

Dani rubbed the back of her neck in a vain
attempt to soothe the stiffness there but forced
herself to stop when she realized Marc was
watching her. "Look, one doesn't necessarily
negate the other. Think about it this way: If he
isn't psychic and **did** have to spend time studying and hunting each victim, we have several
instances where he couldn't possibly have
known in advance where his prey would be, because the women were somehow outside their
normal routine. If, on the other hand, we assume he was so **lucky** because he's psychic and

hunted them that way, then the only victim who doesn't really make sense is Annie LeMott. Who she was made her a dangerous victim, and if he was psychic he should have known that."

"Maybe he couldn't read her," Paris suggested. "Even the strongest psychic isn't a hundred percent."

"As far as we know, that's true," Hollis said. "Plus, some people have shields, either naturally or because they needed at some point in their lives to protect themselves, and even the strongest psychics we know of can't get through walls like that."

Paris nodded. "Exactly. So even if he is psychic, and if he does have **more** bells and whistles than we do, we can't know for sure that he doesn't have some of the same limits. In fact, he must have, given that he's at least nominally human. So he's out trolling, he already has eleven notches on his belt, and if I remember correctly, there was nearly a week between the eleventh victim and Annie. Right?"

Hollis nodded. "Right. Boston was jumpy as hell, and very few women ventured out alone."

"So he hasn't been lucky in that sense. If there's plenty of prey but none of it's vulnerable, unprotected, alone, then this hunter doesn't come out of the dark. And he really, really needs to feed."

Dani said, "I know the animal metaphor fits, but—"

"Sorry. Anyway, he's out hu—trolling and crosses paths with Annie completely by chance." Paris frowned. "Does anybody know what she was doing out alone?"

Nodding again, Hollis said, "She and a friend went to a movie, together. Rode together, sat together in the theater, were careful not to be alone, just as they had been warned to be. Went back to the apartment building where they both lived, together. Approximately a half hour later, a neighbor saw Annie about to take her trash out. That's the last anyone saw of her."

Paris shook her head a little, jolted from the mental exercise of trying to solve a puzzle by the reminder of a young life snuffed out. "Man, you do everything right and then get tripped up by something utterly ordinary."

"Such is life," Hollis noted. "Or fate or

destiny, if you believe in that. Because not only did Annie spend those few precious minutes about ten yards from the safety of the door of her apartment building, but she just **happened** to be exactly the killer's type, he just **happened** to be close enough, and for whatever reason he couldn't know or guess that by grabbing her he was making his first real mistake."

14

AT THIS RATE," Gabriel said with a sigh, "we're gonna be here a long, **long** time."

We can't be here a long time. You said it yourself: Strangers will stand out here. Especially once they know about the victims.

"Yeah, the sheriff's done a good job of keeping his people quiet this long, I have to say." Gabriel studied his map for a moment, then squinted into the distance. "That old textile mill is right in the middle of a neighborhood. No way can I get close in daylight."

My turn tonight, then.

"Right." He put a small check mark beside that particular circled area on his map. "Just about every backyard I see has a dog, so be careful."

Dogs love me.

"They make a lot of noise when you're around. I'm just saying that if you're going to do a little breaking and entering in the dead of night, best not to rouse the neighborhood watch. Okay?"

Yes, Gabriel.

"The meekness does not become you. It's also a rotten lie," he said, moving the map slightly and leaning closer to the Jeep's hood to get a better look. He frowned, then bent to get a laptop out of his backpack and opened it up on top of the map. "You know, this is sort of a weird little place."

Why do you say that? I mean, aside from the obvious serial-killer thing, it seems a perfectly normal small town to me.

"With an awful lot of churches."

Small towns in the South usually do have a lot of churches.

"Uh-huh. With names like Church of the Everlasting Sin?"

You're kidding.

"No."

Hmmm. Maybe that's just the Baptist version of Our Lady of Perpetual Sorrows, something like that.

"I don't think so."

Why not?

He typed rapidly, having no problem carrying on a conversation at the same time. "Every Baptist church I've ever seen has been nice, with polished pews and thick carpet and lots of flowers, and even stained glass. I don't think the Church of the Everlasting Sin is going to have any of that."

Because?

"Because," Gabriel said, "according to this most recent map, the church is presently housed in what used to be an old grain-storage facility, and according to the database we're still compiling on the town, the pastor of the Church of the Everlasting Sin, one Reverend Jedidiah Butler, has locked horns with the town council for the last couple of months. He insists on holding services in the place as it is, and the town wants him to either rehab or rebuild."

Never bet against a town. Unless you have God on your side.

"Yeah, well, I'm not so sure this guy does." Gabriel scowled down at the laptop's screen. "Fifteen years ago, the cops were dogging him out in California. And it wasn't for staging a protest for freedom of religion."

Don't tell me.

"Yep. Seems the good pastor was suspected of killing his wife."

Last night was . . . strange," Dani said, keeping her voice low as she watched people in special protective gear working carefully in and around the roped-off pool.

"Tell me about it," Paris said. "My head is still killing me. Hollis?"

"Yeah, me too." Hollis was frowning. "Is my memory off, or did I hear another voice in there with ours?"

Paris said, "Hard to tell with all the screaming."

"You're clairvoyant and didn't pick it up?"

Paris hesitated, looking at Dani. "Well . . ."

"It was there." Dani looked at the other

two women and managed a smile. "Yeah, same voice. His. I've been thinking about that. That . . . junction of hallways in the dream walk? A bit like the center of a web."

"Another trap," Hollis said.

Dani nodded. "I think about all those women in Boston, the women here—it's like he lays his trap and waits for them to walk into it."

"That's what you feel the symbolism means?" Hollis asked.

"I don't know what I feel, except . . . that something's missing. Something important."

Marc joined them in time to hear what Dani said, but instead of commenting on that, he looked at them one by one and said, "So, is somebody going to tell me what happened last night with the three of you? I can't say for sure about Hollis, but I've never known either Dani or Paris to drink enough to be hungover the next day—and that's what you all look like."

"I'd love to work up some righteous indignation," Paris told him, "but I see them, and I saw me in the mirror this morning, and I couldn't agree more."

"It was a dream walk," Dani said briefly.

"All three of you?"

Dani refused to look at him. "Yes. We thought there was a chance we might find out something."

"Did you?"

It was Hollis who replied, "Another symbolic trap, this one filled with endless hallways and screams. And maybe the voice Dani heard before."

"It was him," Dani said. "But just saying my name, right at the end, before we all came out."

"I don't like that," Hollis said. "I haven't been psychic my whole life, but it doesn't take an expert to know that an evil voice in your mind is not a good thing."

"Maybe I'm just nuts," Dani suggested, not entirely kidding.

Before anyone could respond to that, Shorty joined them to say, "Good news, bad news, and weird news. Good news is, we don't have a body in the pool, the drains, or any of the equipment."

"The bad news?" Marc asked.

"Bad news is, what we do have is more of

what we found here on Wednesday. Body parts, mostly unidentifiable by sight. We won't know for sure until lab results are in, but I'm guessing there isn't a new victim here."

"And the weird news?" Hollis asked.

Shorty held up a clear plastic bag, and they could all see the silver bracelet it contained. "The weird news is that we have another piece of jewelry, and this one has a name on it. Only the name doesn't seem to belong to any of our victims or to anybody reported missing—as far as I know, anyway."

"What's the name?"

"Audrey."

Marc took the bag and studied the contents for a moment, then passed it on to Dani. "Doesn't mean a thing to me. Any of the rest of you?"

Dani looked at the delicate bracelet, the name of its presumed owner spelled out in pretty, flowing letters. She had never been especially sensitive to objects, and this one told her nothing. "Sorry, I'm drawing a blank." She passed it on to Paris.

And knew immediately that Paris felt something. But her twin merely turned the bagged bracelet in her hands for a moment, then handed it off to Hollis with a shrug.

Dani didn't comment. She waited for Hollis to return the bag to Marc with a shrug of her own and watched him give it back to Shorty.

"Maybe it'll mean something to the lab," Marc said. "Thanks, Shorty." He watched his technician return to the roped-off area around the pool, adding, "Paris, what did you pick up?"

"I'm not so sure I like that you can read me so well," she told him with a frown.

"I'm not reading you. I'm reading Dani— so to speak." He looked at her. "You went tense as soon as Paris touched the bag."

Dani met his gaze briefly, then asked her sister, "What **did** you pick up?"

Still frowning, Paris said, "My abilities seem to be changing too. Instead of a feeling that amounts to little more than a hunch, I saw something this time. I got a weird little flash image of a guy buying flowers. Roses. I think it was at that shop up near the old railroad depot."

"Could you recognize him if you saw him again?" Hollis asked.

"No, I didn't see enough of him. Just his hands reaching for the flowers, and a glimpse of an older lady behind the counter, smiling at him."

"Let's go," Marc said.

It wasn't until they were about halfway to their destination that Hollis spoke from the backseat.

"Look for **her** in the water. Maybe it's as simple as that. A bracelet with a woman's name on it."

"I just hope the name gets us somewhere," Marc said. "Preferably before we find the murdered remains of Shirley Arledge."

He really wanted it to be the same, and it almost was.

Almost.

But the drug he was trying worked only to a point, and after that she really didn't want to cooperate.

She was a screamer. He hated it when she

screamed. It was the quiet sobs, the soft, lady-like pleas, that he expected from Audrey.

He finally resorted to taping her mouth again. It was an imperfect solution, and he was conscious of annoyance with that.

"Audrey, you're making this more difficult than it needs to be," he told her.

She moaned, and her wet eyes begged him.

He enjoyed that for a moment, smiling down at her.

She was ready. Her short hair covering her small, well-shaped head was a rich, dark brown, and the pencil had darkened her eyebrows nicely—though he made a mental note to use the hair color on them next time. He had shaved away the ugly yellow pubic hair and the hair on her legs and armpits as well.

Now to get her thoroughly clean.

He got a bucket filled with hot soapy water. He used the brush first, scrubbing her from her feet to her throat. He used the sink sprayer, with its special long hose, to rinse her body. And even though she was pink and glowing, he used a second bucket of hot soapy water and a soft sponge to wash her down a second time.

He rinsed her again, taking care to shift her as much as possible so that the soapy and then the clear water flowed underneath to reach the places his brush and sponge hadn't.

He used two big, soft bath sheets to dry her, taking special care in all the crevices and underneath her. In the process, the table itself was dried, of course, so when he was finally done he used the controls to bring it back to horizontal. Then he used the programmed setting to lower the foot end of the table just a bit.

He stood between her feet and made sure she was looking at him with her wet brown eyes, and began unbuttoning his shirt.

She made a high-pitched mewling sound, and the muscles along her inner thighs twitched in sudden spasms.

"I'm already very clean," he told her. "Because I always am. But I'll rinse myself off first, just so you can be certain nothing dirty is going to touch you, Audrey."

This time a muffled wail escaped her, and her feet and hands jerked as she fought the restraints.

Hands on his belt, he paused. "Now, Audrey—do you really want another shot?"

He could see the delicious indecision in her eyes and savored it. Did she want to be largely insensitive to what was happening to her, but also completely helpless to stop any of it? Or was she willing to risk the terror, pain, and humiliation for the slim chance that she could exert some control over the outcome?

Her eyes closed briefly, and with a sob she went limp, acquiescing.

"That's my girl," he said, smiling as he began to unbuckle his belt.

The time he spent with Audrey was always energizing but draining as well, and he had to plan for regular breaks for himself to eat or nap or just rest for a while.

It was, he had discovered, another way to draw out the experience, to savor it.

It did seem to take a lot out of Audrey, however.

He left the room after their most recent session of lovemaking to take a quick shower, returning clean, dry, and naked; once Audrey had been scrubbed clean initially, he preferred to be naked.

She seemed to be sleeping when he padded silently back in, but when he pulled the tape from her mouth, she flinched and her eyes opened. Eternally wet eyes, pleading eyes, now sunken a bit and surrounded by darkening circles of faintly bruised flesh.

Odd, that. He never struck her face, and yet those circles always appeared toward the end.

As if her eyes were dying first.

"Please," she whispered. "Please don't hurt me anymore. Please let me go. I won't tell anyone. I promise I won't tell anyone. Please—"

"Now, Audrey, we've discussed this. You're not going to tell anyone, we both know that. You don't have to promise me that. And we've discussed your punishment and the need for it."

"But I'm not Audrey. I'm not the one who abandon—"

He reached out a hand swiftly, almost completely encircling her delicate throat. He applied just a little pressure, tightened his fingers only until she began to choke.

He had learned to know and respect his own strength.

"Hush, Audrey," he said gently.

Her eyes grew huge and her naked body jerked. He waited until he was certain she understood, then removed his hand.

She gasped for air and coughed.

"Now, look what you've made me do," he scolded. "I've bruised your throat. So sorry, sweetheart."

She had to try twice before she could whisper. "I'm sorry. I didn't mean—I didn't mean to be bad."

"I know you didn't. Hush, now. Be still while I clean you up."

Jordan met them at Venture Florist and was just getting out of his cruiser when they pulled up. "I checked with the deputies who followed up on those flowers Marie Goode found at her door," he told them. "Since two of our local grocery stores sell flowers in bunches like that, and those seemed the most anonymous places to buy flowers, the guys started there. And they found virtually identical arrangements at both stores, **with** cards identical to the one with the flowers. None of the clerks they've talked to so far remembers ringing up roses anytime in the last few days."

"And there were no prints on the card," Marc said. He looked at Paris, brows raised.

"All I can tell you is what I saw. I'm pretty sure this is the florist, but I'll know for sure once I'm inside. There was an odd arrangement to the right of the register, obviously for Halloween. I hope," she added as they stepped inside.

Dani could see what her sister meant. The small florist shop, filled to bursting with real and silk arrangements and various stuffed animals and vases and other accessories, looked perfectly normal and innocuous.

Except for the tasteful display to the right of the register, which contained, along with bright orange flowers, grinning skulls and black widow spiders.

"This is the place," Paris said.

Miss Patty, who had owned the shop for as long as anybody could remember, emerged from the back room to greet them. "May I help—Why, hello, Sheriff. What can I do for you?" Her clear blue eyes, the single memorable feature in a face as softly wrinkled as old tissue paper, moved alertly from face to face, and she added, "Oh, dear. I expect it's about the murders, then?"

Feeling rather absurdly as though he were talking back to his grammar-school teacher, Marc said, "Miss Patty, you aren't supposed to know about the murders."

"Heavens, Sheriff, everybody knows about them."

Jordan asked, "Then how come nobody's talking?"

Miss Patty smiled at him. "Everybody's talking, Deputy," she said gently. "Just not to you."

"Or to the media?" Marc asked intently.

"Of course not to them. Out of respect to the families. And then, of course, nobody wants reporters and TV crews showing up around here. That wouldn't help you to solve the murders, and it surely would make our lives harder. Now," she continued briskly, "how can I help you?"

"Miss Patty, do you remember selling a dozen roses to—"

Dani.

Once again, she was aware of a stillness inside her, a waiting, a listening. To him. To his voice.

They can't help you. They can't protect you. He can't protect you. Because you're going to come to me. Just like in your dream. It's inevitable. You belong to me, Dani.

"—so I'm afraid I really can't help you, Sheriff. He paid cash, and he was a very ordinary-looking man. I doubt I'd know him again if he walked in the door right now."

Dani was vaguely surprised that nobody seemed at all aware of the voice she had heard so clearly this time. Surprised that nobody was looking at her strangely, or asking why she was breathing so unevenly, because surely she was, surely it was audible to everyone around her.

But no.

Even Paris seemed oblivious, intent on Miss Patty's conversation with Marc.

Patient, Marc said, "Can you tell me how old he was?"

"Well, I never was very good at estimating

age, and I find it's even more difficult as I grow older. If you told me it was my ticket into heaven, the best I could say would be that he was probably a little older than you, Sheriff. About as tall. I suppose he must have worn a hat, or one of those hoodie things, because I can't recall what color his hair was."

She smiled apologetically. "You see, he wasn't in here long at all. Went straight to the refrigerator case and got the roses for himself. We usually have a dozen or two ready, and that day it was red and yellow. He chose the red. He got the card, too, from one of our little cardholders here on the counter. And then he paid me in cash, wished me a good afternoon, and left."

"Miss Patty—"

"We were getting ready for a wedding, Sheriff. Very busy in the back, and so I wasn't really **thinking** about him, you understand. I am sorry. I wish I could help, I really do."

"Thanks anyway, Miss Patty. Oh, and—if you wouldn't mind?"

Her eyes twinkled. "Not talking about this? Of course I won't, Sheriff. You may count on my total discretion."

Outside, Jordan said, "So, who wants to bet me that Miss Patty isn't on the phone in the back room right this minute **not** talking about our visit?"

Nobody took him up on the offer.

15

THE NAME *AUDREY* on a bracelet seemed to mean little, or at least didn't appear to help them narrow their search in any way. Jordan reported three Audreys on the current tax rolls of Prophet County, all of them born in Venture, likely to be buried here, and none having living husbands or living sons.

"Not that I'd expect to find her here anyway," Hollis said. "Unless our killer came home when he came to Venture. And somehow . . . that doesn't feel likely."

"So why did he come here?" Dani said. She rubbed the back of her neck, tired because it had been a very long day and because she hadn't been all that rested to begin with. "Why choose Venture as his latest hunting ground?"

"The sixty-four-thousand-dollar question," Paris agreed. "There has to be something that brought him here, of all places. Something Venture has that every other small town in the South lacks. And we don't have a clue what that is."

Marc got to his feet, saying, "All I know is that I've spent at least an hour longer than I should have in this room today. I need some air. Come on, Dani, I think you do too."

Hollis looked at Paris with mock sadness. "I feel unloved."

"And unwanted," Paris added.

They stared at each other, this time with real frowns.

"Weird," Hollis said. "Déjà vu."

"Yeah, me too."

Dani had no idea what they were talking about. She was fairly certain she wasn't up to sparring with Marc, but she'd also had more than her fill of this conference room and the brutal exercise of trying to put together the puzzle pieces of a monster's insane mind.

She got up and headed for the door, saying only, "If you guys come up with any bright new ideas, sing out."

Paris waved an absent hand, her attention already fixed once again on the open file on the table in front of her.

"At least she's not thinking about Dan or the divorce," Marc offered quietly as they walked down the hall toward the bullpen and main reception areas of the sheriff's department.

"The silver lining?"

"Why not?"

Dani didn't say anything to that until they were out on the sidewalk, both turning automatically toward the distant center of town because it was a pleasant walk on a pleasant late afternoon.

On most days, at least.

"Paris said—" She stopped herself.

"What did Paris say?"

"Nothing. It doesn't matter."

Marc nodded to a passerby who had lifted

a hand in greeting, and said, "Dani, I wish you'd stop censoring your instincts and impulses around me."

She blinked. "Excuse me?"

"You heard me. You did the same thing years ago. Drove me nuts. I couldn't decide if it was me you didn't trust or yourself, and every time I tried to find out, you did your classic avoidance thing and managed to distract me. Somehow."

Dani glanced at him. "Was that what I was doing?"

"Hell, you've known the right buttons to push with me since you were about seventeen."

She cleared her throat. "You probably shouldn't tell me that. I might take advantage."

"Feel free."

It was at least the second time he had said something like that, but more than his matter-of-fact tone made Dani choose not to go down that path with him. Here and now, at least.

She knew damn well she was too tired for **that**. Plus, her head was still throbbing dimly, at least in part because she was trying to shield her mind and wasn't at all sure she could even manage the unfamiliar bit of psychic protection.

That voice. That damn voice. She never wanted to hear it again. And she was terrified it was somehow connected to some part of her deeper than her thoughts.

As if he hadn't expected her to respond, Marc continued, "I was certain it had to do with trust. Then we had that shared experience in one of your vision dreams, and I thought I knew for certain. Because you were gone within a week."

"It wasn't you. I mean, it wasn't about trust."

"Then what was it about?"

Dani wondered vaguely why this seemed easier to talk about as they walked slowly along, not looking at each other. Was that it? Or had everything up to now just made this possible?

"Some things have to happen just the way they happen, Dani. And when they happen." Miranda shrugged. **"No matter what we see or what we dream, the universe has a plan."**

"Dani?"

Was it just a matter of timing? She hesitated, then said, "It was about . . . those monsters I see. Evil people doing terrible things. Horrible events I can't stop. I . . . didn't want to be that girl, not to you."

"That girl?"

"Cassandra." She heard a shaky laugh escape her. "The voice of doom. I never see good things, remember, Marc? I never see happy things. Happy endings. I just see monsters."

"Dani—"

"Paris said that's why I left Venture. That I thought I could take the monsters away with me. All the monsters. So the people I left behind here would be . . . safe. But that's not what happened. Your mother still died of the cancer I saw—**we** saw—take her. And other monsters I saw, like Danny, stayed here. I guess some were always here and always will be. But . . ."

Marc waited.

"But then I came back. And I'm afraid . . . I brought this monster here. Somehow. I brought this evil to Venture."

Marc stopped and turned her to face him, his hands on her shoulders. "Bullshit."

She heard another unsteady laugh escape and hoped it didn't sound as out of control as she felt. "Yeah, that's all I needed to hear, one good, resounding **bullshit**. That'll fix everything."

He was smiling faintly. His hands tightened on her shoulders. "Listen to me. You are not Cassandra. Not the voice of doom. And you did not bring monsters to Venture when you came back here or take them away when you left. The monsters just **are**, Dani. Part of life. The darkness most of us try to keep at bay. The difference is that sometimes you can see them coming, that's all."

"And what good is that if I can't change what I see?" she asked, even as a part of her wondered if that was, for some reason she had yet to fathom, actually happening this time. If she was changing what she had seen, had maybe already changed it.

If she was even making things worse than she had seen.

"The monsters keep winning, Marc."

"Dani—"
"What if this one wins too?"

Saturday, October 11

Roxanne really did like dogs but knew her brother had been right in advising her not to wake the neighborhood with her postmidnight visit, so she took care to be as quiet as possible as she moved toward the abandoned textile mill.

Defunct. The word is defunct.

"And every time you say it," she whispered, "it sounds weirder. But never mind that. Take a gander at the neighborhood and tell me if you sense anything wrong."

Okay, hang on a minute.

She waited in the shadows of what had once been a small gas station of the cozy type seldom seen these days, wondering again why this seemingly prosperous little town could boast so many abandoned buildings. So many defunct businesses. And why it didn't seem to bother anyone to leave the structures standing as is rather than tear them down or repurpose them.

She wasn't quite as suspicious by nature as Gabriel was, but anomalies nagged at her, and this was the biggest one she'd seen in Venture.

Well, barring the serial-killer thing.

I'm not getting anything. In fact, it's damn quiet for a Friday night.

"Saturday morning now," Roxanne pointed out softly as she moved from the shadows and continued on her way.

Either way, it's a bit strange, if you ask me.

"We've both seen most of what there is to see of this town, Gabe, and I didn't notice any nightclubs or bars." She continued to whisper, her voice hardly more than a breath of sound.

They have a multiplex at that mall out by the highway. I guess everybody's there.

"Postmidnight shows? I sort of doubt it, but maybe they're having a film festival or something. Anyway, if that's where they are, let 'em stay there. I don't need anybody's headlights—"

Speaking of. Duck.

She took cover on one side of a tall hedge, just seconds before a quiet car passed her position and turned at the next corner.

Roxanne waited in the shadows through a slow count of ten, then continued on her way. There were streetlights in the area—sort of. Technically, she supposed, since the lights were clearly industrial and likely belonged to the region's power company. But these lights tended to be beside or behind the homes rather than out on the streets, as they were closer to downtown.

So there was plenty of darkness for her to skulk in.

Investigate. Plenty of darkness to investigate in.

"Neither of us is very grammatical." Roxanne paused briefly to get her bearings, then made the final turn that would take her to the hulking building that had once housed a textile mill.

Never mind grammar. You really need to be careful now, Rox. Remember who you're hunting. What you're hunting.

"I know."

Just look for signs, that's all. Find something, and we call in the cavalry. Right?

"Stop worrying. I'm not at all anxious to run into this monster, believe me. Not that I'm his type."

Judging by the victims here, that's not a problem for him anymore. He's making these women into the woman he wants them to be.

"He's sticking to the same body type, though. I'm way too tall." She found the main entrance to the mill—on the other side of a padlocked gate. "Damn. This place has two big steel doors and absolutely no windows; why put a fence around it too?"

Old security. Like everything else abandoned around here, nobody's bothered with it since the last one out locked the gate. Padlock?

"Yeah, big one. Can you get it?"

Of course.

She waited for the telltale click, then removed the open padlock and hooked it on the chain-link fence. Then she paused. "You know, it just occurred to me that since textile mills are filled with big, heavy machinery, they tend to be built on slab foundations. Solid concrete. No basements or under-ground structures of any kind."

Huh. How about that? I never would have—

"Goddammit, Gabe. We're going to have to have another little Come to Jesus talk, you and me."

I don't know what you mean.

"The hell you don't. You pull this protective shit on me one more time, and I'll—"

You'll what?

"Look for another partner."

Yeah, good luck with that. We're stuck with each other, babe. And in the meantime, why don't you check out this place anyway? Because no matter what you suspect about my motives, the truth is that we'd be making a huge mistake in interpreting Dani's dream literally. So we check out every potential hideout for a serial killer who needs space and privacy. Right?

Grudgingly, she said, "Right. But you have seriously got to accept the fact that I can take care of myself."

Okay, okay. But just move, will you? It's nearly dawn.

Roxanne opened the old gate cautiously and was several steps along the broken-concrete walkway to the mill's main doors when she stopped suddenly and turned to scan the darkness behind her.

What?

"That car, the one that passed a few minutes ago."

What about it?

"I've been watching this neighborhood since midnight, and it's the only vehicle I've seen moving."

So?

"I didn't see it turn into a driveway. Plus it was moving slowly and was awfully quiet."

Looking for an address?

"At four in the morning? Do me a favor and sweep the area again, would you? I've got a bad feeling about that car."

Gabriel didn't argue.

Okay. Hang on a second.

Roxanne waited, her uneasiness growing as she visually scanned the area as well as she could in the darkness.

267

Leave, Rox. Now.

"Gabe—"

Get the hell out of there. Don't stop to lock the gate, just go!

Roxanne moved immediately, smoothly drawing her weapon as she stepped through the gate. But as fast as she was, as careful as she was, she never saw or heard him coming, and never even got the chance to assume a defensive posture before powerful hands grabbed her gun arm.

Paris refilled Dani's coffee cup and pushed it across the table to her. "Look, Marc's right, especially about his mother. People get sick. The fact that you dreamed his mother would didn't make it happen—but it may have given her more time, because he used the warning to make damn sure she got to a doctor, pronto."

"That's what he said." Dani wrapped her fingers around the warm cup. "And I pretended to believe him."

"And he pretended to believe that?" Paris shook her head. "He always did know you better than you thought, sweetie."

Dani shrugged. "It was a moment, maybe . . . and then it wasn't. I shut down, or he did. A deputy caught up with us to tell Marc that he was needed back at the station, and we went back. Bad timing, I guess."

"Bad timing." Paris was frowning. "Did you dream last night?"

"Not that I remember." She hadn't slept, too fearful of giving over control of her sleeping mind to the vision dream. Or to the voice that kept getting in.

The only upside, she had decided, was that she seemed better able to shield or cocoon her own mind, since even Paris seemed unaware of the struggle. For the first time, that realization caused Dani a twinge of worry.

It was odd, now that she thought about it, for something so profound happening to her to go unnoticed by her twin.

"So you didn't try to take Marc in?"

Dani dragged her mind back to the conversation. "I told you, I have no intention of doing that. Look what happened the other night with you and Hollis—and both of you are psychic."

"We're both okay. More worried about

you, since you were the one with the nose-bleed."

"Yeah, and that still bugs me. I don't think it was from the strain of taking the two of you in."

"Why not?"

"Because I didn't **feel** any strain at all, not even an effort. I wanted you two with me—and you were. It wasn't until we heard that ungodly scream that I felt . . ."

"What, scared? Because it sure scared the hell out of me."

"No, it wasn't fear. I mean, I was scared, but I was feeling something else."

"Like?"

"I don't know. Pressure? Something like that." **And the voice. The one you barely heard.**

"You got the bends in a dream?"

"Funny. I don't know what it was, obviously."

"But it felt like something outside yourself?"

It was Dani's turn to frown. "Maybe."

"Please don't tell me it was our psychic killer. I mean, I know we all heard his voice, or at least a voice, but he couldn't have actually done anything to you, right? He couldn't have caused the nosebleed?"

Dani's frown deepened. "I don't see how."

"I guess there's no way to know for sure."

"Not unless I bump into him in the next dream." Dani shivered. "I may take you and Hollis in again just for company." Then she shook her head. "Scratch that. You two looked exhausted all day; going into my dream was clearly a bad idea."

"It hasn't hurt me so far."

"And maybe you've just been lucky."

"Too dumb to know better, when we were kids," Paris agreed. "Thing is, we didn't know better. We had a playground inside your head."

"Okay, that sounds really creepy," Dani told her.

"However it sounds, it has had its uses, especially since we signed on with Haven."

"Barely. Twice I've managed to take you into a relevant vision dream. Twice. In more than a year."

"And it was useful both times. I remembered a few details you couldn't, and those details proved helpful to the investigations."

"Didn't change what I saw. It never changes what I see, the outcome."

"How do you know?"

Dani stared at her sister.

"Seriously, how do you know? Dani, maybe what you see is . . . the lesser of two evils. It's like what Miranda told us. Premonitions are tricky beasts: Do you see what happens if you don't intervene, or what happens if you do?"

"That's a hell of a possibility. I mean, that things could be worse than what I see. And you're about as subtle as neon."

Paris sighed. "Just trying to provide a little perspective, that's all. You've gotta get over this idea that you're a prophet—or prophet-ess—of doom, that your ability is entirely negative. It's been dragging at you since we were kids."

"I just . . . For once, I'd like to foresee something positive."

"Maybe the universe doesn't need help with positive. Isn't there some kind of en-tropy theory about how the natural state of things is disintegration?"

Dani stared at her.

"Hey, I consider ideas too. Sometimes. Anyway, maybe what the universe needs help with is keeping everything from falling totally apart. Why show you the happily-ever-afters if what's really needed is help getting there through all the dark stuff along the way?"

"Way to cheer me up, sis."

"You're not getting it." Paris wore an unusually intent expression, and her hazel eyes had darkened almost to brown. "Look, at any given time I might pick up a few facts or bits of information, like the way I did with that bracelet—for all the good it did us. Anyway, those glimmers might or might not help me with an investigation or a problem or, hell, just help me get through the day. But people like you and Miranda and this Quentin we've heard so much about, the universe shows you guys signposts. Not hidden in the scenery the way they are for the rest of us, but lit up and glowing so you can't miss them. And whether those signposts are things to avoid or paths to take, it still gives you a leg up on everybody else."

"Dani, we're all wandering in the dark, and you guys have the lamps." The distant look in her eyes vanished abruptly, and Paris chuck-led. "My metaphor wandered, too, didn't it?"

"Just a little bit." Still, Dani felt better about an ability she had for so many years viewed as usually ugly and depressing. But then she shook her head and added, "Didn't Miranda also say there's a difference between a premonition and a prophecy? That a pre-monition is something you can influence, af-fect, and a prophecy is . . . written in stone? Inevitable no matter what you do to try to change it?"

"Pretty much."

"So how do I know what it is I'm really seeing? A version of the future I help shape or one I can't avoid?"

"I guess you can never really know. Unless you learn how to be a lot more plugged in to the universe than either one of us is so far." Paris eyed her twin, then said, "And we share that neon subtlety. Quit stalling and finish your coffee so we can get to the station."

"I wasn't—"

"Yeah, yeah. If you and Marc don't get things between you sorted out soon, some-body's going to have to knock your heads together. Bad timing or not, we need the two of you functional if we're going to find and stop this killer."

It was a blunt reminder but a welcome one; Dani had discovered since signing on with Haven that being able to use her abilities in positive ways had been slowly changing how she felt about those abilities, and she wanted that to continue.

Needed it to continue.

Especially now.

So she finished her coffee and prepared to return to the sheriff's department with Paris. And it wasn't until they were almost there that she wondered suddenly why Paris had not once, in all this time, asked the question she should have asked about Dani's vision dream.

She had not asked where **she** was.

Because she didn't want to know the answer?

Or because, like Dani, she was afraid she already did?

16

HOLLIS HADN'T EXPECTED to sleep well on Friday night, because the day had been too long and the previous night unusually active, if only on a subconscious level.

There was something amusing in that, she decided. That what had quite probably been a brief dream experience—because they mostly were brief, even if some felt interminable while they were actually happening—could take so much out of one physically.

But dragging her exhausted self around all day Friday had certainly proven the truth of that. It had also convinced Hollis to report in to Bishop before she got ready for bed. And, more important, to hold nothing back.

"You heard the voice too?" Bishop asked.

Sitting on the edge of the bed in her motel room, using the phone on the nightstand because her cell was charging, Hollis frowned at the ice bucket on the dresser. "Yeah, sort of. It was almost more a feeling than a sound."

"What kind of feeling?"

"Pressure," she replied, after thinking about it. "Like something pushing at me. At us. Probably mostly at Dani, since she's the one who woke up with a nosebleed. Or was that from the effort to take Paris and me in?"

"It's difficult for me to even guess," he said slowly. "Her abilities have always been somewhat erratic, I gather, but Miranda felt she was considerably stronger than she seemed, even more than a year ago. I don't recall a nosebleed being reported by her previously."

"Not according to Paris. I have to say, though, that I'm a lot more worried about that voice. Dani seems certain it's the voice—or thoughts, or energy, whatever—of our killer. And even if she hasn't said a whole lot about it, or showed much of what she's feeling, I think she's scared."

"Feeling threatened?"

"Yeah, probably. He told her she couldn't run or hide and that nobody could protect her from him. And he told her **from inside her head.** And not just in her dreams, but when she was awake. Feeling threatened? She ought to be freakin' terrified. I'm not so sure I wouldn't be in bed with the covers pulled over my head if I were in her place."

After a moment Bishop asked, "How **are** you doing?"

Hollis wanted to give him a flip answer, but she had learned the uselessness of that where Bishop was concerned. Just because she wasn't a telepath didn't mean he couldn't read her, even across whatever distance lay between them. So she answered honestly.

"I'm tired and worried. And even though I suppose I should be happy about it, I'm also unnerved that the dead seem to be reaching me a lot easier than they did in the beginning."

"It is a good thing," he reminded her.

"It's a scary thing. I don't think I'm ever going to get used to it, just so you know." She changed the subject abruptly. "Listen, is there any progress in revising that profile? Because we could sure as hell use it."

"You've given me new information," Bishop pointed out. "Wednesday's crime scene, plus the open stalking of Marie Goode, if we assume that's him—"

Hollis interrupted to say, "Trust me, this is hardly the sort of town to have more than one weirdo sneaking around taking pictures of women. That would be stretching coincidence to the snapping point."

"You're assuming the killer takes photos of the murders," Bishop pointed out calmly.

She nodded, half consciously. "Because of the one crime scene we have. Struck me the first time I saw those overhead shots Marc's forensics team got. It was carefully chosen, and not just because it was isolated. The area made a perfect composition for his . . . art. He left us a picture and took one himself, I'd bet on it."

"Then I'd call it more than an assumption," Bishop said. "So he's photographing not only his kill sites but also his potential victims, as he stalks them. That, plus the necklace and bracelet left so conspicuously behind—all are radical departures from his previous M.O. He's leaving traces of himself, possibly even a trail. Add in the virtual certainty now that we're dealing with a psychic mind of unknown ability—"

"And we're screwed?" she finished wryly.

"You need to be careful, Hollis. All of you, but especially you, Dani, and Paris. Because if the need to terrify is at the core of this bastard's sickness—and what little we know about him points that way—then establishing contact with Dani may be teaching him that he has a new tool. A new weapon. It may not be all about a particular look for him, not anymore."

"I'm no profiler, and even I know that's a huge leap in the evolution of a serial killer."

"It may not be an evolution," Bishop said. "He may be . . . devolving. The established personality matrix could be disintegrating."

"Jesus. I didn't know that was possible."

"With the right psychological trigger, almost anything is possible."

"And the right psychological trigger in this case would be . . . ?"

"I have no idea."

Hollis sighed. "Never thought I'd say this, but I would have preferred one of your more enigmatic answers. At least then I could cherish the illusion that **somebody** knew what was going on."

"Sorry to disappoint you." Bishop sighed. "Just be careful, Hollis. I'll get the revised profile to you ASAP. But, in the meantime, don't be too quick to avoid whatever the dead have to tell you. Any trail he leaves, by accident or deliberation, could well take us anywhere—or nowhere; it's almost always true of serials that their victims may be our best leads in finding the killer."

After all that plus the day she'd had, Hollis **really** didn't expect to sleep well. And she didn't, tossing and turning, waking up at least twice to check the clock. And the locks on her door.

Somewhere around three A.M. she finally dropped into an exhausted sleep, the heavy kind that seemed to drag one deeper than dreams. And when she woke from that, it was so sudden that all she could feel at first was the runaway pounding of her heart.

Seconds later, she knew she wasn't alone.

She had left a light burning behind the half-closed bathroom door, and it provided just enough illumination for her to make out a shape at the foot of her bed.

Her weapon was in the drawer of the nightstand, but instead of reaching for that, Hollis reached for the lamp, never taking her eyes off that faint, indistinct shape.

"He knows who you are."

Hollis froze for an instant, her hand on the lamp's switch, chills chasing one another up and down her spine. At least half-hoping she would see nothing, that the quiet statement had been only in her head, she turned the lamp on.

"He knows who you are," Shirley Arledge repeated. Her face was still, eyes anxious. "He knows what you are."

She was already fading.

"Wait," Hollis said quickly, trying to control her voice, to keep it soft. "Who is he? How can we find him, stop him?"

Shirley Arledge shook her head, and her voice faded even as she did, as she might have replied, "He's tricking you . . ."

Hollis slowly sat up in bed, staring at the place where the spirit of a young woman had stood. Then she turned her head slowly and examined the entire motel room: very ordinary, uninspiring, and a little depressing at—she looked at the clock—five in the morning.

Finally convinced that she was, indeed, alone in her room, she looked down at her bare arms, at the clearly visible gooseflesh.

"No," she murmured. "I am never . . . ever . . . going to get used to this."

Still no sign of Shirley Arledge," Marc reported as he joined the others in the conference room. "And still no sign there was anything violent about her disappearance."

"She's dead," Hollis said.

Everyone else in the room went still, staring at the federal agent, and Hollis offered them a weary smile. "I'm beginning to think there's a trail of bread crumbs in the spirit world leading straight to me. First time a spirit's pulled me out of a sound sleep, though."

"Evolving abilities," Paris said almost absently, frowning a little.

"Are you okay?" Dani asked Hollis.

"I'd love to sleep about twelve hours, but other than that, I'm fine. Frustrated by one more thing that doesn't seem to lead us anywhere, though."

Marc stirred, finally, going to fill up his coffee cup before returning to the table, his every move deliberate. He didn't speak until he was seated at the head of the table. "I gather she didn't tell you anything helpful?"

"She said **he** knew who I was, what I was. And then she said that he was tricking me— or us, I suppose. That he was tricking us. She didn't stick around long enough for more than that." Hollis opened a folder on the table beside her and pulled out a photograph of Shirley Arledge, studying it for a moment before laying it faceup on the table and sliding it toward the center of their group. "No question in my mind: This is the woman I saw around five o'clock this morning. I don't get visitations like that from the living, so I can say with fair certainty that she's dead."

Marc took a swallow of his coffee and then looked at the cup as if he wished there were something other than coffee in it. "Well, shit," he said softly.

"I'm sorry. I wish I could offer you something more useful, but I can't. I can tell you Shirley Arledge died at the hands of this monster. I can tell you his box score is up to at least fifteen now. But I don't know much more about him than I did when I got here. I wish I did, but I don't."

"None of us does," Jordan pointed out. "We have one incredibly gory crime scene with a bloody sign that seems out of character for a killer like this one, but no bodies. So far. Bits and pieces of two victims, but DNA results won't come in for weeks, at least, and only a preliminary match between the fingertip found at the scene and some prints we were able to pull from Becky Huntley's bedroom."

Dani said, "So, probably hers. The fingertip. Way too coincidental if the finger belonged to someone who just happened to visit one of our victims long enough to leave fingerprints in her bedroom." Then she frowned. "Wait. Did Becky and Karen—"

Marc was already shaking his head. "It's preliminary in the case of Shirley Arledge, but as far as we can determine, none of these women knew each other. One more dead end."

Hollis said, "Depressingly common in serial-killer investigations. That's why profiling—still more of an art than a science—is so readily accepted and used by law enforcement. Any tool that offers even the hope of narrowing or focusing the scope of the investigation is better than no tool at all."

"We barely have a profile," Marc pointed out. "Still waiting for your boss's rewrite, but in the meantime what we've got is a killer who's probably a white male, probably between twenty-five and thirty-five, probably from an abusive background, and possibly psychic. Hell, I **probably** passed him on the street sometime this week."

"**If** he's psychic, you didn't shake hands with him," Dani murmured. "Otherwise, you'd have known."

Hollis lifted her brows at the sheriff. "That's your range? Touch?"

"Yeah. If we hadn't already shaken hands,

you could sit next to me and I'd never know you were a medium."

Wryly, Paris said to him, "Care to make a list of everyone you've shaken hands with in Venture?"

"Not really. I don't have a clue how to even start that list."

Jordan looked at the file folders stacked here and there on the table and swore under his breath. "I know we're really just getting started in terms of a time frame for a **typical** serial-killer investigation—and, man, I hate saying every part of that—but does anybody else feel like they're spinning their wheels? A huge task force of law-enforcement person-nel, **including** a team of psychics, has been trying to get a handle on this guy for months, with no luck. Granted, we have a smaller hunting ground here in terms of popula-tion—though not in area—and we don't have media breathing down our necks—"

"Yet," Marc interrupted. "Despite what Miss Patty said, I imagine there are at least a few of our citizens who would welcome TV cameras and microphones shoved in their faces."

"Yeah. But the question stands: What do we have that the task force doesn't?"

"We have Dani's vision dream," Hollis said.

"Which keeps changing," Dani pointed out.

"Only in fairly minor details. The setting is always the same: a warehouse."

"And we're generating that list of warehouses now," Jordan promised. "It's taken more time than I expected to run down some of the property owners, but we're getting there."

"Great." Hollis barely paused. "So there's always a warehouse in the vision. There's always a fire. And, with the roof apparently caving in behind us, we always go down into a basement where we know he's waiting, into what we know is a trap. Interesting that the bait is always the same. Far as I know, Miranda's in Boston with Bishop."

"Which was," Marc said, "this killer's hunting ground. And we're **sure** it's the same killer."

It was a question.

Hollis nodded. "We're sure. The psychics

who tracked him here are sure, and Bishop's sure—and that's good enough for me. Even if the murders here **are** getting different in ways that don't make sense. Unless Bishop is right again, and this killer's needs and rituals are falling apart rather than evolving."

"I gather that'll be part of the revised profile," Marc said.

"That seems to be the way Bishop is thinking." Hollis frowned. "At least, that was my take."

Dani raised her voice slightly to say, "Can I just ask the question we're all avoiding?"

Hollis nodded, with an expression that said she knew what was coming. "Might as well."

"Okay. If we're right and this guy is psychic, if that's how he managed to hunt so successfully in Boston, then how do we know he isn't at least a step ahead of us here?"

"We don't," Marc said.

"No, we don't. If anything, we have some evidence that he is . . . playing with us. Leaving signs behind when he never has before."

Hollis said, "That might not be deliberate. It could just be him coming apart."

"But what if it is deliberate? He didn't want the spotlight in Boston, but maybe, looking back, something inside him liked the attention. Maybe now he wants to prove he's smarter than everybody hunting him."

"Maybe," Marc agreed. "And maybe that's a difference we can use to our advantage."

"He's tricking you," Hollis murmured, repeating what Shirley Arledge had told her in the predawn hours. "I'm not the one usually advising caution, but I think we'd better be careful if we even get the chance to play this guy's game. We'd better be very careful."

Tell me again why I shouldn't clean his clock?" Gabriel demanded.

"With all due respect, Gabe, I wouldn't try it if I were you." The hollow cell connection did nothing to hide the dryness in John Garrett's voice. "As good as you are—he's better."

"I'm willing to test that theory."

"It isn't a theory. And the last thing any of us needs is you tangling with Bishop. Just don't, okay? He had good reason for ap-

proaching Roxanne when and how he did. I
agree with his reason. Roxanne agrees with
his reason."

**I do, you know. Three more steps the way
I was going, and I would have tripped that
motion-sensor floodlight. And roused the
neighborhood canine watch. And Bishop
could hardly stop me any other way without
alerting those same dogs. Right?**

"Well, I—"

"Gabe. Let it go."

Gabriel was a stubborn man but hardly a
stupid one. "If you say so, John. But I don't
have to like it."

"I never expect miracles."

"Yeah, yeah." Gabriel kept his gaze fixed
on Bishop, who stood some yards away and
out of earshot in this remote spot overlooking
Venture.

**He's a telepath, Gabe. Do you really think
there's such a thing as "out of earshot" where
he's concerned?**

Bishop turned his head and raised an eye-
brow at Gabriel, then once again directed his
attention to the town.

"Shit."

John, neither present nor telepathic, had nevertheless spent enough time with psychics in recent years to be able to pick up on non-verbal communication—even at an extreme distance. "Something I should know about?" he asked calmly.

"No. Just remembering why I don't like working around telepaths, that's all."

"You can trust him, Gabe."

"With all due respect, John," Gabriel said, deliberately using his employer's earlier words, "I'll make up my own mind about that."

"Fair enough. But on this particular job, your orders include following his lead as you would mine."

"You sure about that? Running a parallel investigation with the police is one thing, and we've done it before. But this time we're hunting an honest-to-God monster, and the sooner everybody involved puts their heads together and compares notes, the better our chances of tracking him down before some-body else dies."

"And do you honestly believe either Bishop or I would do anything to deliberately sidetrack an investigation or delay for even one moment the capture of such an animal?"

"No. I don't believe that." It wasn't a grudging admission so much as it was an uneasy one. "But somebody always has an agenda, and Bishop's reputation preceded him."

"Meaning?"

"You know exactly what it means. He never puts all his cards on the table, John, and I'm betting he hasn't this time. Whether he and Miranda have seen something he's hoping to avoid, or he's just convinced he has a better plan than the rest of us, he's going to keep it to himself."

"None of us wants Dani's vision to come true," John reminded him.

"I know that. And if I were in Bishop's place, with a vision warning me of that particular dire outcome, I'd make damn sure my wife and partner was safe under lock and key, and far away. I got no problem with that."

"But?"

"But he shouldn't be here. He was part of the vision, too, and every player we put within the killer's reach makes it that much more likely that what Dani saw is going to happen."

"Maybe. Or maybe the right person in the right place is all that's needed to change the outcome."

"John, how many times have you and Maggie told us to be careful where premonitions are involved, because we can't know our actions won't produce something worse? Hell, it's practically our mantra."

There was a brief silence, and then John said, "Sometimes things have to get worse before they get better."

"What the hell is that supposed to mean?"

"It means work with Bishop, Gabe. You and Roxanne. Keep every sense open, and stay on your toes. And please try to remember that we're all on the same side, okay? Check in daily."

"Right." Gabriel slowly closed his phone and wasn't much surprised to see that Bishop was already crossing the space between them.

He waited until the other man was close before speaking. "So what now, Chief?" The title held a faint note of mockery rather than respect. "More warehouses?"

"No," Bishop said. "Now we watch Dani."

17

DANI STARED AT THE formidable list of warehouses, storage facilities, and any other isolated building that might provide the space and privacy a murderous serial killer might need, and drew a deep breath.

"Damn," Paris said before she could.

Nodding, Dani said, "I had no idea. And I never realized how many of these places have been locked up and abandoned for years."

"Decades," Marc said. "My deputies check the doors during patrols—when they remember to. But we don't have vandals to speak of, and unless there are complaints . . . In all honesty, these places are easy to forget unless you're staring right at one of them."

Hollis chewed on a thumbnail briefly as she studied her copy of the list. "I know big abandoned buildings are difficult to repurpose, but I'd think some of these would have been somewhere along the way. That or torn down to make way for new construction."

"I might have an answer for that." Jordan was going over a different list, frowning. "Marc, take a look at this. And tell me how in the hell we didn't know about it."

Dani waited until Marc had the list in hand and began to frown himself to ask, "What is it?"

"Looks like about eighty percent of these old buildings have been bought up by a properties-management company."

Dryly, Hollis said, "I don't see much management involved. Wait a minute. The **same** company?"

Marc grunted an assent, then said, "Huh. How about that. The properties-management company is owned by a church."

"A church?" Paris asked. "A single church?"

"Yeah. The Church of the Everlasting Sin."

They all exchanged glances, then Hollis said, "I did a quick recon when I first got here to get the lay of the land, and one thing definitely caught my attention. The Church of the Everlasting Sin. It's currently being housed here in Venture in that onetime grain-storage facility, right?"

"That's the one," Marc confirmed.

"It didn't appear to me to be very wealthy. To say the least."

Jordan looked baffled. "At the last town council meeting, Reverend Butler claimed he couldn't afford to rehab the place. But if his church owns all these other properties . . ."

Hollis moved to the other end of the conference table, where her laptop lay open and ready. She sat down and typed rapidly, then sat back and waited, her gaze fixed on the screen.

While they waited, presumably for more information, Dani said, "I know I've been away for a while, but as I remember it, the churches in the area have always been sort of . . . bland. I mean, just straight-up Protestant, mostly Baptist, nothing out of the ordinary."

"We get the occasional outside-the-mainstream church," Marc said. "A small block building goes up, or a trailer, or an old storefront gets a new sign painted on the window. Nothing as extreme as snake-handling, say, or Satanism, but there's been talk—forgive the pun—of speaking in tongues, and we've had complaints from neighbors when the worshipping got a little loud on Sunday. Most of those churches don't seem to stick around long, even though they have congregations."

"Maybe the congregations aren't large enough to support the churches," Dani offered.

"Could be. All I know is, one day they're there, and the next they aren't. The Church of the Everlasting Sin, though, that one has stuck around. At least ten years, I'd say."

"No wonder I don't remember it," Dani murmured.

Marc nodded. "You wouldn't. Reverend Butler set up shop the summer after you left Venture."

She refused to be dragged back into the past, saying only, "I can't imagine he'd have much of a congregation. Unless it's just an ordinary Baptist-type church with an unusual name?"

"I'm not sure what it is, to be honest with you, but the congregation is sizable. We've had a few complaints, especially in recent years, about some of their practices, but nothing I've been able to get any real evidence on." Marc shrugged. "It's a tight-knit congregation, I can tell you that much. And you seldom see any one of them out alone. It's a bit weird, actually."

"Creepy," Jordan translated. "Far as I can tell, you **never** see one out alone. Well, except for the reverend. Marc, weren't there some rumors about him when he first got here?"

"Yeah, that he killed his wife."

"False rumors?" Dani ventured.

"Depends on your point of view. When I became sheriff, I checked into his background, and what I found was mostly vague except for that single bit of his history. His wife died under mysterious circumstances about fifteen years ago. Investigators were pretty sure in their own minds that he did it, apparently to collect the insurance, but there was never enough evidence to arrest him, much less convict him. Then he got involved with his church and more or less dropped off the map as far as the police were concerned."

Paris said, "I guess it's too much to hope he could be our killer here?"

"He's the wrong age according to the most recent profile we have, he isn't psychic, and as far as I can remember he was in Venture all summer."

"So that would be no," Paris murmured.

"Pretty much," Marc told her. "Which isn't to say he might not know something that could be helpful. Especially since his church seems to own most of the abandoned warehouses and other derelict buildings in Venture."

"Well," Hollis said, "the Church of the Everlasting Sin is wealthy, whether this particular congregation is or not." She was frowning at the screen of her laptop. "The IRS has its suspicions of Reverend Butler even if the police couldn't prove theirs, but it appears he has a very good accountant—in Atlanta—and they haven't been able to pin anything on him. But the church, now that's something different."

"How so?" Paris asked. "I've heard a few wild rumors, but—"

"Maybe not so wild. Says here that the Church of the Everlasting Sin first made an appearance about twenty-five years ago, out west. Gossip had it that among their practices was some kind of supposed cleansing ritual that involved screaming at members—including children—in order to scare the sin out of them."

"I've heard that here," Marc admitted. "But we could never find any evidence of abuse, and neither could Social Services."

"Couldn't find much out west either, according to the FBI files," Hollis told them. "The Bureau was called in initially because a former member charged that the church kidnapped his children, took them across state lines to another—well, they call them parishes, apparently. So what you've got here in Venture is a parish of the Church of the Everlasting Sin. Anyway, turned out the man's estranged wife, still a member of the church, had the kids with her and eventually won legal custody."

Jordan said, "But the FBI kept the case file open?"

"Looks like. Over the years, they had reports from some of the watchdog groups that monitor cults, and complaints from quite a few former members, but so far nothing they could take to court."

"Sounds familiar," Marc said.

"Yeah, only this church doesn't seem to be building its wealth through its members, like most cults do. Nobody signs over their properties or businesses—in fact, that's forbidden. Members are expected to tithe, but no more."

"So how can they afford to buy up all the property here?" Jordan asked.

Hollis scrolled through a few pages, reading intently, then said, "It's one of the reasons the IRS is suspicious. It **looks** like they use the member contributions to purchase land and other properties, and the member businesses provide donations of goods and services to keep the church and all its parishes running."

Marc said, "Jordan, I can think of at least three local businesses owned and operated by members of Reverend Butler's church; let's see if we can put together a list of the rest." As his chief deputy nodded and left the room, he added, "Not that I see how any of this might help us track a killer."

Quietly, Hollis said, "Well, here's the thing. The church owns an awful lot of the seemingly abandoned warehouselike structures in Venture, yes. The church, in fact, owns lots of those kinds of buildings in other parishes around the country. In plenty of small towns probably like this one. And in quite a few cities. Portland, Kansas City, Cleveland, Baltimore, Knoxville."

It was Paris who guessed "Boston?"

"Boston."

The smell of bleach stung his nostrils, but he breathed it in deeply anyway. He liked the smell of bleach. It was clean.

He liked things to be clean.

His worktable had been scrubbed down, and after he poured the bleach onto the stainless-steel surface, he let it remain there for a while, thoroughly disinfecting, before rinsing it off.

In the meantime, he went to his trophy

wall, studying the pictures, enjoying them. All the different candid shots, taken without their knowledge, as they went about their day.

Each individual board told the mundane story of a life.

Walking. Shopping. Getting the mail. Going to church. Pausing on the sidewalk to speak to a friend. Walking a dog. Kissing a husband. Working in a garden.

"This is your life," he murmured, and chuckled.

Such ordinary, sad little lives they led.

Until he transformed them, of course.

First Becky. Then Karen. Then Shirley. All taken from their bland lives and transformed.

He knew they weren't really Audrey.

He wasn't crazy, after all.

They came into his hands someone else, someone boring and uninteresting. Someone the world would have failed to notice if not for his work. Nobodies.

He made them Somebody.

He made them Audrey.

Standing before the first board, he reached out and touched one of the two central images, an eight-by-ten he had taken himself, the record of all his preparations.

Becky as Audrey. Naked on his worktable, her dark hair glossy, her brown eyes staring into the camera's lens, because he had turned her head just so before taking the picture.

Brown eyes filled with terror.

He savored that, the power swelling within him, his body stirring, hardening. He unzipped his pants and freed himself but kept his gaze on the photos.

The other central image was the final shot of Becky as Audrey, when he had finished his work. He touched that lightly, his index finger slowly stroking the image of her, all laid open on his table, her breasts and sex removed and her torso slit from throat to crotch, the cold fluorescent lights above making her exposed organs glisten.

Her eyes were closed for the final shot.

He always closed them for that, because while he enjoyed dying eyes, dead eyes bothered him.

Haunted him—or would, if he let them. But he didn't believe in ghosts. Didn't believe in an afterlife. That's why he worked so hard to make this life fit him, because every moment, every second, had to count.

He stroked the picture a moment longer, feeling himself hardening even more, then moved to the second of his trophy boards.

Karen as Audrey. Same pose, same terrified brown eyes staring into the camera's lens.

And the same growing sense of power inside himself, the feeling that he could do anything, bend anyone to his will.

Anyone.

The knowledge, the certainty of his own invincibility caught at his breath with its strength. He was so hard he ached but exercised his self-control by touching only the record of his work, not himself.

He touched each of the two central photos, stroked them, savored them. The throbbing of his power spread throughout his body, pounded in his ears, and he could hear his breath coming fast now, not quite panting. His vision began to blur, but he forced himself to move on to the third board.

Shirley as Audrey.

Hers was the most complete transformation yet, and he spent long moments stroking the images, remembering every action, every detail of the process.

"Almost perfect," he whispered.

He took a step back but then leaned forward and braced his hands on either side of the board, his gaze fixed on the central photos, refusing to touch himself. His rigid legs were trembling, and his hips wanted, needed, to thrust, to pound, but he forced himself to remain utterly still. His eyes completely lost focus, his breath rasped, but he was otherwise silent as the memories of Shirley/Audrey's final moments made his hard flesh throb and twitch and finally empty itself in spasms of pleasure.

Teeth gritted, he rode out the waves of release without making a sound. Not because he had to, but because he could.

He was Power, and he could do anything.

The Prophecy said so.

Dani—

"Dani, are you ready to—" Marc broke off, staring at her with a frown. "What is it?"

She pushed herself up from her seat at the conference table. "Nothing. My mind must have wandered. Did Paris and Jordan report back in?"

"Yeah." He was still frowning. "So far they've managed to quietly talk to two of Karen Norvell's fellow tellers from the bank. Only one says she remembers actually seeing a man with a camera last summer, maybe taking pictures of Karen, but she doesn't remember what he looked like. Paris said both women are worried that they didn't take what they thought they knew seriously, that they didn't report it to someone. Guilt, of course. Jordan said it was pretty obvious they were afraid Karen's dead."

Absently, Dani said, "Smart to interview them at home rather than at the bank. But you know the news is bound to break by Monday, don't you? I mean, break publicly in a big way."

He nodded. "We've been damn lucky, but with every Venture citizen we talk to, we knock a few minutes off the clock."

"We can only do what we can do. So where's Hollis? Aren't we off to see the reverend?"

"She's in the bullpen talking to one of my deputies who has in-laws in the congregation of the church. We figured a little inside information couldn't hurt. Dani, what is it you've been trying very hard **not** to tell me all day?"

Paris was right; he read her all too easily.

"It's probably just my imagination."

"The voice? His voice?"

"It's an exaggeration to call it a voice, at least now. A faint echo of a whisper."

"Because you're able to shut him out?"

"I wish I could say yes." Dani shrugged. "But I've only been taught the bare bones of shielding, and since I never needed it, I haven't really practiced. No, I don't think it's anything I'm doing."

"Which is bothering you more than anything else."

"Well, yeah. I should be able to shut out psychic contact from someone else. If that's what this is. Dammit, I just don't—"

Marc put his hands on her shoulders. "Dani. Why do you keep trying to carry all this alone? You aren't Cassandra, but if there's a war coming, you sure as hell can't stop it alone. Let us help. Let me help."

She stared up at him, very aware of his hands, aware of the connection with him that she had tried her best to block ever since that other voice had pushed its way in. Because she didn't want Marc to sense or feel that, not that cold, implacable, evil voice, not in her—even if it wasn't her.

Especially if it wasn't her.

Instinctively, she tried to close off a bit more of herself. "You are helping. One step out of this building, and I'm practically surrounded by your deputies."

"That's an exaggeration. And not what I meant, as you damn well know." He sounded frustrated, and his frown deepened.

"The best thing you can do for me," she said deliberately, "is to keep looking for this killer. And Reverend Butler is a possible lead, right? So let's go. If that was thunder I just heard, we may be in for a storm."

She hoped she was speaking literally and hoped it would only be the weather that would turn violent.

His fingers tightened, and for at least a minute Dani wasn't sure if he was going to let this drop—for now, anyway. But finally he said in a match of the even, deliberate tone she had used, "You of all people should know that none of us can get through this life alone. When you're ready, I'm here, Dani. I always have been."

He released her shoulders and turned away. Dani followed him from the conference room, wishing she didn't feel so strongly that she had just made an awful mistake.

The Reverend Jedidiah Butler was an imposing man, at least in his own mind. To the rest of the world outside his admiring congregation, he was rather average in size and build, could have been any age between forty and sixty, and possessed as his single distinguishing feature a shock of silver hair.

He didn't even boast the sort of booming voice common among Southern preachers, but instead spoke to Marc in the slightly nasal tone of someone with bad allergies.

"Sheriff, I don't understand this visit. As I explained to the town council, I haven't the means to—"

Marc waved that away before the usual

rant could get good and started. Thunder was rolling all around, and since they hadn't been invited inside, he wanted to get this interview over before the storm finally broke.

At least, he hoped it would break. They needed rain in the worst way.

"I'm not here because of the council's concerns, Reverend." He glanced at Dani, saw the almost imperceptible shake of her head, and bit back a sigh.

Well, it had been worth a try, he thought. But even without the benefit of Dani's vision, his own judgment told him this onetime grain-storage facility was unlikely to be the "warehouse" she had seen in her dreams. For one thing, the silo was still standing, and even with that the building was by no stretch of the imagination "huge." It was, however, in need of serious repairs and smelled strongly of chickens.

Besides, having shaken hands with the good reverend on more than one occasion, Marc already knew the man lacked psychic ability or, indeed, any level of perception even as high as simple intuition.

"Then why are you here?" Reverend Butler demanded. "Is it about those murdered women?"

Marc stared at him, not as surprised as he wished he could be, especially after talking to Miss Patty. It was a bit difficult to read anything sinister or even suspicious in a local preacher's knowledge when the local florist shared it. He mentally knocked a few more minutes off the clock in terms of when he could expect the media to descend on Venture.

It was Hollis who stepped forward, offering her I.D. folder and badge for the preacher to see. "What do you know about that, Reverend?" she asked pleasantly.

He studied her I.D. for a long moment, then answered with a show of exaggerated patience. "Everybody **knows** about the murders, Agent Templeton. But out of respect for the families, of course we've kept our distance and our silence. Especially as you and the sheriff haven't seen fit to positively identify the victims."

Marc stopped himself from going on the defensive, though it wasn't easy. "Lab results take time," he said.

"Yes, one of my congregants was the gardener out at the Blanton place. He found the . . . remains."

Marc and Hollis exchanged glances, but all the sheriff said was "Information he was ordered to keep to himself."

"He came to me in confidence, Sheriff, as any troubled soul would." Butler shrugged. "But, as I said, the situation was already being discussed."

Hollis's voice was not quite light when she said, "Just as long as there are no lynch mobs forming up."

"We're God-fearing people, Agent Templeton. Even if we had some idea who this evil killer is—and I assure you we do not—we would never take it upon ourselves to hunt him, far less punish him. That is for the law, and the courts, and God to do."

It was a nice little speech. Dani wondered why she didn't believe it.

Because she was a cynic, probably.

Or maybe it was something else.

She tried to concentrate on the possible something else, not really listening as Marc asked Butler a few routine questions about whether he'd seen or heard anything suspicious during the last few weeks. Instead, against her better judgment, she realized she was listening for that voice again.

His voice.

Because with every second that passed, she became more uneasy, more uncomfortable. She was acutely aware of the urge to look back over her shoulder, behind her, but when she looked she saw nothing but the countryside she recognized.

So what was it she was feeling? Sensing?

The fine hairs on the back of her neck were standing straight up, her hands felt cold, and there was a leaden queasiness in the pit of her stomach. Yet when she looked at Butler, at her surroundings, nothing about him or them seemed responsible for what she felt.

Thunder rumbled louder now, rolling around as it did in the mountains so that it seemed to circle them, and she wondered if that was it. Could it be? She had never been as sensitive to storms as many psychics were, to the point of discomfort, but they did tend to affect—enhance, strengthen?—her normal senses.

So maybe that was all it was. Still, she knew she was trying to listen for something beyond her normal senses and honestly didn't know whether to be relieved or disappointed that she could hear no faintest hint or echo of the whisper that so terrified her.

"Dani?"

She blinked at Marc, then scrambled mentally as she realized the reverend had already turned to go back inside his church and that Marc and Hollis were both looking at her with raised brows.

"Sorry." She got back into the front passenger seat of Marc's car, hoping she hadn't missed anything important.

"Are you okay?" he asked her.

"Fine. My mind just wandered, that's all." She was still listening for that voice but at the same time was aware that what she was feeling physically was very familiar. Pressure. Like in the dream walk. Could that be from the approaching storm?

She reached up surreptitiously to touch her nose, a little surprised to find no blood there. Because the pressure was increasing, and she had to fight the urge to move, to try to somehow get out of the way of whatever it was that was pushing at her, pressing against her.

Nothing. **There's nothing. Just the storm coming. Just my imagination.**

Marc looked at her a moment longer, frowning, then started the car and began to maneuver it down the long, rutted "driveway" that wound through a mile of countryside to the old storage facility.

From the backseat, Hollis said, "I hate storms. But maybe that's why. Because I've never been able to see auras before."

18

DANI TURNED IN her seat, noting as she did that Marc shot a quick glance at the rearview mirror so he could see the agent's face. A face that was, Dani saw, just a little strained and far more pale than was normal for her.

"I gather that wasn't the non sequitur it sounded like?" Dani said.

Hollis was looking at Dani. Or, rather, her gaze seemed to be probing the space about a foot out from Dani's body.

"No. It wasn't a non sequitur. It was . . . completely on topic."

"Which topic?" Marc demanded.

"On the topic of monsters."

Dani forced a laugh. "Who, me?"

"No." Hollis met Dani's eyes finally, her own holding a weirdly flat shine. "Dani, can you shield?"

"A little. Not much, but—"

"Do it. Now. Concentrate."

Dani obeyed without hesitation, closing her eyes and doing her best one more time to remember how she'd been taught to wrap herself in a protective blanket of her own energy. It didn't seem to be getting any easier.

Through gritted teeth, Marc said to Hollis, "What the hell do you see?"

"Something I've never seen before." Hollis's voice was low, tense. "But I believe . . . it's not a normal aura. It's an attack of some kind. Someone or something is trying to get at Dani. Marc—"

He didn't wait for whatever Hollis had been about to say but instantly reached over with one hand and covered both of Dani's cold and tightly clenched ones, holding on even when he felt a jolt, even when she cried out in such pain that it broke something inside him.

Without another sound, Dani went limp.

————

Dani looked around, puzzled for a moment because there was nothing but darkness as far as she could see, and silence, and she had the feeling she was alone here. Perhaps it should have frightened her, but oddly it did not.

She couldn't feel a floor or ground beneath her feet. She couldn't, actually, feel her feet, and when she looked down she couldn't see them, because her body just sort of dissolved into darkness.

That probably should have scared her too.

It probably should have scared her a lot.

"No, you were always more comfortable with this sort of thing than I was," Paris said as she mostly emerged out of the darkness in front of Dani.

"I'm the one who tried to run away from it," Dani pointed out, not as distracted as she should have been by the fact that Paris seemed to have a body only from the navel up.

"It was the stuff out there you were running away from, the stuff you couldn't control. People, relationships. Emotional stuff. The psychic stuff was always easier for you."

"I can't control this."

"Oh, of course you can. You always could."

"Bullshit."

"To paraphrase what you said to Marc, that'll fix things—a good, resounding **bullshit**."

"I didn't tell you what I said to Marc."

"Mmm. Never mind that now. Just remind yourself that you really can control this. Later, when you think about it, when it matters. Don't forget."

"What's happening later?"

"You'll need to know stuff."

"Paris—"

"It's all right, Dani. Some things are meant to happen just the way they happen. We both knew this was one of them, right? We both know that's why you really came home."

For the first time, uneasiness stirred in Dani, cold and deep. "I don't know what you're talking about."

"Of course you do."

"No. I don't."

"I wasn't in your vision dream. Right from the beginning. Before you told anybody. Before you came here. Before you did anything at all to affect what you had seen. I should have been there with you, and I wasn't."

"So? It's one of the things I knew would change."

"No, Dani. It's one of the things you knew wouldn't change. That's why you've been so shut inside yourself. Why you've kept Marc from getting close the way he wants to, and why you even shut me out."

"I never—"

"Dani. The only time you let me in was during the dream walk. Not before then. Not since. Because you were afraid. Because you thought there'd be a moment, somewhere along the way, when you could change things. This one particular thing. If you were strong enough. Quick enough. If you tried hard enough. But that's not the way it works, you know."

"Paris—"

"Miranda said it. No matter what we see or what we dream, the universe has a plan. All this was part of the plan."

"I won't accept that," Dani whispered.

"Afraid you don't really have a choice, sis. Besides, you've already accepted it. We both have. That's why we didn't need to talk about it all these weeks while you were letting me cry on your shoulder, and cried yourself, about the end of my marriage. We both knew that wasn't the only ending we were grieving."

"Paris—"

"I'm glad you came back here after the divorce. Have I told you that? How much it meant to me that you came?"

"You didn't have to say anything. I knew."

"We always do, don't we? The best part about being a twin. All the things we don't have to say."

"There are things we do. Paris—"

"Listen, what Shirley Arledge told Hollis is right: He's tricking you. Look past the trick, Dani. You know the truth, it's there in your vision dream. Just think it through."

"I can't do this by myself."

"You won't be by yourself. A twin is never alone, no matter what." Paris was already drifting back into the darkness. "And you can do what you have to, Dani. When the time comes. You'll know. You'll make the right choice."

"Paris, come back!"

"It's okay." Her voice was faint and fading. "I've got something for you, something you can use. I think it was always supposed to be yours anyway. Come see me before you leave, okay?"

Dani listened as hard as she could, but she couldn't hear her sister anymore.

And the darkness closed in.

Sunday, October 12

Dani resisted opening her eyes for a long time even after she knew she was awake and aware. A part of her wanted to hide, to dive back down into the darkness and search for Paris.

But a stronger part of her knew there was only one way back into that darkness, and willing herself there wasn't it.

She opened her eyes. A hospital room, she thought. Dim and hushed, with machines beeping quietly nearby. There was never a sense of time in a hospital room, Dani had found; there was routine and order, but the nights and the days looked very much alike.

Her own internal clock told her hours had passed, that it was probably at least late Sunday morning.

Which meant she'd been out a long time. She wondered with faint amusement what the doctors had made of her.

Somewhere in the building, a medical paper was probably being drafted.

She was distracted from that thought by the realization that there was a shadowy figure in the far corner of the room, but it was the closer presence she was far, far more aware of.

"Dani . . ."

She turned her head to see Marc beside her hospital bed, holding her hand. He looked incredibly relieved and incredibly weary, older than he had looked yesterday.

We pay such a price.

"How do you feel?" he asked.

Dani considered, then nodded. "Good. I feel good." More than that, really. She felt strong. Stronger than she'd ever felt before, and in a way that was completely unfamiliar to her. It wasn't muscles, it was . . .

Power.

"Dani . . . something's happened."

She nodded again. "I know. Paris."

He didn't seem surprised by her knowledge but offered details. "She isn't dead. At least—The doctors say it's a coma. They can't explain it. But they couldn't explain you either." He shook his head. "They're saying she's showing some brain activity, and as long as that continues, there's hope."

Dani knew. She heard the clock in her head ticking off the remaining days—or hours, or maybe just minutes—of Paris's hope. There was so little time left.

Bishop came out of the shadows to stand at the foot of her bed. "I'm sorry, Dani."

She looked at him. "I never thought we'd meet with those words, even though I dreamed them. Sort of. But I get it. You knew he'd come after one of us."

"Yes. Something Miranda saw. But . . . it could have been either one of you. There was no way for us to be sure."

"Until I started hearing his voice in my head."

Without flinching, Bishop said, "At first I believed he'd choose Paris as one of his victims. When she wasn't a part of your vision dream, not beside you when she should have been, and once Miranda was out of the picture, that seemed the obvious answer."

"You were going to use her. Watch her, follow her. Wait for him to go after her. Bait on a hook."

"I'm sorry," he repeated. "But it seemed our best chance of catching him. It bothered me from the beginning that neither of you really fit his victim profile, but from the beginning here he was veering from that, at least in terms of coloring. I had to assume his ritual was changing in some fundamental way, and that meant it was possible he was choosing victims using some other criteria and then . . . making them fit. Both of you could be made to fit.

"You were still dreaming, and Paris was still missing from that dream. That vision dream. But then the killer's M.O. began to change in drastic, unpredictable ways, and quickly. Very quickly. That . . . neon crime scene. Being a little too obvious in stalking and photographing Marie Goode, a previous victim's jewelry left in her home, plus flowers."

"Too obvious," Dani said, half to herself. "Look at me, look what I'm doing."

Bishop nodded. "Not at all in character for the Boston serial. Not a kind of progression, a kind of evolution, I've ever seen before in a serial killer."

"And yet."

He nodded again. "And yet. We were sure this was the same killer even before we got here, positive in our own minds even without evidence to back that up. Since then, Hollis had seen Becky Huntley, later Shirley Arledge; both of them and Karen Norvell were the right physical type, matching the victims in Boston. And you were hearing that voice, a confirmation of our suspicion that we might be dealing with a psychic killer."

Marc said roughly, "How is that any kind of confirmation of anything?"

Dani looked at him. "I knew," she said simply. "I kept trying to tell myself that I wasn't really hearing an alien voice in my head, that it was just some . . . weird psychic fluke, a leftover echo from one of the doom dreams I couldn't remember anymore. Anything. Anything but the truth. That he was real. That he was here. And that he had found a way to connect with me."

"Which," Bishop said, "caused me to believe that you, not Paris, were his intended target."

"I kept walking into his trap," Dani said. "In the vision dream, no matter what else changed, that never did. I knew it was a trap, always, every time, and every time I walked into it."

"Yes, another sign that you were the one he was focused on. We didn't leave Paris unprotected," Bishop said. "But I thought he'd come after you."

Marc, his voice still harsh, said, "If you knew the bastard was psychic, why didn't you expect **this** kind of attack?"

"Because this kind of attack, a psychic attack, is more rare than hen's teeth," Bishop told him. "It just doesn't happen, especially when there's no blood connection. And he hadn't shown any sign that he had even attempted such a thing before."

"There was no way for you to know," Dani said, her fingers tightening in Marc's. "If our abilities worked that way, we'd have all the answers."

"I'd settle for just one or two I can hang my hat on," Marc told her. "Dammit, Dani, you nearly died. Nothing touched you, nobody laid a finger on you, and **you nearly died**."

There was more than anxiety in his voice, and she heard it and wished she could wrap herself in it and in him and just stop everything else. For a while. Just a while. But the clock in her head refused to stop ticking, and even though she squeezed Marc's hand again, she forced herself to concentrate on what Bishop was saying.

"Which is why an SCU guardian is on the way here to keep watching. Over you."

"I don't need a guardian."

"Dani—"

"But someone else does, if I'm right. This guardian of yours, what's his ability?"

"Her ability. I choose guardians carefully; among other things, she has a shield she can extend around someone else."

"Psychic protection. Good. Then I need her to stand guard over Paris."

Bishop was frowning but nodded immediately. "Done."

He thought he owed her, Dani thought. And she wasn't at all sure he wasn't right about that.

She looked at Marc. "I have a hunch you won't be getting too far away from me for the duration, right?" It was more than a hunch.

She knew.

Marc was nodding. "Bet your ass. But I'm no psychic guardian, Dani. I can't protect you from another attack like this one."

She wasn't so sure about that, but all she said was, "I think he went after Paris a lot harder than he did me. And I think I know why. I'm not sure about the timing of everything, but I get the motive. I think. Anyway, unless the vision dream changes drastically the next time around, I'm there at the end. Paris . . . never was." She looked back at Bishop. "Like you said."

He was silent.

"But Miranda **was** there. Or, at least, I thought she was, even if I never actually saw her. Which, I suppose, should have told me more than it did." Dani didn't pause to explain that, instead asking, "Is she safe?"

Bishop nodded. "I took the threat very seriously. She's as safe as I can possibly make her. She has exceptionally strong shields and is guarded around the clock by other psychics with strong shields. We have several guardians in the unit."

Dani remembered something else. "You're connected, the two of you. Telepathically."

Bishop didn't hesitate. "Yes."

"I'd close that connection, if I were you."

"Easier said than done." He shrugged. "We can narrow the link, but the only thing we've found to shut it down completely severs it."

"Death?"

"Death."

She made a mental note to ask for specifics on that story if they all survived, and said, "Well, my advice is to narrow the link as much as you can. He used the one between Paris and me to attack both of us, and I have a hunch he didn't use all his strength to do it. Hollis warned me just in time, and I was able to deflect him at least a little. But even though my connection with Paris is as much blood as it is psychic, it's also an old one; it hasn't been active in any real sense for years. If yours and Miranda's is as . . . deep as I believe it is, he could use it against the two of you. He knows you're here, so all he has to do is follow the connection back to Miranda."

Half under his breath, Marc said, "You make it sound like a road."

"It is, psychically speaking," Dani told him.

Bishop's mind was moving along a different pathway. "Dani, what do you know about this killer that I don't know?"

She drew a deep breath, and said, "If I'm right, I know the one thing he really, really doesn't want you to know. We're not just dealing with a vicious serial killer who's psychic. This enemy is your enemy. This trap I've seen from the beginning? The one we all walk into even knowing what it is? It's a trap set for you."

19

I'M SORRY ABOUT PARIS," Hollis said to Jordan as they waited in the conference room for the others to arrive.

"Yeah, so am I." He shook his head. "Jesus, it was creepy being with her when it happened. Remember when I said I didn't know if it was a relief or a regret, me not being psychic? Well, I've made up my mind. It's a relief."

Hollis smiled wryly. "We are more vulnerable to negative energy than a nonpsychic is, and it has been a problem in the past. But attacks like that one—they're rare. Very rare. We just haven't found many psychics who can affect other psychics in even minor ways."

"No Jedi mind control, huh?"

"Afraid not. Or, at least, not that I know of." She turned her chair to face the board, where photographs of the three known victims in Venture were pinned, and brooded for a moment in silence. "Bishop has always said that if ever a psychic is born who can completely control his or her abilities, the whole world will change."

Jordan grunted. "Think he ever considered the psychic might be playing for the other team?"

"I never thought about it before, but Bishop wouldn't be Bishop if he didn't consider something from every angle he could find. So I'm guessing it was a possibility in his mind from the get-go. Which could explain at least part of his urgency these last years in putting the unit together and cofounding Haven."

"Building a psychic army?" Jordan suggested, in a tone not quite as light as he'd intended.

Hollis turned her chair around again and smiled at him. "We don't want to take over the world, honest."

Jordan felt his face getting hot. "I know that. Seriously, I do. It's just . . . seeing what that bastard did to Paris, knowing now it's possible to attack someone without laying a finger on them or even being within sight, is . . . scary as hell."

"Yes," Hollis said. "It is." Then she frowned as the trained investigator in her considered the matter. "But . . . we don't actually know he wasn't close enough to see her. You were here in town, right?"

"Yeah. We'd just stopped for coffee after talking to another of the bank tellers. Fruitlessly, before you ask; she wasn't even working last summer when Karen Norvell may or may not have been followed."

"Well, it was a potential lead that had to be explored."

"Even to a dead end. Christ, I hate dead ends. Anyway, we were just coming out of the coffee shop, and I'll swear Paris was completely blindsided. I mean, one minute she was laughing and running through a string of dumb metaphors for fruitless searches, and the next she was on the ground."

"She didn't say anything?"

"Hollis, she was in the middle of a **word**. And then dropped like a stone. I thought she'd been shot and was braced for the sound. But it never came." He frowned as his own words brought a realization. "Wait a minute. Why would our killer attack somebody like that, even assuming he's psychic and could? It's hardly his M.O.—here or in Boston. Way too bloodless a crime for him, I'm thinking."

"Yeah, that's been bugging me."

"Have a theory you want to trot out?"

"Not really."

Jordan sighed. "I can't tell you how much I hate hearing you say that."

"Sorry."

"Uh-huh." After a moment, Jordan added, "We're just whistling in a graveyard here, aren't we?"

"Pretty much."

"Yeah, that's what I thought."

Dani wasn't about to leave the hospital without seeing Paris. The doctors weren't crazy about her leaving at all, but since her vital signs were utterly normal and she politely but firmly insisted she was fine and was ready to leave now, they really didn't have much choice in the matter.

Once she was dressed, Marc and Bishop stuck close, escorting her to the IC unit, where Paris lay hooked up to the machines monitoring her faint life signs.

Bishop's "guardian" was already there, sitting in a chair by the bed, and rose to be introduced simply as Bailey. She was unexpectedly fragile-looking, a tall, slender brunette with large dark eyes so calm and deep they were almost hypnotic.

Dani felt a pang of doubt, but that was quickly erased when she and Bailey shook hands. Dani had never been especially sensitive to other psychics, but she could feel this woman's strength, feel the energy that was like a warm blanket enveloping her.

"Wow," she said.

Bailey smiled faintly. "I won't let anyone or anything get to your sister."

"I believe you." She glanced at the men, and added, "But if you guys wouldn't mind, I'd like a few minutes alone with Paris."

The men exchanged glances and then

moved away with Bailey. But only as far as the doorway, Dani realized, where they could still keep an eye on her and Paris.

Paris . . .

Dani stood by her bed and looked down at her twin for a moment, then took one limp, cool hand in both of hers. "You said to stop by," she said. "At least, I think this is what you meant. Don't worry, Paris. I—"

It was just a tingling at first, barely enough to get her attention. But when Dani stared down at the hand she held, she saw Paris's fingers tighten around hers, and the tingling became something else, something much more powerful.

Dani's first instinct was to pull away, but she fought that and held on, watching her sister's face, hoping to see some flicker of consciousness there.

Nothing. Paris's face remained completely relaxed and without expression, even as her fingers clung to Dani's.

Clung and . . .

When Dani realized what was happening, she tried to pull free of her sister's grip, but it was impossible. There might not have been much more than a spark of consciousness left in Paris, but it was enough to do what she meant to do.

I've got something for you, something you can use. I think it was always supposed to be yours anyway.

It lasted only a few seconds, and then Paris's fingers relaxed. Dani was afraid for a moment that it had been her sister's vital life force that had passed from Paris to her, but the machines monitoring her continued to beep quietly and steadily.

Dani watched her sister breathe for a few moments longer, thinking, remembering, then gently tucked Paris's hand beneath the covers and stepped back away from the bed.

Bailey was there almost instantly, pausing before reclaiming her chair to eye Dani and say calmly, "Try to keep your distance from the machinery in this place."

"Why?"

"You'll see. Don't worry, I'll watch over Paris. Anything that goes after her has to come through me first. And I don't give way without a fight."

"Thank you." Dani didn't understand

343

what she meant about machinery. But Bailey was right. She found out.

Hollis and Jordan sat companionably silent in the conference room of the sheriff's department, their solitude broken only when Dani, Marc, and Bishop arrived—with two newcomers.

Gabriel and Roxanne Wolf were so clearly brother and sister that the information didn't even have to be provided—though Jordan found out later that they were, in fact, fraternal twins. He was tall, lean but obviously powerful, and had shaggy pale-blond hair; she was also tall, slender without being thin, and had pale-blond hair cut shorter than her brother's. They were around thirty, were clearly athletic, and shared eerily identical green eyes of the very rare sort: a bright, almost primary shade that seemed iridescent.

After introductions, the group settled in around the conference table, and Hollis was the first to say, "Dani, I'm sorry about Paris. I hope she pulls out of this."

"I hope we can help her do that," Dani responded.

Jordan said, "You know we're willing, Dani. Anything we can do, say the word."

"It's a question of time." She looked around the table. "I know we're all committed to finding and stopping this monster as soon as possible, before he gets his hands on another woman, but the attack on Paris and me has . . . altered the situation."

"Altered it how?" Gabriel asked.

"Several ways. For one thing, when somebody reaches into your mind with theirs, you get a sense of identity. Or, at least, I did, especially since it wasn't his first visit. And one thing I'm sure of now is that whoever attacked us psychically has more in his game plan than killing women."

"Like what?" Hollis frowned. "By the way, now that I'm seeing auras, yours looks a little weird. Almost . . . metallic."

"I'm not surprised," Dani said.

Jordan was staring at Hollis. "You see auras?"

"Apparently. Seems like every case I'm on

brings a fun new toy for me." She eyed him. "Your aura is surprisingly calm, mostly blue and green."

Jordan had no idea what that meant and decided not to ask. He had a hunch he was better off not knowing.

Dani was saying, "I caught just enough of a glimpse into his mind to know two things: He's brilliant, and he's powerful. And I got the sense that he's been planning this for a long time, months at least. Probably even before Boston."

"Planning what?" Hollis asked again.

"To get more powerful. And to get rid of an enemy he views as very dangerous." Dani nodded toward Bishop.

"Bishop made an enemy," Gabriel murmured. "Fancy that."

"Gabe," his sister said warningly.

Bishop shook his head. "No, he's right. I make plenty of enemies."

"Then what makes this one different?" she asked.

"Ask Dani."

Dani didn't wait to be asked. "All I can tell you is that his plan is somehow focused on

Bishop—and the SCU. And that we're all here because he wants us to be."

Gabriel scowled. "I don't much like being a puppet."

"Then we have at least one thing in common," Bishop told him.

Jordan said, "Okay, maybe a dumb question. Granted, we need to find this bastard before he has time to do any more damage. What does the timeline have to do with Paris? Afraid he'll come back and try to finish the job?"

"I'm afraid he has to."

"Why?"

"Because she has—or had—something he wants. And I think he made his first real mistake in believing he could get what he wanted from her and attack me at the same time. It took more energy than he planned and left him without enough to get the job done."

"I'm still in the dark," Jordan complained.

"He wanted something he could use as a weapon," Dani explained. "Not many psychic abilities can be used that way, but Paris had one of them."

Gabriel sat up straighter. "Her secondary ability?"

Dani glanced at Marc, then nodded. "Yeah. And not so secondary anymore, at least not for me—as we discovered at the hospital. I think the doctors were much more happy about me discharging myself after I shorted out two of their machines."

"Say what?" Jordan's voice was a bit faint.

She hesitated, then held up her right hand, thumb and index finger touching. As she rubbed them together, everyone in the room could hear the crackle of energy, very obviously intensifying with the friction she was creating. When she abruptly separated the two fingers, a visible thread of electricity arced between them.

"I seem to be a better conductor than Paris was," Dani said absently, watching the little light show. "She couldn't sleep with an electric alarm clock on her nightstand, because it would short out while she was sleeping. When she was awake, the only thing she occasionally affected was the odd touchy computer or something like that."

"Wow," Jordan said.

Dani looked at him, then shook her hand slightly. With a couple of pops and crackles, the energy dissipated. "Most of us carry around a static charge at one time or another; the human body is filled with electrical energy. My mind just knows how to channel it now. Focus it, direct it."

"Ah. An honest-to-God weapon. Like a laser?"

"Not that focused."

"Not yet," Bishop murmured.

Without looking at him, Dani said, "It's an ability I'd just as soon have temporarily and give back to Paris as soon as possible. One of Bishop's guardians is at the hospital watching over her, but I think all this guy needs is time to . . . recharge his own energy before he tries again."

Roxanne said, "So you think he targeted Paris deliberately? Because he wanted her ability?"

"I think so."

"How did he find out about it?"

"I don't know for sure. But—"

Marc spoke up, saying, "Paris's ex-husband likes to drink. And he tends to rant about Paris, to anyone who even pretends to be listening, when he drinks. All about Paris, especially the things that spooked him. I'm thinking maybe Dan said the wrong thing to the right person. In fact, I'd bet on it."

Roxanne lifted her brows at Dani. "Your twin married a man named—"

"We pondered the subtext of the names, believe me," Dani told her wryly. "Probably something Freudian about it. Or just unlucky chance—all the way around."

"Moving on," Gabriel murmured.

Dani nodded. "Thank you. Moving on—the point is that I think this guy will try again, and as soon as he regains his strength."

"How do you know he lost it?" Jordan asked.

"Bitter experience. Every psychic I know is drained to some extent when they use their abilities. An attack like that one required an enormous amount of energy, **especially** since he wasn't in physical contact with Paris or apparently even close to either of us. I was out nearly eighteen hours, and that was after he expended most of his energies attacking both of us; I'm betting he's still out."

Gabriel pulled at his earlobe briefly. "So you're saying that Paris's ex did his drunken-rant act in a bar where our killer happened to be? I love a good coincidence, but—"

"Not so much of a coincidence when you think about it," Marc said. "Dan worked for a company in Atlanta. We're a bit far out to be a true bedroom community, but we have more than our share of commuters who live in Venture—and his job involved a lot of travel. All up and down the East Coast. He passed through Boston at least three times last summer."

"All kinds of things lining up now," Roxanne said. "So this serial was laying low in Boston, maybe keeping an eye on the investigation into his murders, maybe just having a scotch between victims, when he heard a drunken salesman in a bar talking about his very talented ex-wife. And it seemed like a good idea to get out of the spotlight up there and head south."

"I think it was a lot more deliberate than that," Dani said. "I can't prove it, because so far there's nothing anybody would consider to be evidence—but I know the sense I got from that voice in my mind. That other personality. He was already focused on Bishop, on the SCU. He was planning on a fight. Maybe he intended to make his stand there in Boston, or maybe he was already on the verge of moving on. Either way, hearing about Paris brought him to Venture. Because Paris was here, and she had a very cool ability he wanted for his very own."

"He's a psychic vampire," Jordan guessed hesitantly, half afraid someone would laugh at him.

But this wasn't a group to easily dismiss the seemingly fantastic.

"There are plenty of energy vampires in the nonpsychic world," Bishop told him. "You probably know at least one yourself. They wear out their friends just having a normal conversation, suck the energy right out of the room."

Jordan frowned. "Actually, I know two people like that. But this guy—am I right in thinking he'd have to have some kind of specialized ability? I mean, to steal another psychic's abilities?"

Listening to the clock ticking louder in her head, Dani said, "Probably. To be honest, I don't really care how he does it. Or why. I just want to find him, and before he has the strength to finish the job he started. He'll go after Paris again, and, guardian or not, he could kill her before he ever realized she no longer has the ability he wants so badly."

Jordan nodded quickly. "So we go back to the warehouses."

"And," Marc said, "start checking property records for the last couple of months. I'm betting he likes his accommodations to be a little more comfortable than a warehouse, wherever he does his dirty work. I doubt he's stayed at one of the motels all these weeks, because it would have been noticed. A rental or a lease is more likely. But we'll send deputies out to check the motels anyway."

"Which will also be noticed," Bishop said.

"It's the weekend and getting late, so maybe not so much. In any case, I figure we've got maybe forty-eight hours max before the news breaks wide open." He eyed Bishop. "And speaking of news, shouldn't you be in Boston, all visible for the Director?"

"The Director had to fly to the West Coast for a few days and is due back in D.C. by Wednesday," Bishop replied. "I've got several of my people wasting time in Boston running a shell game to disguise my absence, so I should be covered until then. If the hunt is still on in Venture, I go back to coming down here as often as I can on a corporate jet that does a regular twice-daily run from Atlanta to Boston and back."

"True commitment," Gabriel said politely. Before anyone could comment, he got to his feet and began unfolding a large map onto the conference table. "Roxanne and I have been checking out warehouses and other likely buildings during the last few days; I think if we compare notes, you'll be able to cross off over half the ones on your list."

20

IT WAS NEARLY MIDNIGHT when Marc parked his cruiser in the driveway of his house a few blocks from the sheriff's department, and Dani was still arguing.

"Marc, I slept for eighteen hours. I—"

"You didn't sleep for eighteen hours, you were out for eighteen hours. Big difference. And," he added before she could interrupt him, "I did **not** sleep."

"I didn't say you shouldn't rest, I said I didn't need to."

"You also said I was your guardian—or words to that effect—and your guardian sticks to you like white on rice. And you stick to him."

"I just feel like I should be doing something to help find the killer," Dani said.

Marc turned off the car and opened his door just enough for the interior light to come on. He looked at her steadily. "Are you afraid to dream this time, is that it?"

"I'm always afraid to dream. But that isn't it. I don't believe the killer has regained enough energy to come after anybody, and it's not like I can plan to have a vision dream, you know that. It happens or it doesn't. Passive, remember? I'm tired of being passive. I need to be doing something, Marc, something useful."

"Listen to me. Everything that can be done is being done. Everybody who's not absolutely dead on their feet is out in teams searching buildings or at the station combing through property records. The only thing you or I could add would be two more pairs of tired eyes. We both need a break, Dani."

She really couldn't argue with that truth—or didn't want to. But she did say mildly, "All my stuff is at Paris's house."

"And all my stuff is here. Come on, I'll find you something to sleep in for tonight, and we can go by her place in the morning so you can change."

"What, you mean there aren't any bits of female clothing left behind by overnight guests? I thought every man had a drawer full of those."

"Fishing, Dani?"

She got out of the car, waiting until he joined her on the walkway to say dryly, "Of course I was fishing. Since when was I ever subtle about stuff like this?"

"Stuff like this?"

She decided it was probably a good thing for him that she really was tired, because otherwise she would have picked up something and hit him instead of replying with the simple truth. "Continuing the process of reconnecting."

He stared at her, one brow lifting.

"I'm really too tired to play games," she confessed. "And that is what we've been doing the last few days. Isn't it?"

His front porch light was on, and he stood there at the door, keys in hand, and looked down at her steadily. "That depends. Are you planning on sticking around this time?"

"I thought I would." She hadn't realized she was going to say it until she did.

"Then," Marc said as he unlocked the door, "we're definitely reconnecting."

She followed him into the house, struck immediately by the fact that he had totally re-done it; a decade before, this had been the house left to him by his parents, but now it was unquestionably Marc, an uncluttered, clean-lined Craftsman, both masculine and sophisticated.

"Nice," she told him, looking around.

"Well, the eighties look sort of dated the place. And I really didn't like dark green and pink as a color combo."

"It's not my favorite either." She cleared her throat, allowing herself to become aware of the tension between them. The very deliberate choice surprised her, not because she made it but because she was able to.

Huh. It's like opening a door. A weird kind of control I've never had before. Was I shielding without even thinking about it?

Or just suppressing until I had the time and energy to deal?

"I know it's late," Marc said. "But I have some ice cream from Smith's in the freezer. If that's still the ritual."

"It is." She went with him into the bright kitchen and was quickly sharing with him a bowl of the best homemade vanilla ice cream in the world.

"This alone could have brought me back to Venture," she told him.

"Mmm. I thought it took a vision. And a threat to Paris."

"I didn't know the threat was to her."

"I think on some level you did." Marc shrugged. "But either way, you knew something bad was coming here. And you came back to help."

Dani put down her spoon and looked at him steadily. "You're wondering if I would have come back here eventually, without the vision."

Lightly, he said, "Is this more of Paris's abilities? Are you clairvoyant now?"

Without answering that directly, she said,

"It doesn't take a clairvoyant to see the obvious. Marc, I like to think I would have matured enough at some point, even without a vision, to stop running away from who I am. But all I really know for sure is what I told you before. There's nobody waiting for me back in Atlanta. There never has been."

For a moment she didn't think he was going to respond, and then he said, "I don't have a drawer filled with bits of clothing left behind by overnight guests. I haven't been a monk, Dani, but . . . there was never anybody I wanted to bring home. Not since the beautiful assistant left the magic show."

Dani didn't know who moved first and didn't really care. All she knew was that the instant his arms closed around her and his mouth covered hers was the first time she truly felt she had come home.

It was the nightmare brought to life, Dani thought.

The vision.

The smell of blood turned her stomach, the thick, acrid smoke burned her eyes, and what had been for so long a wispy, dreamlike memory was now jarring, throat-clogging reality. For just an instant she was paralyzed.

It was all coming true.

Despite everything she had done, everything she had **tried** to do, despite all the warnings, once again it was all—

Oh, shit. Not again.

"Dani?" Roxanne appeared at her side, seemingly out of the smoke, gun drawn, vivid green eyes sharp even squinted against the stench. "Where is it?"

Huh. This is new. But I guess . . .

"Dani, you're all we've got. You're all **they've** got. Do you understand that? Which way?"

Wish I could see something in all this smoke. Something to tell me where this building is.

It seemed easier this time for her to concentrate on the stench of blood she knew none of the others could smell. A blood trail that was all they had to guide them.

Well, that and this vision. Why do I keep going through the motions? There must be a reason.

She nearly gagged, then pointed. "That way. Toward the back. But . . ."

"But what?"

"Down. Lower. There's a basement level." Stairs. She remembered stairs. Going down them. Down into corridors everywhere, and— No, wait. That wasn't this vision. That had been during the dream-walking.

Hadn't it?

Hallways in every direction, brightly lit, featureless but almost humming with energy.

Energy?

"It isn't on the blueprints."

"I know." She dragged her mind back, wasting an instant to wonder how she could do that and yet couldn't seem to deviate from the vision-dream script.

I told you all this before, dammit. No, wait—I told Hollis all this before. So where is she? And why is somebody else speaking her lines?

"Bad place to get trapped in a burning building," Roxanne noted. "The roof could fall in on us. Easily."

Exactly her lines.

Bishop appeared out of the smoke as suddenly as Roxanne had, weapon in hand, his face stone, eyes haunted. "We have to hurry."

"Yeah," Roxanne replied, "we get that. Burning building. Maniacal killer. Good seriously outnumbered by evil. Bad situation." Her words and tone were flippant, but her gaze on his face was anything but, intent and measuring.

It was always Hollis before. Why isn't it now?

"You forgot potential victim in maniacal killer's hands," he said, not even trying to match her tone.

"Never. Dani, did you see the basement, or are you feeling it?"

Oh, right—I have Paris's abilities.

"Stairs. I saw them." The weight on her shoulders felt like the world, too heavy to cast aside, so maybe that was what was pressing her down. Or . . . "And what I feel now . . . He's lower. He's underneath us."

"Then we look for stairs."

Dani coughed. She was trying to think, trying to remember. But dreams recalled were such dim, insubstantial things, even vision dreams sometimes, and there was no way for her to be **sure** she was remembering clearly.

Dammit, why do I keep going through the motions? Why don't I just lead the way to the damn stairs?

And where the hell is Hollis?

Why is that different this time?

Is it me?

What in God's name did I do?

She was overwhelmingly conscious of precious time passing and looked at her wrist, at the absurdly childish Mickey Mouse watch with its bright red band and cartoon face that told her it was 4:17 P.M. on Monday . . . October 13.

What? Oh, my God. That's tomorrow.

Why, dammit?

What the hell happened to change the date?

"Dani?"

She shook off the momentary confusion. "The stairs aren't where you'd expect them to be," she said, coughing again. "They're in a small room or office, something like that. Not a hallway. Hallways—"

"What?"

The instant of certainty was fleeting but absolute and gave the term **déjà vu** a whole new meaning for Dani.

Jesus, it's like I'm stuck in a loop—

"The basement is divided," she heard herself say. "By a solid wall. Two big rooms. And accessed from this main level by two different stairways, one at each side of the building, in the back."

Two traps. Not one.

No . . . two parts to one trap.

"What kind of crazy-ass design is that?" Roxanne demanded.

"If we get out of this alive, you can ask the architect." The smell of blood was almost overpowering, but Dani's headache was—

She didn't have a headache this time around.

Okay, I'm definitely stronger now, but—

A trap with two parts . . .

Tomorrow! How can it be so soon?

What happened to change the date? Is it because we found—or will find—the warehouse quicker this time? Because Paris was able to transfer her abilities to me?

No, wait . . .

Bishop said potential victim.

God. Oh, God.
Where's Hollis?

Marc appeared out of the smoke as abruptly as the other two had and took her hand in his free one. In his other hand was a big revolver.

Right gun this time. Déjà vu.

"Where to now?" he asked. "I can't see shit for all this smoke."

Roxanne replied to his question. "Dani is guiding us."

He looked down at her, his expression calm but his eyes holding something as intimate as a caress.

Wow. Never knew a man could make love with just his eyes before. How about that?

Marc said, "I always knew the beautiful assistant was the real wizard. Like the man behind the curtain. Where to, Dani?"

The same—yet not. Why does it keep changing?

It was Bishop who said, "You don't know which side they're in."

"No. I'm sorry." She felt as if she'd been apologizing to this man since she met him. Hell, she had been.

That isn't right. He apologized to me.

The first words he said to me were an apology. Because of Paris. Because he used Paris as bait.

Bait . . .

Am I figuring out the trap?

Or am I part of it?

Roxanne was frowning. To Bishop, she said, "Great. Wonderful. You're psychically blind, Gabe and I are useless except to hold guns, and we're in a huge burning building without a freakin' map."

"Which is why Dani is here." Those pale sentry eyes were fixed on her face.

Dani felt a little dizzy but oddly confident as well. "All I know is that he's down there somewhere."

"And Hollis?"

Hollis. Oh, my God.

She's the potential victim.

The monster has her.

"Dani?" Bishop's face was even more strained.

Hollis. He asked about Hollis.

And she had an answer for him. Of sorts. "She isn't dead. She's bait, you know that. She was always bait, to lure you."

367

"And you," Bishop said.

To lure me?

To lure us.

Always bait, to lure us. But he only ever wanted to catch one of us. He just wanted you distracted, disarmed—

"We have to go, now," she heard herself say urgently. "He won't wait, not this time."

The conversation had taken only brief minutes, but even so the smoke was thicker, the crackling roar of the fire louder, and the heat growing ever more intense.

"We're running out of time on every level," Marc said, his fingers tightening around Dani's. "The storm may roll around us like the last few have done, so we can't count on rain. It's been dry as hell for weeks, and this place is going up like a match. I've called it in."

Bishop swore under his breath. "Marc—"

"Don't worry, they know it's a hostage situation, and they won't come in. But they can damn well aim their hoses outside and try to save the nearby property." He paused, then added, "Am I the only one who suspects this bastard planned out every last detail, including this place being a tinderbox?"

Roxanne said, "No, you aren't the only one. We're on **his** timetable, just like he wants."

Bishop turned and started toward the rear of the building and the south corner. "I'll go down on this side. You three head for the east corner."

Dani wondered if instinct was guiding him as well, but all she said, to Roxanne, was, "He doesn't care whose timetable we're on."

"I noticed that. Why do I get the feeling he blames himself for this mess?"

"He couldn't have known—"

"According to everything I've heard about him, he certainly could have known. Maybe he did. Part of this, at least. Something that might have stopped things before it got this far. Come on, let's go."

Dani and Marc followed, but she had to ask, "Do you believe it's his fault?"

Roxanne paused for only an instant, looking back over her shoulder—

And for an instant, Dani saw Paris instead.

And then Hollis.

And then Miranda.

And when Roxanne replied, she sounded like an eerie blend of four different voices.

"He played God one time too many. He thinks he can stop the prophecy. And we're paying the price for his arrogance."

We're paying the price.

We are.

Prophecy? What prophecy?

Dani held on to Marc's hand even tighter as they followed the other woman. She could hardly breathe, her throat tighter despite the fact that, as they reached the rear half of the building, the smoke wasn't nearly as thick. They very quickly discovered, in the back of what might once have been a small office, a door that opened smoothly and silently to reveal a stairwell.

The stairwell was already lighted.

"Bingo," Roxanne said.

Useless to warn them. We all know it's a trap. Why are we just walking into it?

Wait.

I know this. The trap was the whole idea.

It wasn't about killing women. Not here, not in Venture. That was only . . . window dressing.

That was the first part of the trap, to lure . . . us.

Us. Bishop because he's the threat and had to be . . . disarmed. Paris because he wanted her ability. And now he knows it's mine, so the trap is for me.

This trap was always for me.

Roxanne shifted her weapon to a steady two-handed grip and sent Dani and Marc a quick look. "Ready?"

Dani didn't spare the energy to wonder how anyone on earth could ever be ready for this. Instead, she just nodded.

Marc squeezed her hand, then released it and took a half step closer to Roxanne, saying to Dani, "Stay behind me. You're the only one of us without a gun."

"She doesn't need a gun," Roxanne said.

At least I know now why I don't need a gun. If she means what I think she means.

"Maybe not, but I still want her behind me," Marc said in a tone that not many would have argued with. "Let's go if we're going."

Roxanne had only taken one step when a thunderous crash sounded behind them and a new wave of almost intolerable heat threatened to shove them bodily into the stairwell.

The roof was falling in.

They exchanged glances and then, without emotion, Roxanne said, "Close the door behind us."

Oh, shit.

It always ends this way.

Dani gathered all the courage she could find, and if her response wasn't as emotionless as the other woman's, at least it was steady.

"Right," she said, and closed the door behind them as they began their descent into hell.

21

THIS IS ONE MORNING when I definitely need more than donuts, with or without sprinkles," Hollis said with a yawn as she climbed out of Jordan's cruiser in the parking lot of a small, moderately busy café one street back from Main in downtown Venture. "I just can't pull all-nighters like I used to."

"Join the club." He shut the door on his side and stretched to ease stiff muscles, then glanced toward the café and groaned. "Oh, hell, here comes Matt Condrey."

"Friend of yours?" she asked, amused as

she watched a sturdy bearded man about the same age as the chief deputy weaving among cars to quickly make his way toward Jordan.

"It's a myth that men don't gossip," Jordan said, mostly from the side of his mouth. "Because here comes the worst gossip in Prophet County. Bet you ten bucks the first words out of his mouth will be to ask why we haven't arrested anybody for the murders the public isn't supposed to know about yet."

"I don't think I'll take that bet. Meet you inside."

"Yeah, leave me to my doom. Thanks very much. You're a cruel woman." He raised his voice to add, "Hey, Matt. Something I can do for you?"

"Jordan, you and the sheriff have got to do something about those teenagers parking out at my place every weekend. I mean, I understand hormones, but . . ."

I should have taken the bet. Still amused, Hollis set out on her own wandering path among the cars and around the building to the side entrance. It was not the most obvious location for a "front" door and was in fact one that would have hurt most businesses, but Jordan had told her this place made the best biscuits and gravy in four counties—and in the South, that was saying something.

Customers find your door when they really, really like what you're selling them, even if you make them walk around overgrown shrubbery and wedge themselves in between improbably placed stacks of lumber, presumably for some reno project as yet unstarted.

"Ow!" And get stung by bees—

Hollis stared at the object she found sticking in her thigh and for an instant was aware of nothing except total incomprehension.

Then she got it.

She had time only to wish with all her heart and soul that she had taken the bet with Jordan and remained with him back at the car to collect her winnings.

And then the world spun wildly on its axis, and everything went black.

Dani turned off Marc's portable phone and set it back on its base, seeing her fingers tremble. "Dammit. Bishop said Hollis and Jordan had gone out to get breakfast. Jordan called in not two minutes ago. Somebody stopped him in the restaurant's parking lot to ask about something totally unimportant. Hollis went on. When he got inside, she was just . . . gone. No evidence of a struggle. Nobody saw anything."

"It never fails to amaze me how nobody sees anything when something completely extraordinary happens," Marc said, handing her a cup of coffee. "And yet how many UFOs do you suppose get reported every year?"

Dani appreciated the effort but refused to be sidetracked. "Why the hell didn't I see this coming? Oh, yeah, I forgot—**I did**."

"Don't be so hard on yourself."

"Marc, I should have known how it would go. The vision kept changing, and every time the signposts were all but jumping up and down to get my attention. The different watches, warning me from the very beginning that time was important, that there was less of it than I thought. The baited trap, inescapable, unavoidable, waiting for us at the end of this. The sequence of potential victims baiting that trap, shifting easily no matter what I did, as if it hardly mattered which of them was there, Miranda or Paris or Hollis—"

"What?" he asked when she broke off.

"That was the biggest signpost of all," she said slowly. "And I kept missing it."

"Dani, what are you talking about?"

"The bait. It was Miranda even after Bishop made sure she was out of reach, even though it never felt right to me. That was bait for him, to keep him in this—and separated from Miranda. His half of the trap. That's why he always leaves us in the vision dream, why he always goes alone into one side of the trap."

"Separated from everybody else," Marc said. "Weakened strategically."

"Exactly. That's partly what the trap— what this whole setup—was designed to do."

"And the other part? The other side?"

"The side with the teeth. The side intended to capture prey for a psychic killer with his eye on someone else's abilities."

"Why a trap at all?" Marc said. "Why not just take what he wanted? The attack on you and Paris was nearly successful, so why not try that again?"

She frowned. "I think . . . I feel . . . his abilities are limited, just like every psychic's are. So for him to be able to steal someone else's abilities, maybe the conditions have to be right. Electromagnetic fields. Energy. That's how he was able to try to take Paris's abilities, because there was a storm threatening, and he was able somehow to tap into that. He needed the energy.

"And that explains the storm in my vision dream. It's part of the trap. He needs energy outside himself in order to attack any of us."

"It makes sense," Marc admitted. "Must have frustrated the hell out of him that the weather didn't cooperate. He leaves Boston knowing the hunters are on his trail, comes here to take Paris's abilities—and can't. You know, that could have been what triggered your first vision dream. He tried to get at Paris."

"And wasn't strong enough to register with either of us—consciously," Dani agreed. "But my subconscious got it. And my abilities took over, trying to warn me. While he was figuring out what he needed, I was dreaming about a trap."

"Maybe that's why the murders here were so vicious," Marc offered. "That was him, just pissed. No rain for weeks, no storms— no energy to attack in the way he needed to attack to get what he wanted."

"And once his attack was delayed, then he knew he'd have to do something about the psychic hunters on his trail. I was right. He knew Bishop would be here, probably wanted him to be here. Bishop—specifically him. And specifically here, **with** Miranda far away and as separated from Bishop as she could be while both of them are still alive."

"That connection of theirs?"

"That connection," Dani said. "Like Paris and me, Bishop has another half. Together, he and Miranda are incredibly powerful. Alone, either one is a lot more vulnerable. The killer had to know Bishop would be on his trail. And because the bastard had to wait for conditions to be right, or wait to be able to create them himself, then he had to make damn sure his enemy was as weakened as pos-sible."

"So he took away Bishop's other half. Without even lifting a finger against her."

"I think so." Dani drew a breath and let it out slowly. "I think even Bishop has been playing into the killer's hands, reacting exactly as he was expected to react."

Marc was frowning. "Wait a minute. Wasn't it your vision that **caused** Bishop to make sure his wife was protected and far away?"

"Yeah," Dani replied. "How about that. It's like Miranda says. Premonitions are tricky beasts."

It was the chill that woke her, Hollis realized. She lay on a cold table in a room that was cold in every sense. She didn't open her eyes at first, because she was very afraid she knew what she would see and wanted to delay being forced to deal with that.

She had faced death more than once, and it wasn't getting any easier.

I've got to get a different job.

What had happened? She'd gone with Jordan to get breakfast, and . . . and what? She dimly recalled a distraction but couldn't remember what it was. Then something stung her leg, she reached down, and she found herself holding some kind of dart.

Shit. No wonder there were no signs of a struggle where the women disappeared. He's using drugs.

And just like with all the other women, Hollis had apparently been exactly where the killer expected her to be, and he had been ready for her.

Not that the discovery was a hell of a lot of help to Hollis now, except to provide the answer to one of the questions that had nagged at her.

And to give her a couple more minutes' grace before facing the inevitable. But just a couple, and by then Hollis was wide-awake behind her closed eyes and could hear him, somewhere nearby, humming.

The monster had her.

And if there was anything they knew about him, it was that her chances of survival had just dropped to something close to zero.

The best part about facing death, Hollis had discovered, was that after the first moments of skin-crawling, soul-shivering terror, it was curiously liberating, at least for her. A kind of survival mode kicked in, and all her concentration and energy went into whatever effort was required to better her chances.

She did **not** want to die.

It was, perhaps not coincidentally, also exactly the right state of mind necessary for the best use of her mediumistic abilities. So Hollis wasn't terribly surprised, when she finally opened her eyes, to see Becky Huntley bending over her.

"Be very still," Becky whispered. "And you can't get loose anyway, we all tried our best. He thinks you're still out. As soon as he knows you're awake, he'll want to get started on you. And you don't want that."

Instantly, Hollis closed her eyes again and forced her body to go limp, and it wasn't just because it was still unsettling to her, this absurdly easy communication with the dead.

Is there anything else you can tell me, Becky? She knew she didn't have to ask out loud, which was a good thing but also still strange to her.

"We'll try to help. But . . . we don't have much energy. Karen is so sad because she wanted to be a mother, and Shirley can't believe it's over for her. And he's . . . he's not human anymore, Hollis. Do you think he knows there's a hell? Do you think it would matter to him?"

Not if he isn't human anymore . . .

But Hollis wasn't sure about that, so she didn't dismiss the information. Any bit of knowledge could be a tool, a weapon that could save her life.

If she figured out how to use it.

And when to use it.

"Your friends are trying to find you," Becky told her. "We think there's a chance . . . maybe. If Dani remembers what she can do."

Without asking what that was, Hollis merely thought, **Go remind her, will you?**

"She wouldn't see me. Or hear me. Just the way he can't see or hear me. I'll try to make him see me, because it might take some of his attention off you, but so far it's taken more energy than I have, than any of us has, to break through. Be very still, Hollis. He's coming over here. Try not to let him know you're awake."

Oh, Christ.

———

Dani said, "I don't think he caused or altered my premonition. I could be wrong about that—easily—but I don't think so. I think he had targeted Paris, and when I showed up, when he realized, then he decided it could work to his advantage."

"That sounds an awful lot like luck."

"No, I don't think he leaves much to chance. His original plan was to take Paris's abilities, especially the one that let her channel energy. The one ability that can become a weapon in the right hands. Or the wrong ones. He wanted that potential weapon. That never changed; he just added to the blueprint." She shook her head. "But I meant what I said: I don't really care how he's doing this, or why, not now. I just want to find him and stop him, hopefully before he hurts Hollis and before he has a chance to go after Paris again."

"All right. Look, we both know following the paper trail and searching warehouses is going to take longer than Hollis has, probably longer than Paris has. So why don't we take a shortcut?"

"What kind of shortcut?"

"Dream-walk."

"Marc . . . we might not have gotten much sleep last night, but we did get some, and I can't do anything in my dreams unless it's a natural sleep. Trust me, I'm about as far from sleep as I've ever been in my life."

"I don't think you have to sleep, Dani. Not anymore—and maybe you never did. I may not know a lot about psychic abilities, but one thing I do know is that psychics have been putting themselves into trances for a **long** time in order to tap into their abilities."

"I've never been able to do that. I was taught all the right meditation techniques, we all are at Haven. It works for a lot of psychics. But I could never put myself into a trance."

"How hard did you try? Be honest."

She hesitated. "I don't know. I mean . . . I thought I was trying, but . . ."

"But you were still running. Then. Not now. And now you have every reason in the world to put everything you have into the effort. I'm betting that'll be more than enough." He took her hand and led her into the living room and to the sofa. "I'll help."

"How? Have you ever tried this before?"

"No. But **my** passive psychic ability, remember, is to recognize the abilities in others. I have a hunch that it isn't quite as passive as I've always believed it to be—or else it's just evolving because I've used it so much more lately. Or because of the connection with you. No way to know for sure, but for whatever reason, I think I may be able to help you focus and channel."

She didn't have a clue if it would work, but the clock in her head was ticking louder; a glance at the clock on some of his electronics in the room told her it was now 9:05.

Paris and Hollis were both running out of time.

"Okay," she said. "Meditation techniques. Deep cleansing breaths—"

"Screw all that," Marc said. He took her other hand and held them, half turned toward her so that they faced each other. He was smiling slightly. "Energy follows intent; I think if you want something badly enough, you find it. Just close your eyes and think about Hollis and places monsters might hide."

Dani would never have believed it could be that simple, but she closed her eyes, very conscious of him and of the connection between them that their night together had quite definitely intensified, and did exactly what he suggested.

She thought of Hollis and where monsters might hide.

Unlike all her past experiences, this time the transition was effortless and almost instant. She wasn't sitting across from Marc in his living room, she was standing beside him on Main Street in Venture. A very recognizable Main Street, with noise and people and cars, and only one slight peculiarity.

"I meant to ask years ago," Marc said. "Why is there always so much purple?" He was studying a purple fire hydrant plunked down improbably in the middle of the sidewalk near them and not far from where three purple cars were parked.

"I like purple." She'd never really thought

about it but supposed that was as good a reason as any other. It was, after all, her dream world.

Marc shrugged philosophically. "Works for me. Why are we in downtown, though? Oh, wait—you did this before, years ago. Picked a recognizable landmark to start off from. Said it anchored you."

"Yeah. And now that it has . . . I need to know where Hollis is. I need to know where monsters hide." It wasn't like she was making a wish of a magic lamp but rather telling her own mind, her dream self, how her energy needed to be directed.

And, either because of the need driving her or simply because so much else had changed, the familiar scenery around them shifted in a rush of color and sound, and they found themselves in another not-so-familiar but recognizable spot on the very edge of Prophet County.

"Shit," Marc said. "This is no warehouse. It was an asylum, back in the days when they were called that. And didn't somebody try to run a hotel from here when we were kids?"

"I think so. Didn't last long, though. Marc, the basement of that building has to be huge."

"Searching it won't be a cinch and won't be quick," he agreed. "We'd better get back and get started."

She hesitated for just a moment. "I want to run in there and start looking for Hollis. Stupid, since it's my dream. She'd be there, the way I want her to be. Unhurt. Not being held by a monster."

Marc's fingers tightened around hers. "We need to get back, Dani. We need to gather up the others and figure out how to cover the ground we have to cover. And if I remember right, dream-walking always takes more real time than you expect, doesn't it?"

"Yeah. Yeah, it does."

"Then we should go."

"You're right. Of course, you're right. I can't stop time, can I? Maybe here, but not for real."

"We'll beat time," he assured her.

Dani wondered if he was right, but there wasn't really time—ironically—to ponder it.

"Okay," she said. "Back home . . ." And

didn't realize until much later that by "home" she meant Marc's.

Hollis thought she might have fooled him the first time he checked on her, but when he came back again, he stuck a pin in her arm.

There was no warning and no way for her to feign unconsciousness when the jabbing pain caused her to flinch and catch her breath.

"Ah. So you are awake. I thought you might have been playing possum, Audrey. So naughty. I'll have to punish you for that."

Audrey? So the name on the bracelet did mean something. Christ, the last time an evil serial killer was convinced I was another woman, it was Audra. What is it with me and variations of that name?

Since he knew she was awake, she opened her eyes slowly, blinking at the brightness of lights that hadn't bothered her when Becky had leaned over her.

She wondered if that meant something.

"Hello, sweetheart," he said softly, his mouth almost caressing the words.

She didn't have a clue who he was, just

what he was, and it wasn't the first time she found herself wondering how it was that monsters could look so goddamn **normal**.

Like the "regular guy" neighbor next door.

Something evil dressed in human clothing.

He was not a tall man or an especially short man. Average height, average build, bland coloring. But his small, neutral eyes were . . . curiously shiny, almost metallic, and he didn't seem to blink very often.

Other than that, he just looked . . . normal.

Don't get distracted by what he looks like, dammit. If you want to survive this, work to make it happen. You have before, you can again. You've got fucking nine lives, just like a cat.

Quentin said so.

Of course, he also said you'd used up at least seven of them, and that was a few months back. . . .

"Hi." She didn't try to fake a smile at her captor but did go for a quizzical expression. "So I'm . . . Audrey? Cool. Hey, have you ever considered that there really is a hell?"

———

Jordan offered Dani and Marc a sick smile when they met up outside the sheriff's department, and his first words were, "Christ, I don't know how I could have lost her."

Marc shook his head. "Don't blame yourself. If Dani's right, this bastard's been a step ahead of us all the way."

Dani was looking at Bishop, understanding now that the haunted expression with which she was so familiar through her repeated vision dreams came not from a threat to his wife but from the certain knowledge that his maneuvering, his determination to hunt this particular killer, had placed one of his team directly in harm's way.

"Will it be worth it?" she asked him, not sure if it was curiosity or something else that drove her to. "If Hollis pays with her life, will it be worth it?"

"I don't know." He drew a breath, and his wide shoulders shifted as though under a heavy burden. "If we find this monster, catch it . . . cage it . . . kill it . . . How many other lives might be saved? I don't know. This time, I don't know."

Gabriel said, "We can discuss ethics later. Right now I say we move. Dani, you're sure about this old mental hospital?"

"I'm sure." She looked again at Bishop. "Your guardian. Has she—"

"Reported in ten minutes ago." His voice was steady, like his gaze. "It's not looking good for Paris, Dani, but not from any outside threat. Brain activity has dropped to minimal levels, and some of her other vital functions have been deteriorating. Her doctors say you might want to be there."

The pull to be with her sister, her twin, was inexpressibly strong, but Dani wavered for only an instant.

"And you can do what you have to, Dani. When the time comes. You'll know. You'll make the right choice."

"I have to do this," she said, as much to herself as to anyone else. "I have to. Paris knows that."

Marc took her hand, saying only, "Let's go."

It was 12:35.

———

Hollis coughed and tried desperately to draw air into her bruised throat.

"Watch that mouth," her captor said sternly. "One more thing I have to punish you for, Audrey."

Okay, bad idea. Very bad idea. Note to self: Maniacal serial killer does not like smart-ass questions.

Oh, Jesus, I'm scared. . . .

22

BETWEEN THE TIME Marc had called from his house and their arrival at the sheriff's department, someone had managed to produce original blueprints for the old mental hospital, blueprints they unrolled on the hood of Marc's cruiser when they parked all the vehicles at the base of the long driveway.

It was 1:15.

"I gather we think this guy's expecting us," Jordan commented as they studied the plans.

Dani was frowning down at them, wishing she could remember more details from the vision dream when she wasn't actually in the middle of it. Wasn't there supposed to be a storm?

That thought had barely crossed her mind when she heard distant thunder, right on cue.

Sometimes she thought the universe had a sense of humor.

This wasn't one of those times.

"We have to assume he is," Marc replied to Jordan. "Dani believes this was his goal all along, to collect himself a few psychics. Divide and conquer, so to speak, and build up his own résumé. He probably wanted to start with Paris because her ability could be used as a weapon, but . . ."

Dani finished, "But I think he wants any ability he can grab." She eyed the darkening sky uneasily.

Gabriel was checking his weapon, and said with a grunt, "He'll be disappointed in Rox and me. Each of us is psychic only when we're asleep. A bit like Dani used to be. Hell. Dani—"

"Sorry."

"You're shocking all of us," Jordan said, shifting just a bit to put another inch of space between his arm and hers. "All except Marc, that is."

Dani and Marc exchanged glances, and she said, "Yeah, we noticed that. Sorry for the static discharge, guys. I don't know if it's the coming storm or . . . well, whatever we find in there, but I can't seem to control it very well right now."

Roxanne said, "As intense as this is, I'm not surprised." She took a closer look at the plans, and added, "Two main buildings, both presumably with basements. We split up to search?"

Marc was nodding. "No other way to cover the ground, not if we need to hurry. And we do. Dani, do you sense anything from the buildings?"

She frowned, concentrating, then winced. "General pain and sadness, old echoes. This was not a positive place at any stage of its life."

"Bishop? Are you getting anything?"

He shook his head. "Miranda and I have each closed down the connection between us as far as we could. Without that, I'm at less than half strength. And the weather affects me more without the benefit of her shields. I can barely read Jordan, and he's broadcasting like a beacon."

Jordan blinked. "I am?"

"You are. Remind me to talk to you about shielding, if we have a minute at the end of this."

"You mean if we're still standing at the end of this? Because I got the impression that wasn't likely."

"Don't be a pessimist," Marc said. "Dani, if you don't have strong feelings about it one way or the other, I'm picking the front building for you, me, and Bishop. Gabriel, Roxanne, and Jordan will take the one in the back."

Roxanne exchanged a look with her brother, and then said to Marc, "I need to be with you guys."

"Why?"

"Because if this monster is bent on collecting psychics, each group needs at least one nonpsychic with a gun ready who won't be affected by any kind of mental attack. That'll be me. When I'm awake, I have zero psychic abilities."

"My ability is passive," Marc pointed out.

"It's evolved. Probably the connection with Dani. And, trust me, if this guy is collecting neat abilities, he'll want yours; being able to identify another psychic can come in mighty handy when those are the folks hunting you."

"She has a point," Dani said.

"Meant to tell you," Bishop murmured. "Right now you're also a bit like a conduit for Dani. Which means he could get to her through you."

"And vice versa," Dani said.

Bishop nodded.

Jordan said, "The rear building is quite a bit smaller than the one in front, so I think Gabriel and I can search it fairly quickly alone. That is—Dani, are you sure it's a basement?"

"All I know is that I don't remember seeing any windows," she told him.

Jordan sighed. "We'll hurry."

"Yeah, I would."

"Marc, if we do meet up with this guy, then what are our orders?"

"Shoot to kill."

Jordan blinked again. "That always sounds

so melodramatic in movies. In real life, not so much. What if he isn't armed?"

"He is. Armed and dangerous. That is my official statement as sheriff of Prophet County." Marc looked at his chief deputy steadily. "We couldn't come out here in force, and we're short on time. Hollis is in there, probably being tortured. It's a monster, Jordan. If you see one, shoot it."

"Copy that," Jordan said.

Marc looked at the others. "Okay, then. Roxanne, you're with us."

"Copy that," she said.

By the time they reached the buildings, moving cautiously, the storm was upon them. And it was a very dangerous storm for an area that hadn't seen any decent rain for weeks: It was a dry electrical storm.

The raw energy swirling all around them didn't do much for Dani's control; when she reached for a metal door handle, the sparks ignited a clump of long grass growing wild at its base.

"Damn," she said.

"Let me." Bishop brushed past her, ignoring the skittering of sparks that danced across the arm of his leather jacket, and paused only to stamp out the little fire before going to work on the lock.

Worried, Dani said to Marc, "If all this energy is feeding him the way it's feeding me, this is worse than a trap. The deeper we go into this building, the easier it'll be to contain energy, focus it. The walls, the ceilings, the floors, everything will help. Help him, if he's been practicing his control. But I haven't been practicing. I don't know if I can control this. At all."

"Make it a weapon," Roxanne suggested, her own at the ready. "Dunno if it's lethal, but you could sure surprise the hell out of somebody." She followed Bishop into the building.

"She's right," Marc said. "I know you don't want to carry a gun, so use what you've got."

"You're getting more psychic all the time." When he questioned silently with a lifted brow, she added, "The gun thing. We haven't discussed it. Out loud, anyway."

They eased into the building behind the

other two, and as she looked around, Dani saw absolutely nothing that looked familiar.

And nothing that looked like a warehouse.

They had entered through a huge kitchen and from there found their way out into the central area of what appeared to be the ground floor.

It was a strange and uneasy mix of Victorian hospital and Art Deco hotel decor—the furnishings still in place, brass fixtures, and dusty velvet draperies cloaking all the windows so that the space was dim and filled with shadows.

"Creepy place," Roxanne said. "Big creepy place. How we doing on time?"

Dani didn't have to look at a clock or watch. "We're running out of it. Hollis is running out of it. And I don't see a damn thing that looks familiar."

"One plus is that the building isn't on fire," Marc said. "A symbolic representation of energy, maybe?"

"Maybe," Dani agreed.

"This place could take a lightning hit yet and go up like a match." Roxanne shrugged.

"I say expect the worst and then you can only be surprised pleasantly. We split up?"

Marc looked at Dani, then nodded. "Have to. We're looking for stairs down. But nobody goes down alone. Understand?"

Bishop and Roxanne both nodded and went in separate directions.

"Marc, this isn't the vision."

"Is that such a surprise? You said yourself it had been changing all along. Maybe this is just the final version."

"I guess. But if so much changed, or was symbolic and not literal, then are we still looking for a basement?"

He considered. "If I remember correctly, you said the only constants were that we all knew we were going down into a trap and that the building was falling in behind us."

"Pretty much."

"Sounds like a very final trap. Doom. Maybe that's why it was all so . . . elaborate. The burning building, with smoke preventing you from being able to tell much about it. Going down into a basement to face a killer. Maybe it was only the signposts that mattered. Maybe the rest was just your mind conjuring the worst sort of trap it could imagine."

Despite the closed stuffiness of the space around them, Dani shivered. "Maybe. I hate fire. Scares the hell out of me."

"There you go, then."

"Okay. But—"

"Listen." He touched her cheek with his free hand. "I don't want you to leave yourself open to any sort of attack, with this guy probably ready for us and lurking around somewhere, but can you forget about the vision for just a minute and feel what this building is telling you? Because it's talking to me."

As soon as she stopped trying to recall the vision, as soon as she let her mind go quiet, Dani heard the building loud and clear.

"Basement. There is a basement."

"Yeah. With a cold and slimy monster as tenant."

"Guys." Roxanne appeared suddenly in a hallway to their left. "This way. Bishop's found the stairs."

In less than a minute they were there, looking down at welcoming lights.

"Well," Dani said, "that's the same. But why make a trap so obviously a trap? I would have expected something a lot more subtle from him."

"Maybe that's why he made it obvious," Marc said. "Doesn't really change anything, though."

Dani nodded agreement. "I can feel Hollis now."

"Is she—" Bishop stopped himself.

"She's alive," Dani said. "But . . . hurting. Let's go."

They went down the stairs very cautiously but at the bottom found only a central area from which stretched several long corridors with blank, featureless doors.

"Shit," Dani whispered. "This does look familiar." But not from her vision. From the dream walk with Paris and Hollis. Worse, there was too much iron and steel in this place, too many hard, reflective surfaces that could easily help channel and focus any kind of energy.

"Solitary?" Roxanne was tense, alert.

"Probably," Marc said, and added, "We are **not** splitting up down here."

Very familiar.

Dani felt herself move toward the middle corridor, following a pull so strong she was vaguely surprised not to see an actual rope stretched out before her. "This way. At the end, I think."

"Dani, wait—"

But she was already three steps into the corridor, and even though Marc and the others followed quickly, she was well ahead of them and isolated by just enough space when they all saw her aura become not only visible but also begin to shimmer in a rainbow of colors.

"Dani—"

"I know," she said. Her hands moved out to her sides, almost as if she explored an enclosure. "He's coming after me. I'm just not sure . . . how he's able to do this. I don't hear his voice . . . the way I did before." She drew a quick breath, and Marc saw her pale. "We have to get to Hollis. Now. I might be able to . . . keep him occupied . . . just long enough."

He tried to get to her, but the aura surrounding her began to crackle and spark, and Marc quickly drew back his hand, afraid he would only hurt her more. "Move," he said to the other two.

But Dani had no intention of waiting there and was already moving herself, slowly, carrying the live-energy cloud with her.

At first Marc thought the energy was draining her, but she turned her head slightly and sent him a quick, clear look, and he realized in that instant what she was doing.

"Make it a weapon."

It was dangerous, what she was doing. Potentially deadly. Because a conduit could only accept and channel so much energy without being destroyed in the process.

He didn't know where she was drawing the energy **from**, though he guessed it was the storm still feeding her, even this far underground. Clearly, she'd been right in believing this place would help contain energy.

Hell, maybe the bastard had chosen his trap well, knowing he could use it, having had the time these last weeks to test his little energy nexus.

Dani had no time for experiments or theories or practice. All she had was her instincts and desperation. All Marc had was the certainty that she was risking her life, and there wasn't a damn thing he could do to stop it.

Bishop had managed to slip past Dani without disturbing her crackling aura, but when he reached the door, there was—nothing. No knob or handle, no lock, just a featureless expanse of solid steel.

He looked back at the others and shook his head grimly.

Nobody had brought anything with which to batter down a door, there was no lock to pick, and even hinges weren't visible, much less accessible.

As she reached the end of the hallway, Dani said very quietly, "I'll get the door. Just—move fast once I do. I don't know what will happen if I—Just move fast."

"Dani, for God's sake, be careful," Marc said, just as quietly. He thought he was braced for anything, but in the last few seconds, as the energy cloud intensified and she visibly gathered herself, he saw two of her inside that aura.

"Oh, Christ," he said.

The sound was like an explosion. Was an

explosion. A literal wave of pure raw energy surged forward from Dani with an eerie silence that made the thunderous **craa-aack!** of the door blowing inward all the more deafening.

Marc followed Bishop and Roxanne to the doorway of the room but not into it, remaining in the corridor, his arm around Dani as she sagged abruptly against him, all her energy spent.

What he saw was more than a little surprising, and from their frozen positions he knew the others were just as stunned by the scene that greeted them.

A very ordinary-looking man most anyone would have passed on the street without a glance cowered in the far corner of the room, what looked like a scalpel in his hand as he slashed wildly at the air around him, making guttural sounds that might have been rage— or terror. He appeared to be fighting, or attempting to defend himself, but whatever his weirdly flat, shiny eyes detected as a threat was invisible to the newcomers.

But to their immense relief, in the center

of the room, strapped to a stainless-steel table that was tilted about forty-five degrees up at the head, was Hollis.

She was more than a little bruised and battered, and it was clear the monster had begun to cut her clothing off before he was . . . interrupted . . . but she was very much alive.

"Hollis?" Bishop's normally cool voice was unsteady.

She turned her head and looked at him, and her swollen lips smiled, if only a little. "Boss, I want a raise. Either that or a new job."

"What the hell did you do to him?" Roxanne asked, her gaze fixed on the desperately struggling monster.

"You can't see them, but I have a posse in the room. All his victims have come to visit their murderer. And lemme tell you, they're pissed. Right now, they're telling him all about hell. In Technicolor."

Bishop gestured for Roxanne to keep her gun on the monster and holstered his own weapon as he went to free Hollis.

"**All** his victims?"

"Well, most of 'em. I got scared and opened a lot of doors." She winced slightly. "Ow."

Roxanne said, "I may have to shoot him just to get the scalpel away from him."

"Feel free," Marc said. Then he looked at Dani. "Are you okay? That looked—"

"Paris helped. Right at the end."

"Is she . . . ?"

"She's gone." Dani didn't know when she had started to cry, but she couldn't seem to stop. She felt empty and knew it wasn't because of what she had done, but what she had lost. "I think she just stuck around as long as she did so she could help."

It wasn't much solace to Dani to remind herself that, deep down, she and Paris had both known, for weeks, that this was going to happen. It didn't help to recognize that they had, at least, been granted the time to begin to say good-bye.

Half of her had been torn away, or nearly half; Paris had given her twin her abilities, even her life force, and Dani felt that too. She knew she was not quite as alone as others would perceive her to be.

That didn't help either.

"I'm sorry. God, Dani, I'm so sorry."

"Yeah, me too." She tried for a smile and

knew it was no more than a shadow. "Even if I knew all along it would happen."

"Did you?"

"I knew. Paris knew too. That's why she gave me her abilities when she could."

"He came after you instead of her."

"Maybe he tried to get to Paris first and found the guardian. Or maybe he intended to go after me all along. But I think I surprised him, maybe even hurt him. I don't think he realized that I could learn so fast to channel energy. Neither did I, really."

She looked at the monster that had taken so much from her, from so many people, and even through her numb sense of loss, an uneasiness stirred. "I don't think . . ."

"What?" Marc asked.

"I'm too tired to reach out, really, but what I feel from this monster is . . . it's sick and evil, but . . . I just don't think—"

"Christ, look over there," Roxanne said, nodding toward the wall where photo collections detailed the stalking and torturing of his victims. "I don't think we'll have any problem convincing a jury this is our killer. Assuming it even gets to trial. Want my take, I say he picked this place because the universe told him it was where he belonged. In an asylum."

Dani avoided looking at the trophies, but she could feel herself frowning. "I wonder if this monster was ever human."

"Dani?" Marc's arm tightened around her.

She realized he didn't have to ask the question for her to know what it was. "Out there in the hallway . . . what I felt during that attack. It was never from this room. It was never **in** this room, Marc."

"What do you mean?"

"This is the killer, I know that." Even exhausted and aching, she knew that, felt that. "There are so many dark and twisted things inside him it's like worms. Maggots." She closed her eyes briefly, trying to shut off the unwelcome information. "Audrey . . ."

"His mother." Hollis, freed from her stainless-steel prison and cautiously testing her bruises, said, "His victims got an earful about her by the end. She doted on him. In a very unnatural way."

Dani shook her head. "He was born twisted; she just made him worse."

"Yeah. Well, before they started putting

the fear of hell into him a while ago, one of his victims told me we might want to take a look into the room closest to this one. She seemed to think we were in for a surprise."

Even before they began exploring, they had a baffling mystery on their hands, because when Marc touched the killer he was able to confirm what Dani had already sensed.

"He's not psychic."

"Maybe burned out?" Roxanne suggested. "That last attack against Dani was a fierce one. Maybe too much for him?"

Still surprisingly calm, Hollis said, "If you're talking about whatever energy blew the door in, I doubt he had anything to do with it. He was fully occupied, believe me, for at least ten or fifteen minutes before you guys got here."

"I don't think this . . . man . . . was ever psychic," Marc said, half consciously brushing his hands together after touching the killer. "I've been able to pick up latent psychic ability, but from him I get nothing at all."

They looked at one another, and Hollis said, "I say we look for whatever Becky thought would surprise us."

They found it about ten minutes later while exploring the rooms nearest his torture chamber. The now seemingly catatonic monster remained cuffed and under the watchful eyes and ready weapons of Gabriel and Roxanne.

It was a neat and scrupulously clean room, as small and unadorned as a monk's cell. Just a cot, a metal chair and desk, and an unfinished pine wardrobe, where his clothing was folded precisely.

"He kept a scrapbook of his own life," Bishop said, finding it in one of the desk drawers. He used his pen to turn several pages back. "Born . . . Carl Brewster, ordinarily enough. Not much about his early life here, just his birth certificate and what look like some school records. Enough to help us know where to look for more information about him. Pages of doodles the psychologists are going to have a field day with, including the word **Prophecy** written over and over again."

"Just that word?" Dani asked.

"Looks like. Then the newspaper clippings start. No way to tell just from this what the ultimate trigger was, but it looks like we were right about the Boston murders being his first. There are no clippings or information about earlier murders here."

"When did his mother die?" Dani asked.

Bishop continued to page through the scrapbook, finally stopping about halfway through. "Yeah, that could be it. Her obituary is here. She died last spring, after a long illness."

"Domineering she might have been," Hollis said, "but she was probably his leash and held him back as long as she was alive. Once she was gone, there was no one to stop him."

Marc said, "What sickens me is that he'll probably live out his life in a prison cell more comfortable than this one, with psychologists, cops, and profilers lining up to try to figure out what makes him tick."

"It might help catch the next one," Bishop reminded him.

"I know, I know. Still."

Before he could say anything else, Jordan appeared in the doorway, holding a manila envelope in his gloved hand. "Guys, look at this. And please tell me it doesn't mean what I think it means." He came into the room, crossed to the bed, and emptied the envelope.

Photographs.

"Of me," Hollis said.

"Yeah." Jordan looked at her steadily. "He apparently had a little workroom across the hall where he liked to cut up the pictures. I found this lying on a table in there, all ready for him. Notice anything unusual?"

But Dani saw it first. "They're dated. All taken with a digital camera. And . . . some are dated more than a year ago."

"The bastard hunted me for over a year?" Hollis was too bewildered to be angry about it. For now, at least.

"I don't think so." Jordan showed them the envelope. "This was mailed to him at a post office box here in Venture. Mailed **from** Washington, D.C. Postmarked two days ago."

"He was here two days ago," Marc said slowly.

"Yeah. There are also several empty envelopes in there. D.C. and New York post-marks. Different dates, but all during the past month."

They looked at one another, several things and possibilities falling into place.

"A trained monster," Bishop said. "Or maybe just . . . a tool. A puppet. But not the puppetmaster."

"That's why it felt different," Dani said slowly. "Why I didn't feel the same energy in his—his torture chamber that I felt out in the hallway. Because he wasn't responsible for the attack. Marc was right, the killer was never psychic. His wasn't the voice in my head."

"He was bait too," Bishop said slowly.

Dani nodded. "The bait to draw us. If you want to trap the monster hunters, you have to provide a monster. Find one. Uncage one. Or create one. Every time we hit a wall in the investigation, another little fact or detail or possible lead would be dangled in front of us. To keep us asking questions, to keep us off balance. To keep us moving, always toward the trap."

"He didn't catch anything in his trap," Jordan pointed out. "Did he?"

"He didn't get Paris's ability," Dani said. "But this attack . . . it was different. It was stronger, more focused. He may have gained something, even if it wasn't a new ability. The experience alone could have given him something of value to him."

"You said you thought you hurt him," Marc reminded her.

"It felt like I did. A sense of pain, of frustration. But . . . it wasn't a crippling injury. There was still the echo of a very strong, distinct presence, a personality—especially right at the end, when I discharged all that energy. He knew he'd lost . . . this round."

Jordan said, "Shit. This round?"

"It isn't over," Marc said.

Epilogue

SENATOR ABE LEMOTT turned from the window and looked at the man in his visitor's chair. "So that's it?"

Bishop said, "The monster who killed your daughter will spend the remainder of his pathetic life screaming at the walls, babbling about some prophecy he probably created when his own acts became too evil even for him. We may never know; whatever was left of his mind got broken there at the end. Or maybe a long time before the end."

"And the monster who pulled his strings? The cold, calculating mind behind him?"

"We never saw him," Bishop said. "Even though we believe he was close enough, more than once, to watch. Close enough to affect some of us. Close enough to hunt and possibly even capture the . . . prey . . . for his pet killer."

LaMott's mouth twisted. "Like feeding a spider."

"Yes."

"So who spun the web?"

"So far we haven't found so much as a trace of evidence that he even exists. Except, of course, that we know he does."

"What else do you know?"

"I believe I know where to start looking for him."

Senator LeMott smiled. "That's good, Bishop. That's very good indeed."

About the Author

KAY HOOPER is the award-winning author of **Sleeping with Fear, Hunting Fear, Chill of Fear, Touching Evil, Whisper of Evil, Sense of Evil, Once a Thief, Always a Thief,** the Shadows trilogy, and other novels. She lives in North Carolina, where she is at work on her next book.